Rubyville

A Place in My Heart

BOOK FOUR

Deborah Ann Dykeman

Copyright © 2016 Deborah Ann Dykeman

Cover design by Julia Ryan / www.DesignByJulia.com
Cover image © Alex Gukalov / Shutterstock

All rights reserved.
No portion of this book may be reproduced in any form whatsoever.
All Scripture quotations are taken from the King James Version.
All emphasis in Scripture was added by the author.

Scripture quotations in Author's Note are from Bible Gateway (NASB)
biblegateway.com

Drifting With You (Richard and Evelyn's Song)
Written by Deborah Ann Dykeman, © 2016

This book is a work of fiction. Characters, names, places and incidents are based on the author's imagination or used fictitiously. While some of the events mentioned in this book have occurred, and some places are actual locations, they are still used by the author for fiction only. No intent has been made to write a historically correct account. Any resemblance to real life is entirely coincidental.

ISBN: 1537096826

ISBN-13: 978-1537096827

Books in the Rubyville Series

A Place to Call Home

A Place of Refuge

A Place to Heal

A Place in My Heart

COMING SOON

Love Defined Series

Also by Deborah Ann Dykeman

To Thee I'm Wed

Dedication

This book is for all those looking for answers in this world today. There *is* hope, love, and justice. Seek Him and His Word.

Acknowledgements

Julia Ryan and Britta Ann Meadows...there are no words to say for all that you have done for me with this series!
You have made my dream come true; you have made it a reality and it is finally tangible.

Alyssa Lynn...your input and editing has been a tremendous help. Your insight has been priceless.

Thank you, thank you, and thank you!

And to my Heavenly Father, for these gifts You have given me...
I pray Your Word comes through and You are glorified.

Psalm 118:24

Chapter One

Rubyville, Kansas
March 1948

EVELYN SHOVED AWAY FROM the kitchen table and walked to the white, steel cabinet upon the wall. She took a glass from the shelf and went to the refrigerator, sliding the pitcher of milk out and giving it a little shake.

"Evelyn, dear, have you finished your homework yet?" Helen's voice called from the front room.

Evelyn rolled her eyes, filling the glass to the rim and setting the foaming tumbler upon the enameled table top. "I'm almost done, Mama…just getting some milk to go with another piece of cake."

"*Another* piece of cake?" Helen's high pitch preceded her into the kitchen. "I served you a fairly large slice at supper." Helen entered the room and set her hands upon her gray, wool-clad hips. Her red nails glared against her porcelain fingers. "Do you really think you should, my dear?" She smiled, red lips matching her nails and the counter tops in the newly fitted kitchen. She gave her seventeen-year-old daughter a wink. "You have the senior prom coming up with Mr. Darby, and you want to look your best for him…*and* fit into your dress, don't you?"

Evelyn glanced down at her long, thin frame. The plaid skirt she wore ended at shapely calves, followed by narrow feet in brown and white saddle shoes. She looked back at her mother and sighed. "Mama, I would delight in a few extra pounds here and there. The only thing that distinguishes me from a young man is the long hair."

Helen shook her perfectly coiffed blonde head. "I only meant that your dress has already been purchased." She sat down at the table and crossed her legs, one elbow upon the white and red top. "If you would quit your daily jaunts through the brush by the river you might have a hope of having a more *feminine* figure."

Evelyn plopped on the seat of the chair. "Well, Aaron likes my figure just the way it is."

Helen raised a brow. "And why would Mr. Darby comment on your figure in *any* way?"

Evelyn slid the cake plate over to her mother. "Would you cut me a nice *big* piece, please? You are so much better at it than I am." She gave her mother a wink and picked up her pencil as she went back to the paper before her.

Helen lifted the dome lid off the pedestal plate and set it on the table. "I will cut you a *small* piece just as soon as you answer my question. Please tell me why Mr. Darby would be talking about your figure." Helen stood and went to another cabinet, taking a plate from the shelf. She grabbed a fork and knife on her way back to the table.

Evelyn dropped the pencil. "Mama, you don't have to snap your cap. He has just complimented me…thinks I'm pretty…that's all." She shrugged one shoulder. "He hasn't mentioned anything that he shouldn't have."

Helen sat back down and waved the serrated knife at her daughter. "I was married at one time, if you remember. I know what kind of things young men say."

"Well, my father must have been more interesting than Aaron. He's as pure as the driven snow. There's nothing killer-diller about *Mr. Darby*, I can assure you, Mama." Evelyn went back to her paper.

Helen sliced through the chocolate cake, laid a moderate piece on the plate, and set it before her daughter.

Evelyn stared at the serving. "Jeepers! There's certainly *nothing* killer-diller about *that* slice of cake."

Helen placed a hand on her hip and gave a huff. "I cannot understand half of what you say. Surely the other children at school don't converse in that manner."

Evelyn put her elbow on the table and stared at her mother. "Would you have wanted to be referred to as a *child* when you were my age? Speaking of manners, do I get a fork?"

Helen shook her head and fetched a fork. "Certainly. I can't have my daughter eating with her hands. Especially if she refuses to be called a child." She laughed. "And no, I wouldn't have liked to have been called a child at your age, either. I thought I was pretty sophisticated." She sliced a tiny bite from the cake and popped it in her mouth. She chewed and swallowed before adding, "Just make sure that both of you remain *as pure as the driven snow.* There's plenty of time *after* you're married to learn all the *intimate* things about a person."

"Believe me, Mama...that won't be a problem for me." She put a big bite of cake in her mouth and chewed. "The thought of Aaron and me doing anything more intimate than sitting on the river's edge and fishing just about gives me the shivers." She complied with an exaggerated motion of her shoulders.

Helen covered her smile with her hand. "How many times have I asked you not to talk with your mouth full of food? It is very unladylike."

Evelyn gave a big swallow and gulped down half her milk. "I don't remember the number of times, Mama." She brushed at the corners of her mouth, shaking her head to refuse the napkin her mother held out. "But I'm always polite when I'm with other people. That's what counts." She slammed her book shut.

Helen sighed with a shake of her head. "I suppose that's about the best I can ask of you. In time you will mature and understand the importance of acting like a lady at *all* times, not just when you are around others. You never want to be a hypocrite, my dear."

Evelyn finished her cake and drank the last of her milk. "I don't think I'm a hypocrite...just a bit more relaxed than you. You've always been rather uptight about things I don't think are very important."

Helen crossed her arms. "Oh really? Do you care to share some of those *things* you think I'm uptight about?"

Evelyn stood and took her plate and glass to the porcelain sink. "You are always fussing about my hair, the way I dress, my education..." She sighed. "The list just seems to go on and on sometimes. Rather like I will never be good enough to be your daughter, and most certainly not a wife or mother."

Helen frowned. "I don't mean to be critical. I just want you to be the very best person you can be. I want to encourage you to dress properly, wear your hair in an attractive style, and not do things that make you look—"

"Make *you* look poorly, Mama. *You* don't want to look bad." Evelyn leaned one hip against the sink and crossed her arms. "I think you are always trying so hard because you brought me up without a father. You don't want people to talk…to think you might have done a less than perfect job of raising me."

Helen crossed her legs and swung one foot. "That is just not the case, Evelyn. Everyone around here knows that your father died when you were a baby. They never even met him. This town has no expectations of him at all."

"Just of fatherhood in general." Evelyn walked to her mother and stood behind her, wrapping her arms around her shoulders. "I love you, Mama. I think you did an amazing job of raising me. I just want you to enjoy it, before it's all gone…that's all."

"All gone? What are you talking about now?" Helen twisted to look at Evelyn.

Evelyn patted her mother's shoulders. "Nothing, Mama…I don't want to get into an argument. It seems as though we bicker every time we are together for more than a few minutes." She walked to the kitchen door and took a coat from the hook on the wall.

"Where are you going? It is like pitch out there, not to mention the wind is blowing a gale again." Helen shivered. "The March wind has such a lonely sound."

"I think that's just the coyotes calling." Evelyn gave her mother a sassy grin. "I will be back in a few minutes. I have some verses to memorize for the senior play and I want to clear my head of all that homework before I begin." She blew her mother a kiss and opened the door, her hand on the screen.

Helen stood, placing the dome over the cake. "You are such a strange child. I will never understand how your mind works."

"I'll be back." Evelyn fluttered her fingers at her mom, letting the screen door bang shut behind her.

"Evelyn!" Helen shut the door after her daughter.

Evelyn chuckled. *Whoops! Love you, Mama!*

"WELL, IF IT ISN'T Evelyn *Barton* Hanover." Cynthia sauntered toward Evelyn, her slim hips swinging in her tweed skirt. She stopped beside Evelyn and watched as the redhead opened her locker door.

"Good morning, Cynthia." Evelyn's words were clipped as she looked down at the petite fellow student. "Won't you be late for class if you stand there and gawk at me?"

The black-haired girl waved a hand. "My next class is Mrs. Teter's. You know how she is…be tardy, sleep in class…just as long as you study and do well on the test. She's probably the most favorite teacher at the school."

Evelyn pushed in one book and grabbed another from the small, metal space. "Yes, Mrs. Teter is *everyone's* most favorite for those reasons. She's also very nice and a great teacher. But I wouldn't push her too much."

Cynthia giggled, a high tinkle sound in the crowded hall of students. "You are such a worry wart." She gripped her books in front of her red sweater and leaned one shoulder against the lockers. She looked at Evelyn's head. "That bow really looks good in your hair. It must be very difficult to find colors that don't clash with that red."

Evelyn leveled her eyes at Cynthia as she shut her locker door. "Since your mother runs the only dress shop in Rubyville, you must be an expert on colors and what matches. After all, you spend every minute you aren't in school or church working there." Evelyn turned and walked away.

Cynthia ran after her. "Well…at least *I'm* doing something with my life after graduation. I'm not marrying some local yokel and having a passel of children. I'm leaving this quaint little town and getting an education so I can take over my mother's business someday."

Evelyn raised a brow. "You're going to come back to this *quaint little town?*"

"Not all of us are *Bartons*, you know. We have to make our own way in this life." Cynthia raised her chin in the air. "I'm happy to not have everything handed to me. I'll appreciate it more." Cynthia and her upturned nose made their way down the hall.

Evelyn shook her head and stared after the young woman. "Just keep telling yourself that, Cynthia, dear."

"She can be such a stinker, that Cynthia Rowe!" Molly Johnson nudged her cousin's shoulder and gave her a smile. "She is very jealous that you're marrying the absolute *best bachelor* in Rubyville. She's had a crush on Aaron Darby for years."

Evelyn sighed. "I know...and I would deliver him in a box with a lovely bow tied on top if my mother would only let me." She glanced at her cute cousin. Two blue slides, placed on each side of her head, kept the curly, brown hair from her face. "But I think I like Aaron too much to do that to him."

Molly widened her eyes. "You'd better like him! Aren't you two supposed to be married this summer?"

"That's what Mama is hoping and praying for." Evelyn opened the door to her class and waved.

Molly returned the gesture. "See you during lunch, cuz."

The ringing of the bell cleared the hallway and Evelyn sighed as she turned and faced the classroom. *I don't really understand how another year of arithmetic is going to benefit me, but here I am! Just a few more weeks of trying to figure out the unknown...concerning school, anyway!*

EVELYN PULLED THE FRONT of her wool coat together and buttoned it. "It was nice of you to take some time off from the mercantile and walk me home, Aaron, but it really isn't necessary."

The tall, thin young man smiled down, his straight brown hair falling into his eyes. He brushed it back and tucked Evelyn's school books under his arm. "I tell you every time I walk you home that it's something I look forward to. I mean, I can't do it every day, of course, but when I have a chance, I'll be here." His green eyes softened as his gaze swept over her face. "I thought we might stop by the hotel and have a cup of hot cocoa." He searched the gray sky, dark clouds changing shapes. "We could be in for a storm, but not until later."

Evelyn narrowed her eyes at the sky above. "I hope it's not snow. I'm tired of cold weather."

Aaron placed a hand at her back. "Well then, a hot cup of cocoa will be just right, won't it?"

Evelyn scooted away. "I really think it's best that you don't show signs of affection where people can see us. You know it makes me uncomfortable."

"Yes, holding your hand, taking your elbow, kissing your cheek…" He shook his head. "They all make you uncomfortable. Everyone knows we are to be married, Evelyn. They probably expect us to show some kind of affection."

"Well…I'd rather not." Evelyn stopped and looked up at Aaron. "You *do know* that Cynthia Rowe has a crush on you…and has for awhile now."

Aaron blushed and continued walking. "Yes, and she is becoming rather a pest. She spends most of every Saturday popping into the mercantile for something or other. If it wasn't such a busy day I would ask my father to handle Saturdays."

Evelyn jogged up to Aaron and kept pace with his long legs. "Have you thought about asking her out on a date?"

Aaron stopped and gaped down at Evelyn. "Why would I do that when I'm in love with you and marrying you in a few months?" He shook his head. "I've loved you for most of my life, and you know that. Why do you not understand?"

Evelyn sighed. "We aren't officially engaged, Aaron."

"Only because you keep turning down my proposal each time I ask and you won't set a date. Everyone in Rubyville expects it. Your mother is thrilled—"

"I know my mother is thrilled. She's talked about us being married for years now." Evelyn scowled and thrust her hands into the pockets of the coat. "As if *her* wanting me to marry you should make it happen." She flung one arm out. "As if everyone in Rubyville should have input into whom I marry." She stomped her foot. "It should be *my* decision."

Aaron brushed back his hair and looked down the empty sidewalk in front of the two-storied brick addition of the school. "I thought we had this all worked out, Evelyn. As soon as you graduate in a couple of months, we are going to be married. I purchased that nice little house next to the mercantile for us to live in."

"I know all that!" she sputtered and scowled. "But those are *your* plans, not mine. I keep telling you that you are more like a brother to me, Aaron. I love you…but like a brother, not a husband."

"You can't know that. You've never been married. You will come to love me in time…just as I love you." He reached out and put a hand on her shoulder. "You'll see."

Evelyn ducked away and crossed the street, her breaths showing as white puffs.

Aaron looked each way of the dirt road and followed Evelyn. "You are being silly. Can't you see that you have everything right here in Rubyville? All your family lives here…this is your home. I will be a good husband to you and I will take very good care of you, Evelyn."

Evelyn spun around, her eyes flashing. "I *love* Rubyville and I *love* my family…but that doesn't mean I have to stay here forever…or…or not see any other part of the world." She flung out her hands. "I'm young and I want to explore what options I have. That doesn't mean I hate it here. Just that I want to live a little bit before settling down with someone. Why can't you understand that, Aaron?"

He hung his head. "I don't understand it. I can't think of myself living anywhere else, or doing anything else with my life." He looked at her, his green eyes turning to pools. "I want you beside me, Evelyn. In my dreams, you've always been there, working alongside me at the mercantile, taking care of our home, and having our children. We can still go fishing, have picnics together, and enjoy one another just as we always have. That doesn't have to change when we are married."

Evelyn closed her eyes and sighed. "I'm so very tired of arguing about this with you and my mother." She opened her eyes and stared up at the blustery sky, shaking her head. "Neither of you are going to change your minds about my life."

"I know you want adventure and excitement…but you don't have to leave Rubyville for that." He gave her a smile. "It was fairly exciting when the Paine's cow got loose and ran across the hotel porch."

Evelyn returned the smile. "Yes, that did liven up Rubyville for a few hours. Thank goodness it was during the winter." She laughed. "Can you imagine the ruckus it would have caused if guests had been sitting on the porch at the time?"

"There would have been more than a few overturned rockers." Aaron reached out and touched her chin. "You are so pretty with your red cheeks. We'd better have that hot cocoa and get you warmed up."

Evelyn shook her head and took her school books from Aaron. "I'm not feeling well…a bad headache coming on. I'm just going to go home." She gave him a weak smile. "I do appreciate you coming to the school…I just want some time alone. I think really well when I'm walking…by myself." She turned and strode away.

Aaron stood on the sidewalk, his bony shoulders slumped in his too-large jacket. He watched the tall, slender form until she crossed the street, passed the hotel, and entered the park. He shook his head and walked back to the mercantile.

EVELYN DROPPED HER BOOKS upon the table and unbuttoned her wool box coat. "I'm home, Mama!" She hung her coat upon the hook by the kitchen door.

Helen entered the cheery red and white room, her blonde hair tied up in a scarf, a large apron covering her house dress. "I stopped by the mercantile earlier today and Mr. Darby said he was going to take you by the hotel on your way home from school." She glanced at the red, electric clock upon the wall. "You barely had time to walk home."

Evelyn opened the refrigerator. "I finished the milk last night—"

"Yes, and Beth dropped some more off on her way by this morning, as well as some eggs. She was going in to help Ellen at the hotel. They wanted to get some baking done before the weekend." Helen folded the dirty side in of the cloth she held. "I haven't started supper yet. I wanted to finish the dusting first. I thought you would be with Mr. Darby for awhile. He was so excited to see you after school when I spoke with him."

Evelyn set the pitcher of milk on the table and went for a glass. "Are there any cookies left? I'm absolutely famished."

Helen rolled her blue eyes to the ceiling. "Of course there are cookies left. You are the only one that eats them, my dear." She set the dust cloth on the counter and handed Evelyn the cookie tin. "Don't go and spoil your supper."

"I think that's just something all mothers are supposed to say." Evelyn laughed and took four peanut butter cookies from the tin and replaced the lid.

Helen set her hands upon her hips. "Are you going to tell me what happened with Mr. Darby? You can only avoid me so long."

"I told him he should ask Cynthia Rowe out on a date. She's had a crush on him for ages." Evelyn pulled out a chair and sat down.

Helen put one hand to her apron-ruffled chest. "You didn't! How could you be so cruel and tease him like that?"

Evelyn looked at her mother and returned to dipping her cookie in the milk. "I wasn't teasing, Mama. I *really* think he should ask her out. They have much in common and Cynthia adores him."

"And just where would that leave you, my dear?" Helen went to the sink and washed her hands. She dried them on the towel hanging above the porcelain counter.

"It would leave me free to enjoy my life for awhile and not worry about what Aaron wants. Aaron would be happy, Cynthia would be happy…it works for everyone concerned." Evelyn started on her second cookie, bobbing it up and down in the glass.

Helen took a bowl from the cupboard and set it down on the counter with a *clank* that filled the room. "Mr. Darby would certainly *not* be happy!" Helen turned to her daughter. "He's in love with *you*, Evelyn. He can't just switch his feelings to someone else because you say so."

Evelyn popped the last bite of the cookie in her mouth and crossed her arms upon the table. "Exactly, Mama! That's what I keep trying to tell you and Aaron. I can't just love him because you tell me to."

Helen strode to the pantry and returned with the flour canister. "I think you are just being stubborn. You care about that young man and you know it. You just want him to chase after you and make you feel important and loved."

Evelyn looked down at her arms. "I *do* care about Aaron, Mama...and that's why I want what's best for him. Being married to me won't work. We will both be unhappy...he just doesn't know it yet."

Helen cocked her hip and placed a hand upon it. "Every marriage has its ups and downs. No marriage can be perfect. Your love should grow for one another over the years."

Evelyn's eyes slid to her mother. "I agree with you and I understand what you are saying...but how could you know that, Mama? You were only married a couple years."

Helen dropped her hand and faced the counter. She opened the flour canister. "Your father and I were married almost four years, to be exact. It wasn't always perfect, but we worked on our problems...usually."

"Which is the reason father killed himself...he was so happy with you?" Evelyn spoke the words soft and low.

Helen spun around, knocking the canister of flour to the floor. White drifted across the red linoleum like snow. Helen raised her finger, one red nail pointed at Evelyn. "First of all, your father did *not* kill himself. I don't know who told you such a lie."

Evelyn blushed pink and lowered her head. "I found the newspaper clipping in your drawer along with the letter my father wrote to you."

Helen narrowed her eyes. "You were going through my drawers? How could you?"

"I was looking for the scissors the other day. They weren't in the sewing basket," Evelyn shrugged, "so I opened the drawers beside your bed. The paper was right there on top, not hidden or anything."

Helen crossed her arms. "So you took it upon yourself to just read it? What else have you rummaged through, trying to find out information?"

Evelyn sighed. "Nothing, Mama. You know I'm not like that. But the kids at school have always said my father killed himself. It's no secret in Rubyville."

Helen slammed her open palm on the kitchen counter. "Please save me from these small-town gossips and maligners! They would rather share a lie than the truth…because it is far more interesting and does more damage. Just look at all the problems it leads to."

Evelyn bit her lip and took a sip of milk.

Oh, Mama. Is Rubyville really the problem?

Chapter Two

EVELYN PULLED THE COVERS high against her shoulders and snuggled down into her bed. She turned her head, the rag curls digging into her temple. The moonlight streamed across her bed, the bare branches of the trees surrounding the house dark forms against the silver. The wind moaned, rattling a loose window pane. She closed her eyes and cleared her thoughts.

Dear Heavenly Father, here I am again, just like I am every night, begging You to send someone into my life that I can love for all eternity. Someone that loves me just the same. As You and I have discussed before, it's not Aaron. He is a fine young man, and he would be a wonderful husband and father...just not my husband and father to my children. Please help Mama understand that before it's too late. As I've told You before...he doesn't even have to be that handsome. Evelyn rolled her closed eyes. *Alright, it would help if he was a bit handsome and taller than me and that he loved You as I do. I should probably make that last item the most important criteria if I expect help from You.* Evelyn smiled. *But You understand me as no one else does. You have been here every night of my life, ready to listen to me.* She gave a laugh. *Sometimes You listen to me for hours and I'm sure You wish that You weren't God and didn't have to.*

Evelyn's eyes popped open. *I take that last part back. It was blasphemous...but You do understand.*

Evelyn turned on her side, adjusting the rag curls. She rubbed her temple. *I also hate having to wear these silly things each night. I have hair that is stick-straight, as You know, and I should be able to wear it just the way it is. Mama is such a bore when it comes to wanting me to look just the same as everyone else. What is wrong with someone being exactly who they are and not putting on airs? And speaking* of 'airs'...what is wrong with people thinking my father killed himself? If he had taken Your Son, Jesus Christ, as his Savior, he is in Heaven with You, no matter how he died. Helen scratched her head. *I do understand that it is not a good thing to take your own life...that is up to You...but it doesn't change Your Word to us. Just as You say in Acts 16:31, 'Believe on the Lord Jesus Christ, and thou shalt be saved, and thy house.' You don't ask us to spin around three times and wiggle our nose.* Evelyn rolled her eyes again. *There I go...being disrespectful once again. But You understand me, and You know I need You to talk to.*

Evelyn sighed. *Everyone feels sorry for me...sorry that I didn't have a father growing up. What they don't understand is that I had You. You have taken care of me, and Mama has as well. Sure, it would have been lovely to get to know my father, and I do miss him some days. But I will get to know him in Heaven...why can't that be good enough? So anyway...I'd better get some sleep. But remember, please let my father know I miss him and I will be there someday. Please provide me with someone to share my life with and someone for Aaron. I personally think it's Cynthia Rowe...but You know her, and she can be rather stinky at times. But if she will let You, You can work on her as well. Take care of Mama...and please...help her to relax! We are only here for a short time and we should enjoy what we have. Just let her love me as her daughter and not worry so much about my future. It's in Your hands. In Jesus name...Amen.*

Evelyn closed her eyes, smiling with the thought of the future God had planned for her.

THE LATE-MAY SUN GLOWED high in the sky as Evelyn entered the mercantile, the bell giving a cheerful jingle. She walked along the shelves at the front of the store, peeking around the end at the couple conversing at the long walnut counter.

Cynthia patted the back of her perky white hat upon her black hair and laughed at Aaron's comment. She reached across the counter to place her gloved hand upon his arm. "Mr. Darby, you say the funniest things. I could listen to you for hours...just hours."

"Well, Miss Rowe, I think that would be a great waste of your day." Aaron placed the items on the counter into a large paper bag.

"Oh, I don't think it would be a waste at all." Cynthia set her small purse upon the length of wood and took out the proper amount of coins.

Evelyn sauntered up to the counter and braced her jean-clad hip upon it, leaning one elbow on the scratched, dark wood. "Well, if it isn't Cynthia Rowe." Evelyn gave her a smile and turned to Aaron.

Aaron grinned. "I didn't think I would get to see you until tonight. I thought you would be doing all those things women do to get ready for the prom."

Cynthia chuckled, her eyes sweeping over Evelyn, from scuffed saddle shoes to scarf-covered hair. "I don't think Evelyn knows what needs to be done to get ready for a dance. You may be taking her just as she is now." She tittered once more.

Evelyn smiled. "Now, now… don't you be worrying that empty head of yours, Cynthia." She raised a brow. "You must remember the beautiful dress your mother made for me? You may have even sewn some of it yourself."

Cynthia snapped her purse shut and hung the short handle over her arm. She reached for the brown bag.

Evelyn turned to Aaron. "I really think you should help *Miss* Rowe with her groceries, Aaron. That is probably much too heavy for her."

Aaron stuttered and stumbled over his words, looking between the two young women. "Well, there is no one to watch the store…I think she has…do you have…" Aaron turned to Cynthia, his face mottled red.

Cynthia smiled. "I'm just walking over to mother's shop. I told her I would help with a couple dresses needed for a wedding next weekend before I…" she glanced at Evelyn, "get ready for my date. I'm sure I will be alright."

Evelyn grabbed the bag. "I know Aaron doesn't mind a bit. It will give him a chance to breathe some fresh air after being inside this stuffy building all day." She nodded with her head to get Aaron from behind the counter. She met him at the end and deposited the bag in his arms. "I will watch the store."

"But, I really shouldn't leave—"

Evelyn patted Aaron's shoulder. "I'll be just fine. If someone needs something that I can't handle, well, they will just have to wait for you. That's all there is to it." Evelyn walked to the double doors at the front of the store and opened one, waving them through. "I'm sure you won't be long."

"No, no I won't be long. I will walk Miss Rowe right over and then I'll return." Aaron waited until Cynthia reached the steps leading to the storefront. He leaned over and whispered against Evelyn's ear. "I don't know what you're doing, Evelyn, but it won't make me change my mind about you."

Evelyn shrugged. "Whatever you say…it's just good that you are helping someone in need." She waved him through the door. "Go on now…you don't want to wait until there are a flood of customers. I can handle one or two with no problem…but…" she raised a brow.

Aaron gritted his teeth. "I will be talking with you when I return."

"I'll be here," she sang out. "Good-bye Cynthia…and thanks so much for the lovely work you did on my dress. I'm sure I'll be the Belle of the Ball."

Cynthia threw a dark glance over her shoulder, then smiled at Aaron as he came alongside her.

Evelyn rolled her eyes skyward. *I'm really not a very nice person at times, Father. But if a job needs to be done…you might as well get it over with. I just wish Cynthia Rowe didn't rattle my bones the way she does.*

EVELYN SPUN IN FRONT of the long mirror, the full skirt of the pink princess dress lifting with the motion. She stopped and cocked her head to one side, adjusting the short puff sleeves. Evelyn smiled at her reflection. "If you could only see me now, *Miss* Rowe. I think you would be whistling a different tune."

Helen's voice carried up the stairs. "Evelyn, dear, Mr. Darby is here. You don't want to keep him waiting."

"I will be right down, Mama," Evelyn replied. She glanced back at the mirror, smoothing the hair from her temples into the small pink roses positioned at the sides of her head. Her hands fluffed the printed netting of the gown and grabbed the matching shawl from her bed as she rushed from the room.

She took a deep breath at the top of the stairs and attempted a regal descent. Her smile widened as she noticed Aaron's eyes light up. *Success!*

Aaron held out his hand as she reached the bottom step. "You are beautiful, Miss Hanover...absolutely beautiful." His green eyes swept over her, pausing at her chest. "I...I have a corsage for you...but maybe...maybe your mother should—"

Helen held out her hand. "I would be delighted to pin it for you, Mr. Darby." She took the tiny bouquet of flowers out of the box. "Look at this, Evelyn. I've never seen such a pretty array of flowers, and they match your dress perfectly." She pinned the flowers just below Evelyn's left collarbone and stepped back to admire the display.

Evelyn smoothed a petal. "Thank you, Aaron...they are very pretty. You remembered that I love roses." She tilted her head and sniffed. "They smell lovely, too."

"You didn't need the roses, you already smelled good before that..." Aaron cleared his throat and looked away. "Maybe we should be going. We don't want to be late, after all."

Evelyn smiled. "No, we wouldn't want that." She gave her mother a hug. "Thank you for the beautiful dress, Mama. I really feel like a princess in it."

Helen patted her daughter's back. "You are beautiful, my dear. Much prettier than those blue jeans you insist on wearing around the house." She gave a wink and opened the front door. "Now scoot, you two. Be sure to be home before midnight."

Evelyn raised a red brow and looked at Aaron. "Another whole hour granted. Whatever will we do with the time?"

Aaron stammered and blushed. "Thank...thank you, Mrs. Hanover. I'll be sure to have her home on time."

Helen smiled. "I know you will, Mr. Darby. I would trust my daughter with no one else."

"EVERY TIME I RIDE with you in this auto, I'm amazed at how well you take care of it, Aaron Darby. Why, it looks brand new." Evelyn slid her hand over the blue-upholstered seat. "You've had it for a long time now."

Aaron patted the dashboard. "Four years and counting. I think I can get a lot of use out of this old Plymouth. They're a great automobile in my opinion, especially this '39 model. It's built to last." He turned the long vehicle from the road leading to Rubyville and accelerated. "But your mother's automobile is the best one in town. It's a real beauty, I must say."

Evelyn nodded. "She loves her convertibles. I was a bit disappointed when she purchased the one she has now. I hate the grill on the front. It looks like someone gritting their teeth."

Aaron chuckled. "It's an automobile, not a person. How can it 'grit its teeth'?"

Evelyn shrugged. "I don't know, but it just looks mean to me. I adored her old Chrysler New Yorker. It just looked friendlier somehow. But the red interior is so pretty on this newest one." She rolled her eyes. "Excuse me, Mama calls it red tartan plaid. " She laughed as she watched the fields fly by.

"Well, for a girl, you sure have an opinion on automobiles." Aaron glanced at her. "Or are you just trying to keep the conversation from what you did this afternoon at the mercantile?"

Evelyn dropped her jaw and widened her eyes. "Now why would I do that? I didn't do a thing wrong today at the mercantile. Cynthia needed help, and you know it, Aaron Darby."

Aaron turned his eyes back to the road. "*Helping* her wasn't what I was talking about. Pushing us together at every opportunity is the problem." He gave her a sideways look. "You know what you're doing. I told you I wasn't interested."

"Well, you should be. Not only does she adore you, she knows all about running a business in Rubyville. You both are the perfect match." She laid a hand on Aaron's arm. "If you were married to Cynthia, we *all* could be friends. She wouldn't always be trying to push me aside to get to you."

Aaron shrugged her hand away and brushed at his temple. "*We* are on a date right now…just you and me. Please let me enjoy it, Evelyn. I don't know why you keep bringing this up."

Evelyn crossed her hands in her lap among the pink billows of material. "Actually, *I* didn't bring it up...*you* did. I was very content to talk about automobiles all the way to the dance."

Aaron smiled. "Alright, I will give you that." He looked at her, his eyes caressing her face. "I just wanted to say once again how beautiful you are tonight. You will be the prettiest girl there, I'm sure." He turned back to the road. "Just remember that you're already taken. You know us getting married is the right thing to do. Our parents are happy about it and I think you would be excited if you would just allow it." He looked away from the road once again. "I love you, Evelyn. We are going to be very happy together. We will have the very best kind of marriage...one formed out of a very long and special friendship."

Evelyn sighed. "If you say so. I will try to not bring it up again." She raised a finger at him. "But just remember. I love you as well, but like a brother. It's going to take me a long time to think differently of you, Aaron Darby." She clasped her hands once again. "And you need to keep your eyes on the road, not me. We are going to be a big pile in the ditch, and I know *that* will ruin your plans."

Aaron laughed. "I will, if you slide a bit closer. You seem *very* far away."

Evelyn lifted her chin. "I'm perfectly fine where I am. You need to concentrate on your driving. We aren't married yet, and we shouldn't be doing things to tempt you." She stared out the window and mumbled, "If Cynthia were here, she would be sitting in your lap, no invitation needed."

"What was that?" Aaron tilted his head toward her.

"Nothing...just humming a little tune. I can't wait to hear the music tonight." Evelyn fluffed the skirt of her dress and loudly hummed.

"Well, it should be good. I've heard the band before and they were great." He signaled and turned at the stop sign. "I'm rather excited to be going to your prom, since I didn't attend mine."

"I told you to go, if you remember. Your senior prom only happens once." She sighed and stared out the window. "I wish our school had a big enough gymnasium to hold the prom attendees." Her eyes slid to Aaron. "But it *is* exciting to get out of Rubyville for the evening." Her eyes twinkled. "I wonder how many people will be there. Several of the girls, Cynthia included, were going with young men from Emporia."

Aaron nodded. "Yes, I heard all about Bill Caruthers this afternoon."

Evelyn laughed. "Cynthia was obviously trying to make you jealous."

Aaron gave her a smile. "Well, it didn't work. I'm very happy for Cynthia and Bill, and I hope they have a very long and fruitful life together."

Evelyn pursed her lips and shook her head. "I wouldn't count on it, my friend." She looked down at her corsage and adjusted the ribbon. "You know, I really love Rubyville and I'm happy that I grew up there. But," she gave a little frown, "there are times I just wish for a little more."

"More what?"

She shrugged. "I don't even know. I have a beautiful house to live in, family and friends, and a church that I love attending. That all should be enough...but it just isn't at times."

Aaron slowed as he neared a curve. "I know it's more than sufficient for me. I don't ever want to live anywhere else on this old earth. I have everything I need right in Rubyville, Kansas." He gave her a wink. "And soon, it will be even better."

Evelyn rolled her eyes and leaned her elbow on the armrest. "Don't you want to see other places...just visit? Aren't you curious about the ocean or the mountains?"

"Not really. I read about them in school. I don't see the need to go there just to see them. Too many choices make a person discontent with what they have." He grinned at her. "I keep telling you I'm very content with everything in my life."

Evelyn wrinkled the side of her mouth. "I know, I know." She raised her hand and propped her chin in the palm. "I just want to try a bit of everything. It's hot in Kansas in the summer, but I bet it's even hotter in the desert. Lake George was beautiful when we visited a few years ago, the water deep and cold. I cannot even imagine what the ocean must be like. And the Adirondack Mountains were so pretty and green, roads twisting among the trees. The Rocky Mountains must be spectacular."

Aaron shrugged. "We can have a plan to visit all those places at some point in time. Maybe each summer we can travel to a different destination. It will be a learning experience for our children, too."

Evelyn smiled. "That would be nice…better than never seeing them."

"A little excitement in that reply would be welcome." Aaron turned into a large, crowded parking lot and found a space for the blue Plymouth.

Evelyn leaned forward, her eyes scanning the automobiles and the brightly-dressed girls. She turned to Aaron and laid a hand on his arm, her green eyes dancing. "Isn't this just swell? There are *so* many people here!"

Aaron gulped. "I see that. I didn't know it was going to be such a big deal." His eyes slid to her. "We can always just grab a soda. The drive over was really nice, and I bet the drive back will be just as good, if not better."

Evelyn leaned back and stared at her date. "Don't be a fat-head, Aaron Darby! This is the best night ever! I can't wait to get in there. I don't have to be home until midnight and I intend to have *fun*." She gestured to her door. "Now you had better let me out before I just do it myself. That won't be ladylike at all."

Aaron adjusted his black bow tie and took a deep breath. "Alright…but just remember, if it weren't for you, I'd be headed back to Rubyville right now."

Chapter Three

RICHARD KING INSERTED A finger into the turndown collar of his shirt and pulled it from his damp neck. He raised his voice over the music and leaned down slightly toward his friend. "I bet it's about one hundred degrees in here. I'm dressed up like a penguin and about to keel over. I can't believe I agreed to be a third wheel for you."

Bill Caruthers looked his friend up and down. "You *are* spiffy in my old duds. Nice bow tie." He nodded his head toward the corner of the large gymnasium. "There's a fan over there. Stand in front of it for awhile. I'll wait here for Cynthia…you know how long it takes a girl to go to the powder room."

"Sounds good to me." Richard's blue eyes scanned the crowded room. "It'll give me a chance to see what the options are."

"Christopher Columbus! Look at the dish that just came in." Bill nodded toward the double doors at the end of the room. "I haven't seen hair that color…*ever*."

"What are you looking at, buddy? There must be fifty girls in this room." Richard raised his chiseled chin, looking over the couples dancing.

"The redhead with the rather dopey fellow. She's wearing a pink dress."

Richard stuffed his hands into his pockets, scrunching the black jacket he wore. "You know I find carrot-tops unattractive. They are physically unappealing and they usually have a rotten attitude to go along with the hair. I'll be in the corner, waiting for a blonde or brunette to interest me."

Bill shrugged. "Suit yourself. But if I wasn't here with Cynthia, I would get to know that one. I bet she has green peepers that will grab the soul right out of you."

Richard chuckled. "You never cease to amaze me, my friend. Every girl is better than the last one."

Bill grinned. "Life is good, isn't it?"

Richard shook his head and made his way around the perimeter of the room. He stopped near the fan and sighed. *Finally, a breath of air! Whoever thought of putting on all these clothes, gathering a bunch of sweating bodies in one room, and then dancing must have been crazy! There has to be better ways to spend an evening with a girl.* He smoothed back his blond hair and wiped the perspiration from his brow.

He watched as Cynthia returned to Bill, sliding an arm through his. She looked up at him, her pretty face powdered white, red lips smiling. The blue dress she wore complimented her black hair. *Now there's an option. Petite, with black hair...and a nice face too. You can't beat that. Maybe I'll sneak in a few dances with her while Bill is off sampling this fine assortment of dancing 'butterflies'.* He smirked, his eyes flitting from one pretty girl to the next.

He leaned one shoulder against the wall as he noticed the dopey fellow and redhead stop to talk with Bill and Cynthia. The black-haired girl blushed and pulled her arm from Bill's, laying it against her ruffled bodice. She laughed, gazing up at the tall, stick-thin fellow. She moved closer to him, laying her hand upon his arm. He moved away, placing a large hand upon the redhead's back. The redhead stepped forward. She smiled when Bill said something. *Change your partners and do-si-do.*

Richard grinned as he watched the exchange and then felt his heart triple beat as the green eyes turned to him. *Jeepers! Bill was right. Those eyes are like nothing I've ever seen. They've snatched my very heart away...from across the room.* He felt his heart begin to thud, echoing through his head. *Wow!*

"I'VE NEVER SEEN YOU look so handsome, Mr. Darby," Cynthia gushed as she placed her hand upon Aaron's arm. "You really should dress up more often."

Aaron slid his hand to Evelyn's back. "That would be rather inappropriate at the mercantile, Miss Rowe."

Evelyn moved forward. "It's very nice to meet you, Mr. Caruthers. Aaron here was just telling me that Cynthia spoke of you incessantly when she was in the mercantile earlier."

Bill glanced at Cynthia and raised a brow. "I will have to give Miss Rowe more interesting topics to discuss with others. I'm afraid I'm rather a bore in certain areas. My friend over there is always saying so." He nodded to the corner where Richard stood.

Evelyn smiled as her eyes followed the gesture. Her breath caught as she tracked the long length of the blond-haired man leaning against the wall. He was ruggedly handsome, with a sharp jaw line leading to high cheekbones in a tanned face. The small dent in his chin took her breath. She pulled her eyes away and looked at her date. "I would love some punch, Aaron. It's incredibly hot in here." She fanned her face with her hand as her eyes wandered back to the tall man in the corner.

Cynthia's eyes sparked. "I'll go with you, Mr. Darby. I'm rather parched myself."

Bill stared at his date. "I would be delighted to get you something, Miss Rowe. Mr. Darby and I will return in just a moment."

Cynthia waved a hand at Bill. "Don't be silly. Mr. Darby won't mind a bit if I go with him." She smiled at Aaron. "We'll be right back." She looped her arm through Aaron's and pulled him to the punch table.

Evelyn raised her brows and clasped her hands. "Cynthia Rowe can be quite *persuasive* when she wants to be." *Or just plain obnoxious.*

Bill tilted his head. "If I didn't know any better, I would tell you to be careful with your date."

Evelyn laughed. "And I could say the same to you." She looked over at her date and Cynthia at the punch table. "But no worries with me and Aaron. We have been friends for a *very* long time. We are more like brother and sister." *And if I have anything to say about it, we'll stay that way.*

Bill grinned. "Really?" he replied slowly, stretching out the word. "Then you wouldn't deny me a dance?" He looked out over the crowd. "This is a slow one. It will give me a chance to get to know you better."

"I would be delighted, Mr. Caruthers." Evelyn smiled and followed him into the crowd of dancers. They took position and began to move slowly to the music. She glanced over Bill's right shoulder, and the slate-blue eyes of the handsome man in the corner captured her own and her heart beat faster.

"Jeepers, you're tall for a woman."

His comment pulled her back. She looked at him across the small space between their bodies. "Yes, but it has its advantages. All the women in my family are tall."

"Well, it looks good on you." He cleared his throat. "I would assume you are a senior."

"Yes, I will graduate in just a couple of weeks." Evelyn gave him a smile, her eyes seeming to find the tall man in the corner each time she glanced over the shoulder of her dance partner. "What about you?"

"A couple of weeks, as well. Richard and I have great plans for our summer of freedom." He laughed.

"Richard? Is he the friend in the corner?" Evelyn's eyes slid there once again. The corner was empty. Her heart dropped as her eyes sought to focus on the crowd as they continued to twirl. *Where'd he go?*

"Yes, he is. We have been pretty much inseparable for most of our lives. He keeps me from making too many bad decisions. Much more level-headed than I, I hate to say." The music ended and a drum beat began. Bill shook his head as he let go of her hand. "I'm going to have to sit this one out, doll. I love this Benny Goodman tune, but it's too fast for me."

"Wait! I know this song...I *love* this!" Evelyn's eyes sparkled as she looked at her former dance partner, clasping her hands in front of her chest. "Won't you give it a try? We can dance slowly."

"May *I* have this dance?"

Evelyn turned at the sound of the voice, catching the slate-blue eyes as they swept over her.

The handsome face gave a slow smile. "Do you know the Lindy Hop?"

Evelyn laughed. "I sure do, if practicing in front of my bedroom mirror counts!"

"Let's see if it does." The dimple in the strong chin deepened as he smiled and pulled her into the dance.

CYNTHIA CROSSED HER ARMS and drummed her nails. "I didn't know our *Miss Hanover* could dance so well."

"Yes, it seems she has some talents I was unaware of." Aaron observed the tall couple on the dance floor, just one of a few dancing to the popular tune. The other couples had formed a large circle, clapping and encouraging the dancers. "She *is* really good."

Bill sauntered over to the pair watching the dancers. "Richard has been into jive for awhile now. He'll be happy to have found someone to share his hobby." Bill took out his handkerchief and mopped his brow. "They're a good-looking couple."

Aaron shot him a dark glance. "That won't be possible. Miss Hanover and I are to be married this summer...next month to be exact."

Cynthia put a hand to her chest with a gasp. "Next month...why Evelyn doesn't even have a ring yet."

"She will." Aaron narrowed his eyes as the music ended.

THE LAUGHING COUPLE WALKED over to the trio as the band leader announced they would be taking a fifteen-minute break.

"That was so much fun!" Evelyn laughed, breathing heavily as she patted her jaw line with the back of her hand.

"Better than in front of the mirror?" Richard gave her a wink, perspiration dripping along the sides of his face.

"*Much* better!" Evelyn blushed further on her pink face.

"You two were cookin' with helium. You just about cleared the dance floor and had the place to yourselves." Bill smiled and looked down at Cynthia. "Why don't we get some more punch while the band is taking a break?" He offered his arm.

Richard's eyes slid to the stern lines of Aaron's face and then to Evelyn. "Well, thank you for the dance, Miss...?" He raised one golden brow.

"Miss Hanover, Evelyn Barton Hanover," she supplied, looking down at her clasped hands. "You are more than welcome...I haven't had so much fun in...in ages." She glanced up. "You are very good."

He gave her a wink. "Lots of practice." He scanned the room. "I'm going to step outside for a few minutes and see if it's any cooler out there." He nodded to the couple and walked away.

Evelyn's eyes followed him as long as she could without turning her head. She looked at Aaron. "Have you had a chance to dance yet?"

He stared at her. "Of course not. How would I have been able to, with my date…my *fiancé*…out on the dance floor with other men?"

Evelyn bit her lip. "I'm sorry, Aaron. I just assumed you would ask another girl to dance if I was asked by someone else. You know I don't go to many dances. This is rather new for me."

"You sure wouldn't know it. I didn't realize you could dance the Lindy Hop." Aaron gave her a smile. "I'm not angry with you…just disappointed, I guess. But you looked really good out there. You can really cut a rug, as they say."

Evelyn smiled. "Thank you." Her eyes swept the room. "I'm going to the powder room to freshen up a bit. I'll be right back." She glided away, the skirt of her pink dress billowing around her.

She opened the door and walked to the long counter, grateful that the small room was empty. She looked at her reflection in the mirror and gasped. Her hair hung in ringlets down her back and over her shoulders, the tight rag curls long since gone. Her eyes sparkled in the harsh light of the room, complimenting her rosy cheeks. *Why, I look almost pretty, red hair and all.* She dampened a towel and pressed the cool cloth to her temple and cheeks, then over her throat. She smoothed the bodice of the dress and straightened the limp roses in her corsage.

Blue eyes beckoned her and the handsome face flashed into her head. Her heart began to beat rapidly, and she placed one hand there.

He's the one, Father! I know he is!

RICHARD UNTIED THE BLACK bow tie at his neck and stripped it from his collar. *I'll have to have Bill tie that again, I suppose.* He unbuttoned the top few buttons of his white shirt as he reached his automobile in the high school parking lot. He opened the door of the black Ford and tossed his jacket and bow tie upon the worn seat. Slamming the door shut, he propped one foot on the running board and braced his elbow on the roof of the 1932 two-door. His hands smoothed the back of his damp hair as he looked up at the stars twinkling over the three-storied brick building. *Oh Father, you do have a sense of humor. The first girl that I've taken a shine to, and she's a redhead.*

He grinned. *But she sure can swing a wing. And she's not too hard on the eyes, either.* He shook his head and braced his chin on the back of his hand. *She's downright gorgeous, as a matter of fact. Those green peepers just about snatched my soul, just like old Bill said they would.*

He closed his eyes, bringing Evelyn's face to mind. *Rosy cheeks that you just want to reach out and touch, that long neck just beckoning a kiss…* his eyes flashed open and he quickly scanned the parked automobiles. *You're headed for trouble, Richard King.*

"Here you are!" Bill sauntered up, opening and closing his black jacket. "It feels good out here. It's stifling in that gymnasium." He looked up at his friend. "You aren't leaving already are you… after just one dance?"

Richard flashed Bill a grin. "We were really knockin' it out, weren't we?"

Bill placed his hands on his hips. "You were, and that boyfriend of hers wasn't too happy about it. You should have seen the look on his face."

Richard chuckled. "I was much too busy looking at hers. She's gorgeous…absolutely gorgeous."

Bill shook his head. "You're clobbered already! Don't go and do that, Richard, old pal. Nothing good will come of it. That dish is spoken for. The drip she's with was telling Cynthia and me that they're getting married next month."

Richard dropped his foot from the running board and straightened. "Next month! Why she's not even wearing a ring."

"That's what Cynthia pointed out and he assured her that she would have one soon. You're on a track going nowhere." Bill scratched the back of his head. "I can see your interest…but you need to ask someone else to dance. She's taken."

Richard shoved his hands in his pockets and scuffed his foot on the ground. "I know you're going to think I'm crazy…but I'm going to marry that girl. I'd do it tonight if I could."

Bill grabbed his friend by the shoulders and looked up at him. "I'd slap some sense into you if I thought it would help! You *are* crazy! You can't just up and marry a girl you just met! You won't even graduate high school for a couple of weeks. I know your home life hasn't been the best over the years, but getting married to someone you don't know won't make *that* any better." He let go of Richard's shoulders and set his hands on his hips once more. He paced the length of the black Ford. "You don't even know her."

Richard opened the door and retrieved his bow tie and jacket from the seat. He placed the strip of material around his neck and buttoned his shirt. "Hey, tie this for me. I'm going back in."

Bill smacked his forehead. "You can't even tie your own bow tie but you're going to get married." He flashed his hand up and down in front of Richard. "The duds you're wearing are mine. You don't have a thing to your name besides that old jalopy you rattle around in." He pointed to the automobile.

Richard tilted his head. "Tie it please. I don't have all night."

"No, you have the rest of your life, and you're going to mess it all up in just *one* night!" Bill reached up and worked on the black tie.

"You should lower your voice. You're going to draw attention over here." Richard's lips twitched with his words.

"I should have the police lock you up. Keep you from making the mistake of your life." Bill pulled the ends of the bow, straightening it.

"I haven't asked her to marry me *yet*." Richard lowered his gaze.

Bill stepped back and shook his finger up at his friend. "And don't be doing it!"

"You're the one that pointed her out. I'm just taking your advice." Richard shrugged into his jacket.

"Yes, I said she was cute and *I* thought of taking a few spins around the floor with her. That's all! We have plans for this summer and they don't include a wife!" Bill lowered his voice. "Do you hear me?"

Richard chuckled. "I hear you." He headed toward the large building.

Bill rushed up to him and met him stride for stride, his shorter legs working overtime. "Where are you going…what are you doing?"

Richard gestured to the double doors. "I'm going to go back in there and find Miss Hanover...see if she will dance with me again."

"That's fine," Bill raised a finger and shook it at Richard, "but no conversations about marriage, or setting up a home together, having children, being in love—"

Richard stopped and grabbed Bill by the shoulders. "Relax, old pal. I'm the level-headed one...remember? I'm not going to do anything stupid."

Bill gulped and reached out, patting Richard's cheek. "Alright...I'm going to have to trust you on this one."

Richard grabbed Bill's wrist. "And stop that. People are going to think we're nuts."

Bill pulled at his wide, black satin lapels. "They wouldn't be far from the truth. At least one of us *is*."

Chapter Four

AARON TILTED HIS HEAD and spoke low against Evelyn's ear. "You're not having a bit of fun, are you?"

Evelyn sighed and pulled her eyes away from the tall, blond-haired man dancing with Cynthia. She pasted a smile on her face. "I'm having a wonderful time…just tired, I guess." Her eyes found the large clock upon the wall. "We had better start for home pretty soon. I don't want to be late."

"You won't be late. Your mother trusts me." Aaron gripped her waist tighter, as he laid his cheek against her hair. "You are probably worn out after that dance with Mr. King."

Evelyn pulled away, adjusting his hand upon her back. "Mr. King?"

Aaron nodded to where Cynthia danced. "Yes, the one you danced the Lindy Hop with. Cynthia told me his name was Richard King."

Well, Cynthia Rowe, for once you have some information that I care to hear. Evelyn smiled. "I don't think one fast dance wore me out."

Aaron rubbed his hand along her back. "I'm just happy you decided to spend the evening with me. It's been really nice being so close to you for so long."

Evelyn pulled away and clapped her hands with the other couples as the music ended. "You have been rather possessive all evening. I really couldn't accept any other invitations to dance."

Aaron smiled down at her. "That's just as it should be."

The band began playing again and Aaron reached for her.

"Excuse me, Miss Hanover. May I have this dance? I think this one will be much *calmer* than the last one." Richard lifted a corner of his mouth, his blue eyes darkening as he gazed at her.

Aaron took her hand in his. "Miss Hanover is with me tonight, Mr. King. We were just about to leave."

Evelyn's eyes looked up at Aaron and then slid to Richard as her heart beat quickened. "I would love to, Mr. King." She placed her hand in his. She looked down at his long, tanned fingers as they wrapped around her palm. *Oh my...his hand is so warm.* Her gaze slowly lifted to his eyes and she was pulled into their blue depths.

Richard smiled down at her, his right arm sliding around her waist as she placed her hand upon his upper right arm. He swung her into the melee of couples, leaving Aaron at the edge of the dance floor, a scowl upon his face. "Are you alright, Miss Hanover?"

She gave him a wide smile, her eyes sparkling. "I'm just fine...better than I have been all night."

He grinned. "Me too." His hand slid further along her back, his hand splaying across it.

Evelyn's breath hitched as the shivers traveled through her body. She moved her hand to his shoulder and stepped closer. "This new song is beautiful. I think it's going to be a favorite of mine."

Richard pressed her closer and spoke softly against her cheek. "I'm not familiar with the words. Do you know them?"

Evelyn swallowed and began singing along with the band. "I'm drifting...drifting...drifting away...drifting with you, to a place that is new. I'm drifting...drifting...drifting away...drifting with you, on an ocean so blue. Our lives are as one...have only begun. Let me hold you now, until the setting sun. I'm drifting...drifting...drifting away. Please follow me dear, to a place that is near. I'll love you 'til then, until eternity ends. I'm drift—"

She looked up at him and then dropped her gaze. "Well, that's how it goes. I got a little carried away...you probably didn't want me to sing as much as I did."

His eyes slid to her lips. "That was beautiful. You have a very good voice."

Her cheeks blushed pink. "It must be from all the years singing in our church choir. I love music."

Richard guided her to the center of the dance floor with sweeping circles in time with the band. His hand moved over her back, bringing her close to his long form. His dark eyes swept over her face and as the song came to a close, he lowered his head and pressed his lips against hers.

Evelyn closed her eyes and melted into him, her left hand going to the back of his neck. *My first kiss! It's so much better than I ever dreamed it would be. My heart feels as though it will stop beating, and then I fear it won't slow down. His lips are so soft and warm! I never want it to end!*

Richard pulled back and spoke against her lips, the kiss lingering there. "He's coming. I've kept you hidden so far, but we'd better start clapping ferociously for the band." He let her go and put his hands together as Aaron gained their section of the dance floor.

"Evelyn, we need to leave now so you are home on time." Aaron's eyes hardened as he looked at Richard. "Your friend Bill was looking for you a few minutes ago. It seemed urgent."

Richard's lips twitched and his eyes slid over Evelyn's face. "Thank you for letting me know...*kind sir.* Where is *home*, Miss Hanover?"

Aaron took Evelyn's hand and started walking. She turned back and called, "Rubyville. It's not hard to find."

RICHARD SHOVED HIS HANDS into his pockets and watched as Aaron pulled Evelyn from the room. She paused at the double doors, looking back, her eyes searching for him. He lifted one long arm in farewell and she flashed him a brilliant smile. *Rubyville has to be wonderful if you are there, Miss Hanover.* He took his hands from his pockets and weaved in and out of the dancers.

Bill met him just outside the doors. "You're still single, aren't you?"

Richard laughed. "For now. Do you know where Rubyville is?"

"Of course...that's where Cynthia's from. I picked her up and I'll be taking her home." Bill frowned. "It's a cute place, but not too big. Why do you ask?"

Richard clapped his hand upon Bill's shoulder. "I'd like to ride along when you take Miss Rowe home tonight."

Bill gaped at his friend. "What? That will kind of ruin the plans I had for Cynthia and me."

Richard gripped the shoulder. "You need to leave that girl alone. She has eyes only for that drip with Miss Hanover. Seems strange to me, but that's the way of it. You don't want to be messing with someone else's wife, old pal."

"Wife? What are you talking about? The only girl that Aaron Darby wants is the one *you're* chasing after, friend." Bill shook his head and shrugged away from Richard's grasp. He brushed the spot where Richard's hand had been. "Keep your mitts off me. You wrinkled my duds."

"So, we need to convince Miss Rowe that Mr. Darby is her perfect match and Miss Hanover is mine…although we don't need to let her in on that part." Richard stripped off his bow tie.

"I'm *not* tying that again tonight." Bill raised a finger at Richard. "So where does that leave me, if you have this all planned out?"

Richard shrugged. "You have the entire summer to figure that one out." Richard took off his jacket and slung it over his shoulder as they walked toward the automobiles. "You seem to attract the dames to you like flies." Richard looked around. "Speaking of which, where *is* your date?"

Bill sighed. "She's in the powder room again. I think she just goes in there to gossip with all the other girls."

"You just figured that one out?" Richard snorted.

They reached Bill's automobile. "Just remember…*you're* in the back seat. I'd like to at least try to hold her hand."

Richard tossed his jacket into the back seat of the 1947 Ford. "Fine by me…I need a nap anyway. You won't even know I'm there." He climbed into the back and sat down. "Remember not to drive like a crazy man in this jalopy. I wouldn't want to get sick." He cranked down the windows.

"You'd better not get sick. This is a brand new car…unlike your pile of rust." Bill slammed the back door shut. "I'm going to wait for Cynthia inside."

Richard shrugged as he unbuttoned his shirt and crossed his arms. He scrunched down on the seat and laid his head against the upholstery. "Even better for me…I can get started on my nap that much sooner."

"ARE YOU GOING TO give me the silent treatment the entire way home, Aaron Darby?" Evelyn draped the shawl across her shoulders and pulled it over her hair to keep the red strands from blowing in the wind.

Aaron's eyes watched as she covered her hair. "Do you want me to shut my window?"

Evelyn shook her head. "No, the air feels lovely. It was very hot in the gymnasium tonight."

"It *was* warm, but most of us weren't cavorting all evening like you were." He gripped the steering wheel, his knuckles white.

Evelyn sighed. "I danced *three* dances with someone other than you."

He nodded. "And two of them were with that Richard King."

Evelyn was thankful for the dark night as she sneaked a smile. "Yes, they were." She stared out the window, Richard's face reflected there. "I haven't been to many dances, but I think you are supposed to dance with others while you're there. That's considered polite."

"Well, I don't know what kind of world we live in if you take your fiancé to a dance and then she is off with other men all evening, being handled by them." He shook his head. "It doesn't seem right to me. But what do I know? I'm just some guy from a little town in the middle of Kansas."

Evelyn rolled her window down further. She closed her eyes and breathed deeply of the cooler night air. "First of all, I wasn't *handled* by anyone. Secondly, I'm not your fiancé, Aaron. Do I need to stand in the park gazebo and make an announcement? Maybe at church tomorrow?"

Aaron shifted down and pulled off the road. He turned to her. "Evelyn, we have to talk about this. We have had an agreement between the two of us for *years* now. I asked you to marry me at *least* two years ago."

Evelyn opened her eyes and twisted to face him. "Yes, you did ask me two years ago. I told you I was only sixteen and I didn't want to think of marrying anyone at that time. I wanted to finish school first."

"So we agreed to wait until you graduated." Aaron set his elbow on the open window.

Evelyn shook her head. "You and my mother kept talking about it and encouraging it, Aaron. But I don't want to marry you. I think God has other plans for me."

Aaron scowled and leaned his temple on his hand. "So now God doesn't want you to marry me, either."

Evelyn smiled. "You've known since we were in grade school together that I talk with God very frequently about my life and the decisions I make. Why wouldn't I consult Him about my future husband?"

"It isn't like He answers you and tells you what to do next." Aaron shook his head.

"I can't believe you just said that, Aaron Darby!" She slapped the seat. "He always answers me."

Aaron snorted and pushed the hair out of his eyes. "Now you are going to say you have long conversations with Him."

Evelyn lowered her head. "Actually I do…pretty much every evening when I go to bed, and often during the day. No, He doesn't physically speak to me in a voice, but through prayer and reading His Word, He guides me and directs me. I know what He expects of me." She shook her head. "I'm very disappointed in you, Aaron. We've attended the same church every Sunday our entire lives. I thought you understood this and wanted to live your life the same way."

Aaron dropped his hand. "I have accepted Christ as my Savior, and I know I'm going to Heaven when I die. I know I should act a certain way and do things in a way pleasing to Him, but sometimes it's just too hard, Evelyn." He looked at her. "Do you really think He cares that much?"

"Oh, I do!" She reached across the seat and took his hand. "He sent His Son to die for us on that cross. He loved us *that* much. Why can't we live our lives to be pleasing to Him? I don't think it's much to ask of us."

Aaron rubbed his brow. "When you word it that way, I do seem selfish." He gripped her hand. "But how do you *know* that God doesn't want us to be married? Maybe you're wrong."

Evelyn smiled. "I *know* that He gave me a friend for life, someone to grow up with and make memories with. He gave me someone I admire and respect and love dearly as a brother. You *are* the brother that I never had. But our memories *together* will end there."

Aaron swallowed deeply and turned away, a tear sliding down his face. "I don't want to live the rest of my life without you in it."

Evelyn grasped his hand. "You don't have to, Aaron. But the relationship will be different." She brushed at her own cheek. "I think…I think there will be a void there for both of us for awhile, but eventually it will be filled with the person God has planned for us to spend the rest of our lives with. Someday, you will understand and thank me for not marrying you."

"I will *never* say those words to you." He cleared his throat, looking up as headlights came up behind them. "I need to get you home. This evening has been about the worse one in my life. I don't need to end it with your mother being upset with me as well." He pulled his hand away and set the automobile into motion.

Evelyn crossed her arms. "Don't you worry…I'm going to have center stage on that one."

BILL SLOWED DOWN AS they came upon the car sitting to the side of the road. He frowned as it pulled out and sped down the road, spewing dust and dirt. "I was going to see if they needed some help, but I guess all is well."

Cynthia narrowed her eyes. "I can't be completely sure, but I think that's Aaron Darby's Plymouth."

Richard popped up and braced his arms on the back of the front seat. "Maybe they had a flat tire."

Bill shrugged. "Everything seems fine now, whoever it was. The turn for Rubyville is just up ahead." Bill turned slightly and looked his friend in the eye. "A little privacy, please."

Richard rolled his eyes and sat back, clasping his hands behind his neck. "As slow as you've been driving I'm surprised it's not almost morning."

"Some of us had plans for the evening…and they didn't include a chaperone." Bill winked at Cynthia.

Cynthia giggled. "The only plans I had were to go to the prom and have a wonderful time…which I did."

Bill turned into Rubyville and followed the dirt road to Cynthia's house, a small, one story with a side porch. He parked out front and turned to Richard. "I'm going to walk Miss Rowe to the door."

"I'll be here. I'd like a little tour of Rubyville before we leave." Richard smiled. "You know, so I will know where everything is when I return." He opened the back door on the driver's side and got out as Bill helped Cynthia from the automobile. "Nice to meet you, Miss Rowe."

Cynthia gave him a smile as she looped her arm through Bill's. "Same to you, Mr. King."

Richard walked around the nose of the Ford and slid into the front seat. He shut the door and rolled down the window, resting his arm there. He watched as Bill leaned forward and tried to steal a kiss, Cynthia ducking her head. Richard chuckled. *You never change.*

Bill returned, whistling as he stepped into the vehicle. He shut his door and put the auto into gear. "I'm going to be your best friend."

"You *are* my best friend." Richard smiled, drumming his hand on the outside of the Ford.

"Be careful of the paint there. I don't want you scratching it." Bill turned, passing the two-storied brick school building. "I found out from Cynthia where your Miss Hanover lives."

Richard grinned. "That was smart thinking. Why didn't I come up with that idea?"

Bill laughed. "Because you've been muddle-headed all evening…ever since you danced the Lindy Hop with that redhead."

Richard nodded. "But even in my most muddle-headed moments I can usually out-think you."

"You just keep thinking that, old pal." Bill pointed out the window to a large limestone building with a tall steeple. "That's where Cynthia and Miss Hanover attend church, Mr. Darby also. Cynthia was telling me that a William Barton donated the land and had the church built back in the 1800's. She said he was an ancestor of Miss Hanover's…a great-grandfather or something."

Richard leaned down, looking out Bill's window at the tall structure glowing in the moonlight. He turned his head to the right. "Nice big park with a gazebo, but where's Miss Hanover's house?"

"We're getting there. Just be patient. You said you wanted the tour, so I thought I would drive you around the main streets in town." Bill turned south and then west, skirting the park. He drove to the corner and gestured across the street. "There's Mr. Darby's mercantile."

"He owns a store?" Richard shook his head. "No wonder he's such a drip."

"But probably a wealthy drip." Bill glanced at his friend. "At least better off, with more prospects than you."

Richard shrugged. "All the money in the world won't make you happy if you are miserable with the person you're married to."

Bill turned south once again and drove a couple of blocks before heading east. He nodded toward Richard's window. "There's the train depot, and just down the road about a mile or so should be the Hanover place. Cynthia said it was a limestone house…the last one on this road. If you keep going, you get to the river."

"Well, even though I've been hot all evening, a swim doesn't sound good right now. So don't drive too far." Richard smiled and sat straighter on the seat. He smoothed back his wind-blown hair.

Bill shook his head. "What are you doing? You won't be seeing her anymore tonight. It's after midnight."

Richard grinned. "You never know."

Bill slowed down. "What if that Mr. Darby is still there? Maybe we should come back in the daylight." He looked around at the dark landscape. "I don't want to get shot at for trespassing."

Richard gestured at the narrow strip of dirt ahead. "We're on the road. No one should be upset about that."

"Yes, but how many people do you think travel out here this time of night? We may look a little suspicious." Bill shook his head and slowed to a crawl.

"You're going to stall the engine. I could walk faster than what you're driving. We're out here now; I want to see her place. Turn off your lights if you're worried about being spotted." Richard draped one arm out the window, his head leaning out.

"Like that won't look strange." Bill shook his head and shut off the lights, using the moonlight to direct his way. "There it is. Two-storied limestone house with a long front porch...just as Cynthia described."

Richard hung out the window as they passed. "I wonder which room is hers."

"Since all the lights are out, maybe we should just get out of here as quickly as possible before we get into trouble." Bill shook his head. "You get me to do the strangest things."

Richard sat back. "You'd better turn around. That line of trees is getting closer. It must be the river you were talking about."

Bill did a K-turn in the middle of the road and headed west. As soon as they passed the house, he sped up and turned on his lights. "That's all the spy work I care to do for awhile."

"I wonder if she has any siblings. That house is certainly large enough to hold a big family." Richard propped his elbow on the door and looked at the scenery rushing by as they left Rubyville.

"Cynthia said Miss Hanover is an only child. Something about her father dying when she was just a baby and her mother moving here. Miss Hanover and her mother live in that house all alone." Bill glanced at his friend. "Don't go into a decline, old pal. You'll see her again."

"You'd better believe it! The quicker the better...just as soon as I have a plan."

Bill rolled his eyes. "You and your plans."

Chapter Five

HELEN SET A PLATE of eggs and bacon on the table and turned back to the stove. "Do you know anything about a couple of young men driving by the house after you arrived home last night?"

Evelyn pulled the plate towards her and picked up her fork. *Thank You, Father, for this food, and help me this morning. It won't be right to go to services with Mama upset with me. I might not be too happy with her either.*

"Evelyn, did you hear what I asked?" Helen walked to the table and sat down, taking a sip of her coffee.

"I don't know anything about young men driving by." Evelyn cut off a bite of fried egg and popped it in her mouth. "Maybe they were going fishing."

Helen crossed her leg, swinging it back and forth. She drummed her nails upon the table. "I know you need to be quiet when you're fishing, but I don't think driving at a crawl with your headlights off really matters to the fish." She shook her head. "I think they were up to no good. That's what I think."

Evelyn smiled as she picked up a piece of crispy bacon. "What were you doing up, spying on people at that time of night?"

Helen raised a perfectly plucked brow. "After I had waited for you to arrive home safely, I couldn't get to sleep. So I was sitting in front of the window, enjoying the night air, when I heard the tires on the road. They were being pretty sneaky."

Evelyn shrugged. "Maybe they just didn't want to wake anyone up. We *are* the last house on the road. They could have been lost."

Helen nodded. "That may be true. They turned around before they got to the river." She took her cup from the saucer and sipped, looking over the rim at her daughter. "Did you have a nice time last night? Mr. Darby seemed different somehow when he dropped you off."

Evelyn took a deep breath and set her fork upon the plate. "Yes, I had a wonderful time last night. I was asked to dance the Lindy Hop." Her eyes sparkled. "It was so much fun!"

Helen frowned, placing the cup on the saucer. She took a delicate bite of her toast and then brushed the crumbs from the corner of her mouth. "I didn't know that you knew the steps to the Lindy Hop." She looked at her daughter. "I'm fairly certain Mr. Darby wouldn't know them."

Evelyn stared down at her lap. "He doesn't. The young man I danced with was a great hoof…dancer."

Helen crossed her arms. "How many times did you dance with *that* young man?"

"Only two… and another with Cynthia's date." Evelyn's eyes met her mother's. "Aaron wasn't too happy about it."

"I'm sure he wasn't. After all, *you* were his date. I hope you danced with *him*." Helen swung her leg faster.

"I danced all the rest with him, Mama." Evelyn picked up her fork. "I thought it was considered polite to dance with other people when asked."

Helen nodded. "It is, but you usually save certain dances for your date." She smiled. "It's been a very long time since I attended a function like that. I'm sure the rules have changed since I was your age."

Evelyn cleared her throat and pushed the remainder of her eggs around on her plate. "Last night I told Aaron that I would not be marrying him."

Helen gasped. "No wonder he seemed upset. Did you phrase it just like that?"

"No…I told him that I had many happy memories with him and that I would always love him as a brother, but I couldn't marry him." Evelyn looked at her mother. "I didn't want to hurt him, Mama, but I couldn't just keep letting him think I was going to be his wife."

Helen uncrossed her legs and stood. "I think you need to give yourself more time and not make a rash decision about this. Aaron Darby is the perfect match for you. He has a successful business, an automobile that he takes very good care of, a nice house, and he attends the same church that you do."

Evelyn wrinkled her brow. "Then if he is so perfect, why don't you marry him?"

Helen laid a hand upon her chest. "That was a very inappropriate and disrespectful thing to say!"

Evelyn's eyes dropped to her lap. "I'm sorry, Mama. It was." She took a deep breath and leveled her gaze at her mother. "I will *not* be marrying Aaron Darby. He is *not* the man for me to spend the rest of my life with. I hope we can remain friends, but I'm afraid that won't be for a very long time, if it happens."

Helen pulled the edges of her robe together. "You are making a very bad mistake turning him down. I hope you don't regret it." Her eyes moved over the kitchen. "Since you're dressed for church, I'm going to let you clean this up while I get ready."

"Of course." Evelyn pushed back her chair and took her plate to the sink.

Helen walked to the door and turned back. "Does the young man you danced the Lindy Hop with have anything to do with this decision?"

"No, Mama! You know I've tried to discuss this with you and Aaron for years now. You just wouldn't listen to me. I can't marry someone that I don't love, that I'm not attracted to." Evelyn stood behind her mother's vacated chair and gripped the top of it. "I love Aaron only as a brother."

Helen shook her head. "I know you keep saying that. But you don't have a brother, and the only young man you've ever been around on a regular basis is Mr. Darby. I don't think you understand what love is, and I would certainly hope you know nothing about *attraction* for a man. You're much too young." She turned and walked from the kitchen.

Evelyn gaped at her mother's retreating figure. *No, Mama, I don't know exactly what it feels like to love a man. But I know that the feelings I have for Aaron are not what they should be for a man I want to marry. And no, I haven't had an earthly father to love and protect me, but I have my Heavenly Father. He has shown me love and compassion; He has guided me and protected me. A man that understands that relationship with our Heavenly Father will strive to love me in the same way...just as the Bible says he should.*

She picked up her mother's cup and saucer and placed them in the sink as she stared out the window. She put one hand to her chest. *And yes, I know what attraction feels like. I'm not too young if God placed that in my body. I just have to handle it in the correct way, within His boundaries.*

Her eyes closed as she remembered the tall, blond-haired man. His tanned face, chiseled jaw, and cleft in the strong chin as he smiled at her came to mind, those incredible blue eyes looking at only her. She rubbed her throat. *There it goes again. I can hardly catch my breath. I feel warm all over and my head wants to spin with the happiness that is wrapping all around me!* She gripped the porcelain sink and opened her eyes. *Dirty dishes and church...that's my reality for this moment.*

EVELYN AND HER MOTHER entered the foyer of the limestone church, the coolness of the interior sweeping over them. Evelyn breathed deeply of the beeswax and lemon oil used to polish the wood. The large bouquet of peonies adorning the long table in the foyer also emanated a sweet fragrance. She adjusted the little purse on her arm and clutched her Bible closer.

Helen peered into the sanctuary where the morning light streamed from the long windows lining the room. The yellow glow gleamed across the polished wood floor. "We have a nice crowd this morning. I see a couple of visitors as well. It looks like Mama has taken one of them under her wing."

Evelyn smiled. "Grandmama is wonderful about making visitors feel welcome. I often wish I was more like her and not so shy in that area."

Helen patted her daughter's arm. "You do just fine. Let's take our seats while Mrs. Teter is still playing. Our heels make an awful sound on that wood floor and the piano helps to cover it."

Evelyn laughed as she followed her mother into the sanctuary, stepping lightly. She waved discreetly and smiled at classmates as they walked the aisle to the second pew from the front, Annabella Barton's chosen place.

Helen stopped at the end of the pew, gesturing Evelyn to enter first, just as she did every Sunday.

"Good morning, Mrs. Drummond." Evelyn smiled at the pastor's wife as she slid by her mother into the pew.

The older woman returned the greeting. "You *are* going to sing for us this morning, aren't you?"

Helen put a hand on Evelyn's arm. "Of course she is. I've heard her practicing all week."

"It's such a blessing when you minister in song, Evelyn. I don't think I've ever heard a sweeter voice. It is so encouraging when our younger set takes part in the services." Mrs. Drummond turned toward Helen.

Evelyn continued into the pew and smiled at her grandmother. "Good morn…" Evelyn's eyes widened as they focused on the slate-blue eyes of the young man sitting on the other side of her grandmother. She gripped the pew in front of her and sat down, almost missing the hard seat. *Mr. King? What is he doing here…in my church…in Rubyville?* She gulped. *I'm shaking all over and can't breathe… and there goes my heart, about to beat right out of my chest.*

"Good morning, my dear." Annabella slid an arm around her granddaughter's shoulders and gave her a hug. "You are looking very pretty this morning. That straw bonnet and matching purse is just the thing for this May morning."

"Thank…thank you, Grandmama." Evelyn stared straight ahead. "Those must be your peonies at the front of the church. They smell wonderful." She scooted back against the hard back of the pew. *What am I going to say? I want to look at his handsome face so badly! But what if last night was just me thinking it was something it wasn't? What if he really didn't kiss me, and I just really wanted him to—*

"Evelyn, dear, are you alright? I've been trying to introduce you to Mr. King." Annabella wrinkled her brow and looked at her granddaughter. "Your face is very flushed. Are you too warm?"

Evelyn tried to speak and succeeded to croak. "I'm…I'm fine."

"Well, if you say so, my dear." Annabella turned her white head and smiled at the young man seated next to her. "Mr. King, may I introduce you to my granddaughter, Evelyn Hanover?"

Richard stood to his full height and smoothed the front of his suit. He smiled, his blue eyes twinkling. "It's an honor to meet you, Miss Hanover. Your grandmother has been telling me all about you."

Evelyn swallowed around the lump in her throat and slid her eyes up the long length. *Oh my goodness! I'm sorry, Mama, I know you don't like me saying that, and I'm not really, I'm actually thinking it. Oh my goodness, he is even more handsome than he was last night! I can't breathe, I can't think what to say and he's smiling at me and all I want to do is faint. Just faint, right here on the church pew! What would people think of me?* "It's nice to meet you, Mr. King."

Annabella laughed. "We had a lot of time to fill before services began. I came over early just as I do each Sunday morning and Mr. King was here, sitting on the steps of the church. He was a tremendous help with the flowers…getting water for the vases and carrying them for me. I hope your mother doesn't mind, but I invited him to have Sunday dinner with us. Your mother always has plenty and I told Mr. King that he needed to have a good meal before he headed back to Emporia." She smiled up at the young man before turning back to Evelyn. "Can you imagine…driving all the way over from Emporia for church." She laughed. "I told him there must be churches much closer for him to attend, but we love visitors, don't we?"

Evelyn nodded, her eyes sliding to Richard as he sat down. He smiled at her and gave her a wink and she couldn't help but return a smile of her own.

"Good morning!" Pastor Drummond silenced the piano and the chatter with his greeting. "Please stand as we sing the Doxology."

Evelyn set her Bible and purse on the pew and pulled herself to a standing position on trembling legs. She gripped the pew in front of her and prayed she would not faint, concentrating on the words she sang. "Amen" rang out and Evelyn sat down, sighing.

Pastor Drummond continued his morning announcements, thanking Annabella for the lovely flowers from her garden. "It's always a privilege to have Miss Hanover minister to us with song." He beamed a smile at the second pew back. "So, before we sing our hymns this morning, we will have her come up."

Evelyn opened her mouth and floundered like a fish out of water, her eyes wide. *Oh Father, I cannot stand up there and sing...not with Mr. King here. What if I make a mistake, or...or open my mouth and nothing comes out. Yes, that's exactly what's going to happen. I'm going to open my mouth to sing and nothing will come out. Or I'll just collapse behind the pulpit and they'll have to carry me out of here.*

Helen nudged her daughter and frowned.

Evelyn swallowed. *There's a lump in my throat the size of my fist. Cotton, it feels like cotton stuffed in there about to choke me.* She stood and passed in front of her mother, smoothing the skirt of her lavender-flowered dress. *Please, Father, calm my anxious thoughts, and still my beating heart so that I may breathe. Take the fear from me and let this song be for Your honor and glory, Father.* Peace drifted down like the softest petals as she walked to the front of the church. She gained the pulpit and opened the hymnal to the song she and Mrs. Teter had chosen the month before. She smiled at the pianist and turned to the congregation, her eyes seeking Richard's. He gave her a smile and the last bit of fear melted like snow in spring.

RICHARD GAVE EVELYN A smile when her eyes sought his. He watched as her shoulders, so straight and rigid just a moment before, relaxed and her face softened. Her beautiful green eyes swept over the congregation the moment the piano began playing, and she encompassed the crowd with that gesture, drawing them near her. She began singing in her sweet, clear soprano, and he was entranced along with the rest of the people gathered there.

Richard had often heard the hymn that spoke of walking in the garden with the Savior, but never had it sounded so wonderful. *Her voice...but, even more, the reminder of the fellowship we have with You, Lord!*

The last word drifted through the room. Evelyn closed the hymnal and laid it on the pulpit.

Richard sat back. *She has the voice of an angel. I've never heard anything so lovely.* He watched as she walked back to where they were seated and sat down, peace surrounding her every step.

Annabella tilted her head toward him and whispered, "Doesn't she have a beautiful voice? She has been gifted in music since she was a small child."

Richard nodded. "She does…absolutely."

The pastor called out the number for the hymn and asked the congregation to stand.

Richard turned to the page, his thoughts difficult to rein in. *Father, she has to be Your child. She sang that old hymn for You, and You were right there beside her. She is gifted, but what is even more beautiful is her love for You. It flows all around her. Father, how can I ever be good enough for someone like her? Why would she even want to be with someone such as me? I have nothing to offer her. I've been foolish to come here and think she would even give me the time of day.*

He closed the old hymnal, clutching it at his side as he sang the song from memory, his baritone blending in perfect harmony with the redhead he had danced with the night before.

Chapter Six

HELEN KICKED AT A small stone, a frown upon her face. "You should have taken Mr. King up on his offer to drive you home. It's been a very long day for you, Mama."

She helped her mother across the road, nodding to the older man slowing his automobile to allow them to pass. The sound of children playing in the park floated to them on the Sunday afternoon breeze.

Annabella swung the cane ahead of her and stabbed the dirt road. "And miss out on a walk with my daughter? You know how much I adore walking. And as long as God gives me the strength to use these legs, I will. This afternoon I have the added benefit of visiting with you."

They entered the coolness of the park, the large trees lining the perimeter offering shade. Green grass greeted their footsteps. "Hello Miss Barton, Mrs. Hanover," called a little girl from the swings. "Can you see how high I'm flying?" She giggled and pumped her legs faster.

Annabella waved. "Please be careful, Betty. We don't want any broken arms."

Helen harrumphed and crossed her arms. "And now those two are back on my front porch doing heaven only knows what." She looked at her mother and shook her head. "I still can't believe that you asked that young man to dinner at *my* house without consulting me."

Annabella laughed. "Now don't snap your cap, Helen. Isn't that what Evelyn is always saying? When was I supposed to ask you? Mr. King was at the church when I arrived this morning." She stopped for a moment and took a deep breath. "Besides, you have Mr. Darby over almost every Sunday. Since he wasn't at church this morning, I think it worked out just fine."

"Yes, and I wonder why. I'll have to stop by the mercantile tomorrow morning." Helen drummed her fingers on her upper arms. "That Mr. King has a ferocious appetite. I thought I was going to have to cut into that second apple pie."

Annabella picked up her cane and tapped Helen's calf. "You need to simmer down, my dear. Those two are in love and there isn't a thing you are going to do about it."

Helen gasped. "In love? Why, they only met one another last night. Don't say such silly things to get me upset." She took a deep breath and patted the hair from her temple.

Annabella continued walking. "I'm not trying to upset you. But don't run from the truth."

"The truth is that Evelyn needs to marry Mr. Darby. He is the best option for her." Helen raised a hand in the air. "Why, we don't even know this Mr. King."

Annabella bobbed her white head. "I can understand your distress. You've had Evelyn's life planned out for her for many years now."

Helen stared at her mother. "What is that supposed to mean?"

"Just let me finish what I'm trying to say. It takes an old woman longer to formulate the words sometimes." Annabella gestured with her cane to the white gazebo in the park. "I need to sit down a bit before we continue."

Helen helped her mother up the stairs to the encircled space, sitting beside her on the wood bench lining the walls.

"I sure have some memories in this old building." Annabella shook her head. "Some of them not so pleasant. But we can't change the past, can we?"

"Mama, please finish what you were going to say about me planning out Evelyn's life. I don't believe that's true. I think most mothers have a desire to see their children make good decisions and they try to encourage that. I've only done the same." Helen crossed her legs, clasping her hands in her lap.

Annabella patted her daughter's knee. "Please don't take this the wrong way. But you have wanted what *you* have planned for Evelyn, ever since she was a baby." Annabella held up a hand when Helen opened her mouth. "Let me finish." Annabella leaned forward bracing both hands on the cane. "I think Aaron Darby is a wonderful young man. I believe he would have made Evelyn a good husband. He would have taken care of her and loved her all of their days."

"That's exactly what I've been saying." Helen stared at her mother.

Annabella held up one finger. "That would have been fine if Evelyn agreed and *wanted* to be married to Aaron. But she has said for years that she didn't want to do that for many reasons. You just haven't listened, my dear."

"So I'm a selfish mother, pushing *my* wishes on my child?" Helen gaped at Annabella.

"Yes, my dear." Annabella smiled and clasped Helen's hand within her own. "We mothers all do that at some point in our child's life. We think we know best because we have lived our life and experienced so much compared to their years on this earth. That is true to some extent. But living isn't about doing what others want you to do. It's about following God's direction."

"You don't think I have been a godly mother to my daughter?" Helen stared wide-eyed.

Annabella pursed her lips. "Most of the time you have been thinking more about Evelyn's physical needs. Her home, clothing, and the food she eats. You want someone else to come in and take over your duties. You think, and rightly so, that Aaron Darby is the best candidate for the job." Annabella squeezed Helen's hand. "God tells us that He will make sure that we have our physical needs taken care of. Our spiritual needs are what He wants us to concentrate on. After listening to Mr. King this afternoon, I think he will take better care of Evelyn's spiritual needs than what Mr. Darby is capable of doing."

Helen pulled her hand away and stood. She walked to the opposite side of the gazebo and spun around. "And *none* of her physical needs will be taken care of. You heard him, Mama. All he has is that beat up old car. I'm surprised it made it all the way to Rubyville. He hasn't even graduated high school yet."

"But he has a love for the Lord. He seems *very* responsible, and he is not afraid of a little hard work, from what he told us this afternoon. He will take care of Evelyn." Annabella gave a half-smile. "And he loves your daughter, even more than he can see right now." She lowered her voice. "And, Helen, she loves *him*."

Helen slapped her leg. "Please stop saying that! They don't know anything about love. How could they? They met last night, all dressed up and starry-eyed. That doesn't make a marriage, and you know it, Mama."

"No, it doesn't make a marriage, but it sure goes a long way for easing the difficult times." Annabella looked away. "Once, a long time ago, I fell in love. It took me many years to mature, and he as well, and to appreciate the same kind of love I see in the eyes of those two young people sitting on your front porch, at this very moment." She turned to Helen. "I want them to have those years now, together, and not have to wait for them as I did."

Helen slid to the bench behind her. "I can't believe you are telling me to let my seventeen-year-old daughter run off with some man she met twenty-four hours ago. You *have* lost your mind."

"I'm just a crazy old woman." Annabella smiled and struggled to her feet. "Maybe I have lost my mind. But I've seen a lot in my eighty-five years in this old world. And I know if you fight Evelyn on this one…you will lose her." She held her hand out to her daughter. "I had better continue on home before I'm completely tuckered out. That offered ride is sounding better by the minute."

EVELYN GLANCED AT RICHARD, sitting in the chair across from her. "I'm still amazed that my mother agreed to walk home with my grandmother."

Richard sat, one ankle upon his knee, his arms draped upon the wicker chair. "They don't walk together?" His lips twitched as his gaze slid over her face.

Evelyn looked away, her cheeks turning pink. "That's not what I meant. My mother has been determined that I should marry Aaron Darby." She gestured to the line of trees along the road in front of the house. "My mother left us here, alone, while she walked across town." She blushed pinker. "I never thought she would leave us by ourselves."

Richard smiled. "My impression is that your grandmother pushed for us to be here." He made a grand gesture of looking at the wood boards of the porch. "I'm fairly certain our chairs are nailed in place and there is glue applied to the cushions." He watched her smile. "Go ahead, try to stand, I bet you can't."

Evelyn giggled, covering her mouth. "You say the strangest things, Mr. King. You do have the ability to make me laugh."

He grinned. "I'm glad. Laughter eases a lot of hurts." He looked away and ran a finger along his chin.

"Have you suffered a lot of hurts?" Evelyn spoke softly.

He took a deep breath. "No more than anyone else. God gives us each what we can bear...no more. At times, I thought He was wrong," he gave a half-smile, "but it always turned out alright in the end."

"Do you have any brothers or sisters?"

He shook his head. "I was adopted when I was very young. I have no memory of my parents. The couple that took me in..." he stared off, his eyes darkening. He turned back to her and smiled. "Let's just say that they really shouldn't have become parents. They took in another boy and girl after me and they both ran off several years ago." He shrugged. "Maybe I should have, as well."

Evelyn leaned forward in her chair and braced her elbows on her knees. "Why didn't you, if it was so terrible?"

"One thing my parents did for us...and I will be eternally grateful for...is took us to church every Sunday. I don't know why they did, but it was a safe haven for me. I learned that God has a plan for each of us. I believed that He allowed me to be a part of my family for a reason, and I was going to make the best of it until I was on my own. No matter how bad it was." He pressed his lips together. "It was pretty awful at times. My adoptive parents will be accountable for what they did to three children. But I was determined that it would not ruin my life. God was always watching over me."

Evelyn sat back and looked down at her hands. "I'm sorry that you had a rough time growing up. I can't even imagine living in such a way." Her eyes met his. "But I'm very happy to hear that God has been a very important part of your life. He has been the one true constant companion in mine."

The scrunch of tires rolling over dirt and gravel pulled their attention to the gray-blue vehicle coming down the road.

Evelyn took a deep breath. "It looks like Aaron Darby has decided to visit."

Richard's eyes went from the 1939 Plymouth to Evelyn. "Should I sneak out the back way?" He asked the question with a twitch of the lips, his eyes twinkling.

She shook her head. "We aren't doing anything to be ashamed of. You were a visitor at church this morning, and it's very common for us to have visitors over for Sunday dinner after services. Aaron knows that."

Richard raised a brow. "What about a visitor that you danced with the night before?"

Evelyn bit her lower lip and raised a finger at him. "That's the part that could be a problem."

The automobile stopped in front of the house, the roof barely visible over the lilac hedge lining the road.

Evelyn frowned. "That sounds like Mama with him." She stood, smoothing the skirt of her dress. "I hope everything is alright."

Helen passed through the opening in the hedge, Aaron following.

"Look who I found out driving around town. He drove by just as your grandmother and I were leaving the park." Helen laughed and turned back over her shoulder. "It was a good thing too. Mama was getting pretty tired. So, he gave her a ride home and I invited him over for some apple pie to thank him for his consideration."

Aaron stopped in front of the porch, shoving his hands into his pockets. "I'll just go on home. I didn't realize you already had a visitor." His eyes wandered off Evelyn and met Richard's. "It's Mr. King, isn't it?"

Richard stood and held out his right hand. "Yes, Richard King. It looks like you survived the prom."

Aaron glanced down at the tanned hand and slowly pulled his own pale appendage from his pocket. He grasped Richard's hand. "Yes, I survived. Dancing isn't really something I enjoy very much. I probably won't be doing it again anytime soon."

Richard smiled. "Don't let one prom shape your opinion. It can be a lot of fun when you know the dance steps."

Helen's eyes flitted from Aaron to Richard and then Evelyn. "Dear, I think we should have our pie out here on the porch. The weather has been lovely all day, but it's especially nice right now with the evening breeze. Please help me serve." She turned to walk into the house.

Richard cleared his throat. "It *has* been a wonderful day, Mrs. Hanover, but I need to head home. I work for a couple hours before school starts, so I usually turn in pretty early."

Helen swiveled around and pasted a smile on her face. "I'm sorry to hear that, but it *is* a long drive back to Emporia. We do understand…don't we, Evelyn?"

Evelyn nodded, her heart giving a quick stab of disappointment. "Of course, Mr. King. We wouldn't want you to be late for work in the morning."

Richard smiled at Helen. "Thank you for the delicious meal earlier. I haven't had roast that tasty in a long time. The pie was the best I've *ever* had."

"I can cut you another nice big piece for the drive home…or to have later." Evelyn glanced at her mother. "It's even good for breakfast with a glass of cold milk. We have plenty left over." She walked to the front door and opened the screen. "I think your hat is in here as well."

Richard nodded. "It is. I would love another piece of pie." He turned to Aaron. "Enjoy your evening." His eyes went to Helen. "I'll just leave through the back since my automobile is by the garage. Thank you again for everything. It was a very pleasant day for me, getting to know all of you."

Helen clasped her hands before her waist and gave a curt nod. "Evelyn, please be sure to bring Mr. Darby a slice of pie when you return. Remember that he likes a large dollop of whipped cream on it."

"Yes, Mama." Evelyn walked through the door, Richard close behind her.

They crossed the sitting room and entered the kitchen, Evelyn taking the pie from the counter. She set it on the table.

"I'm going to have a long battle ahead where your mother is concerned, aren't I?" Richard went to the line of hooks upon the wall by the door and took his fedora by the crown. He walked to the table and stood close to Evelyn, watching as she sliced the pie and set a large piece on a plate. She wrapped an embroidered napkin around it.

"I'm afraid so, Mr. King. She's had her heart set on me marrying Aaron since I was practically in diapers." She braced her hands upon the back of the chair, staring at the kitchen door leading into the sitting room and the front door beyond. *Please, Mama, just give us a couple minutes to say good-bye.*

Richard tilted his head near her ear. "And are *you* set on marrying Mr. Darby?" He spoke soft and low.

Evelyn slid her eyes closed and sighed quietly with the warm words tickling her cheek. "It always seemed like the right thing to do, even if I didn't want to."

"Do you love him?" Richard stepped closer, giving a quick look toward the door.

Evelyn opened her eyes and looked up at Richard, his face mere inches from hers. The slate-blue eyes traveled over her face, stopping upon her lips. Her breath caught at the intimacy of the caress. She gripped the chair as the kitchen began a slow turn. "No, I don't love him."

"Are you going to marry him?" The words purred against her cheek.

"No...no, I'm not." Her eyes sought the white collar at his tanned neck, his tie loosened. "You smell wonderful." She blushed, her eyes lowering to his wide, brightly-patterned tie. "I'm sorry, that came out wrong."

He grinned, the cleft in his chin deepening. "It must be my aftershave. I have a terrible habit of cutting myself while shaving. I use the stuff by the gallons. It's called Old Spice."

Evelyn took another whiff as her eyes slid back to his face. "Now that you mention it, you do have a slight cut."

His hand went to his chin. "Yes, if you look closely, there is probably more than a few."

"Doesn't it sting?" Her eyes sought the other cuts he had mentioned.

He smiled as he shook his head. "Just for a minute or so after I put on the aftershave. I don't think I've ever had so many questions about shaving. I didn't know it was such a fascinating topic."

Evelyn's eyes shifted toward the door. "I'm sorry. Since I didn't have a father growing up and no grandfather, I don't know much about men shaving, I guess. I never knew there was such a thing as aftershave and that it could smell so good." She turned back to him. "Mama is always telling me I ask too many questions."

"Questions are never bad." His eyes dropped to her lips once more. "As a matter of fact, I have one for you."

"Yes?"

"May I kiss you before I leave? I've thought about it all afternoon." His hand slid over hers resting on the chair. "You see, *you* smell wonderful as well, and I can still remember the way your lips were so soft when I kissed you last night."

Evelyn's eyes widened and she glanced at the door. "I don't want Mama to walk in and see us." She put one hand to her chest as she looked up at him. "But yes, I would really like that."

He slid his hand from hers and cupped her cheek, moving to her neck. He pulled her closer, lowering his lips to hers. He sighed and whispered. "Even better than I remembered."

Evelyn returned the kiss, inhaling deeply of his masculine scent.

"Evelyn," the screen door banged, heels clicking on the wood floor of the sitting room.

Richard clapped his fedora on his head as he gave her a wink, rushing out the kitchen door.

"Is Mr. King just now leaving?" Helen stood with hands on her hips.

Evelyn turned to the sink and watched Richard get into his automobile. "Yes."

Helen frowned and lifted the plate of pie from the table. "Why did you wrap Mr. Darby's pie up like a Christmas package?" She took the napkin from the pie and shook her head. "You also forgot to put the whipped cream on it. Whatever am I going to do with you?" Helen went to the refrigerator.

Evelyn pressed her lips together and dabbed at her warm cheeks. "I thought the napkin would keep the flies from the pie. I was going to put the whipped cream on it after I gave it to Aaron so it would be nice and fresh." *Evelyn Hanover, what a story that is! You should be ashamed of yourself.*

"I'll take care of the whipped cream. You go on out and visit with Mr. Darby. He shouldn't have to sit out there all alone." Helen shooed her daughter away with her hand.

Evelyn walked through the kitchen and into the sitting room.

When will I see you again, Richard King? I barely know you and yet I can't imagine spending a day without you.

Chapter Seven

HELEN KNOCKED ON THE partially open wood door, pushing it back to look inside the room. "I noticed that your light is still on. I wanted to speak with you about today, before you went to bed. But it looks like you are already tucked in for the night. We can talk tomorrow."

Evelyn laid the book on the chenille bedspread and looked at her mother. "I'm still awake…just reading a bit before I turn off the light." She rolled over to her side and patted the bed. "You can sit with me, like you used to when I was a child."

Helen gave a half-smile. "I think you are a little old now for a bedtime story." She sat down at the foot of the bed and crossed her leg, lapping the edges of her robe over her knees.

"I don't think you can ever be too old for a bedtime story." Evelyn propped the side of her face on her hand. "You should have written down your stories. They were very good. That way you could have read them to your grandchildren someday."

"My grandchildren?" Helen raised her chin and crossed her hands in her lap. "Will I have grandchildren one day?"

Evelyn laughed. "I hope so. Isn't that the normal course of things?"

"Yes, it is…if you marry and have a family. But you aren't willing to do that with the man that is best suited for you." Helen's blue eyes slid over the decorations of the bedroom.

"Mama, you didn't come in here to discuss Aaron Darby again, I hope." Evelyn sighed and sat up, drawing her knees against her chest. "I thought I made it very clear to you this morning that I would not be marrying him."

Helen leveled her darkening blue eyes at her daughter. "Yes, that is what you said at breakfast." She brushed a speck off her knee. "I came in here to discuss that young man, *Mr.* King, that you were so infatuated with over dinner." She raised her chin and looked down at Evelyn. "Of course you understand all the reasons that it would be very *inappropriate* for you to encourage him."

"No, I can't think of a single thing that would be wrong." Evelyn jutted her chin, her chest heaving. "You just don't like him, even though you don't know him. You haven't even given him a chance, Mama."

"And I don't plan on giving him one. Neither of us knows him, his background, or his plans for the future. All I've observed is a rather ratty suit and a rusted out automobile."

"It's always about the *things* in life, isn't it, Mama?" Evelyn scowled, gripping her knees tighter. "Did you listen when he was talking about how hard he works? Or that he is graduating as the valedictorian of his class?"

"I heard all that, but that still doesn't make him good husband material for you, my dear. Why can't you see that?" Helen swung her foot back and forth.

"I was rather impressed that he drove all the way out here, to Rubyville, when he was up late last night for the prom. Not many young men would put forth that effort." Evelyn rubbed her brow.

Helen gave a delicate snort. "Many a young man has traveled to great lengths to get a girl that he has set his sights on."

Evelyn raised her hands. "What is so special about me, Mama? I'm an ordinary student, not very attractive with this red hair," she pointed to her rag curled head, "and I don't have very much to offer anyone."

Helen shook her head. "Mr. King thinks you have money, my dear. Which you do, but you shouldn't go around advertising that. It's in poor taste."

Evelyn threw back the covers and sprang to her feet. She faced her mother. "I refuse to think that is the reason for Mr. King's interest in me. The only people that know about my history are those that live here in Rubyville. Our family is not so special that it has reached the society page of places like Emporia or Manhattan, Kansas."

"Don't be so dramatic, my girl." Helen looked away, tapping her red nails upon her knee.

Evelyn walked around the edge of the bed and sat down next to her mother. She took her mother's hand in her own. "I think I love Mr. King, Mama. I know he feels the same about me."

Helen threw back her head and laughed. "You *are* naïve. You met the man last night and spent this afternoon with him. You think you *love* him?" She shook her head. "Don't be ridiculous!"

Tears escaped the green eyes, sliding down the flushed cheeks. "Please don't belittle my feelings for him. I have never felt the way I feel when I am with him. He makes my heart race and all I can think about is him. I want to be with him forever."

"Him, him, him! That's all you've been saying this entire conversation." Helen pulled her hand away and stood, tightening the belt at her waist. "Evelyn Hanover, I refuse to give you permission to proceed with a relationship with that young man. He is beneath you. You need a man that can care for you, provide for you…and one that isn't after your money."

Evelyn shook her head. "I love you, Mama, and I respect you…but you are very wrong about Mr. King. I know it deep down inside. He loves me, just as I love him." Evelyn bowed her head. "If he asks me to marry him, which I pray he does, I will do it."

"If you proceed, you won't have my blessing. There will not be a wedding at our church here in Rubyville. I refuse to go along with this ridiculous scheme of yours." Helen spun around and strode from the bedroom, slamming the door behind her.

Evelyn's shoulders slumped and she covered her face with her hands. *Oh, Mama! Why are you so hateful? Why can't you see that Mr. King is a man of integrity and honor? He doesn't care about my money…he loves me. I know it!*

She dropped her hands and looked up at the ceiling. *Father, please direct my path, show me the way You would have me to go. I want Mama's approval in this, but more than anything, I want Yours. Let me know what to do. Amen.*

Emporia, Kansas

BILL CLAPPED RICHARD ON the back. "That was a great speech you gave. It was a little heavy on the God stuff, but still good. I was beginning to think I was in church."

Richard took the mortarboard from his head. "I know you profess to have taken Jesus Christ as your Savior, but you continually amaze me at your reluctance to accept Him into your life on a regular basis."

Bill shrugged. "I'm going to Heaven someday and that's all that matters. I don't see the point in cramming God and the Bible down other people's throats. If they're interested, they will ask about Him."

"But if all they see is someone as lost as they are, why would they ask?" Richard walked to his automobile and opened the door, tossing his cap and gown on the seat. "People ask questions and want something different in their lives if they see something they want." He shut the door and turned to his friend. "Living the Christian life should make us content and at peace, willing to help and love others."

"Yeah, I hear you. You're just making too big of a deal about it. That's all I'm saying." Bill grinned. "Just relax and enjoy life. Eternity is another time and place."

Richard nodded. "It is. But if I don't put gasoline in my old Ford now, I can't drive it out to Rubyville later. Do you see what I'm saying?" Richard smiled. "I plan on having a full tank of gasoline, ready and waiting, when I head up to Heaven. I want to reap the full rewards and benefits God has planned for me...not just *get by*."

Bill waved his hand. "Enough of the preaching." He set his hands on his hips. "What's this about you heading out to Rubyville again? I thought you said Miss Hanover's mother was less than happy to see your ugly face the last time you were there."

Richard rubbed one tanned cheek. "I'm not that bad-looking." His eyes lowered over the length of Bill's frame. "At least I'm not a shrimp. That can't be too attractive to women."

Bill puffed out his chest. "Great things come in small packages." He eyed his friend. "I don't think it's as much about me being of normal height as it is of you being ridiculously tall."

"Miss Hanover didn't seem to mind." Richard grinned. "As a matter of fact, I think we fit together pretty well when we were dancing. I wasn't bent over breaking my back and she wasn't on tiptoe. A match made in Heaven."

Bill sighed. "Miss Hanover *is* a little tall for my taste, but there were a lot of gorgeous attributes in that long form. I could adapt."

Richard put his hand on his friend's shoulder. "Well, you won't have to worry about that. She's taken."

Bill nodded. "I remember…that Mr. Dotty, Drippy…whatever his name was."

"Mr. Darby." Richard dropped his hand and smoothed back his hair. "You can be rather offensive at times. And no, she's taken by *me*. I have it from Miss Hanover that she does not love Mr. Darby, and she is not going to marry him."

"You found this all out in one afternoon visit?" Bill leaned against the Ford and crossed his arms. "You *are* on a mission."

"Yes, I am. And I found *that* out in just a couple minutes, right before I kissed her." Richard smiled, his eyes looking off into the distance.

Bill turned sideways and stared at his friend. "You kissed her? She actually let you after a couple of dances and a morning at church?" He twitched his head. "Maybe I *should* start attending church more regularly."

"Yes, you should, but not because you want to go around kissing girls." Richard slapped the hood of his automobile. "Well, I'm off. As I said, I'm going to Rubyville and I'm going to visit that gorgeous girl we were talking about."

"It's been a couple weeks since you were out there. What if she doesn't want to see you? What if she decided to marry that guy anyway," Bill shrugged, "because her mother made her. What if she—"

"What if the Rapture occurs tonight?" Richard punched a finger at Bill's shoulder. "*That's* what you should be more concerned with. Are you ready to go?"

Bill smiled with a tilt of his head. "As ready as I'll ever be."

"I was afraid you'd say that. I'll be praying for you. I think your tank is running on empty and you're starting to sputter." Richard walked around the nose of the Ford and hopped in. He lowered his head to talk to Bill out the open passenger window. "I'll let you know when I'm back in town. I'm going to stay in Rubyville tonight and attend services in the morning. I really enjoyed the pastor's message last time." He winked at Bill. "And if I'm really lucky, Evelyn will be singing again. She has a voice like a song bird, my friend."

Bill crossed his arms as Richard started the engine. "You're just looking for another kiss." He leaned an arm on the open window frame. "Where are you going to stay overnight? Just invite yourself to the Hanover's house for tea and crumpets and ask when breakfast is served?"

Richard grinned. "You drove by the hotel when you took Cynthia home. I thought I would stay there. That's why I've been working extra hours the past couple of weeks…saving up gasoline money and for a room. I'm not stupid." He pulled the automobile into gear.

"I think I disagree with that last part. By the way, if you marry her, do I get to be the best man?"

Richard chuckled and started to drive away, causing Bill to jump back with a yelp.

"Ouch!" Bill brushed his arm where it had scraped on the window frame. "You chucklehead! That hurt. And you didn't answer my question."

Richard laughed. "You'll have to wait and see." He revved the engine and raced away, leaving his friend in the dust.

Rubyville, Kansas

"THAT WAS A DELIGHTFUL party for all our graduates." Annabella beamed as she looked out over the crowd of people gathered in the park. "Just think… we had eleven graduates in the class of 1948! My papa would have been so proud. There were years when he thought we would have to close the school down because of lack of students."

"I think there was only three or four of us back when I graduated in 1901." Beth Johnson sighed. "Where have all the years gone? It seems like it was only yesterday." She smiled at her mother. "It *was* a lovely party, Mama Bella." She brushed back her gray hair and smiled at her husband, Daniel. "But I think we had better head on home. Daniel hasn't been feeling well the past few months and the heat of the day seems to make it worse."

Daniel nodded. "I *could* use a little nap."

Annabella waved the couple on. "I appreciate you joining us for as long as you did, Daniel. Life isn't so pleasant when you're not feeling well."

Beth stood and walked over to Evelyn. "I wouldn't have missed seeing my niece in her cap and gown, and receiving her diploma. It's a pretty important day." She leaned over and kissed the top of Evelyn's red head. "I'm very proud of you, my dear." She straightened, pressing one hand at her back. "Do you have any plans for your summer yet?"

Evelyn's eyes slid to Helen. "Not really. Just content to be at home and see what happens. I wouldn't mind giving Ellen some help at the hotel." She turned back to her aunt.

Beth smiled down at Evelyn. "She would be most grateful, I'm sure. Daniel is rarely there these days and I'm not able to be there very often. I know it gets terribly busy during the summer months. Even with the new café in town, the hotel has plenty of diners." She patted the younger woman's shoulder. "Be sure to stop in and visit at the house whenever you are able. I would love the company."

"I will, Aunt Beth." Evelyn reached up and laid her hand over Beth's, giving it a squeeze.

Annabella braced her hands upon her cane and watched her daughter and son-in-law walk slowly from the park. She shook her head. "I have asked Daniel to see Dr. Rundell. The symptoms he is having remind me so much of my father before he passed away. It was his heart. The heat always made it worse."

Helen nodded. "I remember the day well. Dr. Rundell's great-grandson was being born the day you called him to the house to see to Grandpa Barton." She smiled. "Just think…that little baby born that day is now our doctor here in Rubyville."

Annabella gave a wince. "Please don't bring that up. Each time I go into his office, I have to remind myself that he's old enough to *be* a doctor." She sighed. "We are very lucky to have such a family as the Rundells to be caring for us. It's probably very unusual for one family to return to their hometown to practice medicine when life would be more lucrative elsewhere. I know old Dr. Rundell had been a doctor in Kansas City for many years before making Rubyville his home."

"As you said, they have been wonderful to all of us here." Helen picked up her glass from the make-shift table, and took a sip of lemonade. "I think I will talk to Beth about Daniel making an appointment. It can't hurt…and they may get some answers."

"I do think that is best, my dear." Annabella waved a fan before her face. "It has been a beautiful day, but it's time for me to go home as well. Please make sure the rest of the cake is taken back to the hotel. I don't want it left here in the park for any little creatures to eat."

Evelyn winked at her grandmother. "You shouldn't speak of the children in such a manner. What would their parents say?"

Annabella smiled. "Don't be causing any trouble, my dear. Rubyville is blessed with some wonderful families, but I remember when my own grandson kept the school and most of the businesses in constant terror."

"Yes, Georgie kept this old town pretty interesting. You never knew what kind of antics he would be up to." Helen laughed. "That's probably why Daniel is so worn out now. Georgie kept him on his toes all those years."

Molly plopped down on the wooden hotel chair and lifted the curly brown hair from her neck. "You all must be talking about my father." She gestured to a tall, lanky man standing with his arms crossed as he talked with a group of men. "He heard his name and asked me to come see what you all were saying about him." She lowered her head and laughed. "He said it probably wasn't anything good."

Helen turned to her youngest nephew and gave him a little wave. "He knows us all too well."

George Johnson lifted his hand and smiled, shaking his curly, blond head. He turned back to the group of men.

Molly leaned forward and propped her elbows upon the table. "So… what *were* you all saying about Papa?"

Annabella laughed. "Those are stories that are better left for your parents to tell. Your father would never forgive me if I told his fifteen-year-old daughter the things he used to do."

Helen raised a brow as she adjusted the narrow fabric belt at her waist. "Well, I guess I don't feel so honorable in that area. I'm only eleven years older than him and he was a real stinker at times." She looked back at her nephew and shook her head. "He knows it too."

"So what did he do?" Molly raised a hand and propped her chin on it, her eyes twinkling. "Just one story…and make it a good one."

Helen crossed her arms and tilted her head. "Let me think a minute."

Evelyn nudged her mother. "You'd better think fast because he's headed over now."

George sauntered over to the group of women and braced his hands on the back of Helen's chair. "So, *Aunt* Helen, what shenanigans are you up to?"

Helen tilted her head to look at her nephew. "Shenanigans? *Me?* That would be you, Georgie."

He chuckled and looked at his daughter. "Don't believe most of what you hear about me. I was just an innocent little boy and people had a tendency to be very mean to me."

Annabella raised a hand from her cane. "Now just hold on there. I wasn't going to share anything with my great-granddaughter out of respect to you, but if you are going to play innocent—"

"We will just have to start talking." Helen smiled up at George.

Molly repeated her request. "Just one…*please*."

Annabella leaned back in her chair. She shook a finger at Molly. "Mind you, your father was only seven years old at the time, and this is not a trick you should share with your brother Henry. We don't want to give him any ideas."

George rolled his eyes. "Henry doesn't need any help with ideas…believe me."

"Well, he still hasn't topped this one that I'm about to tell." Annabella leaned her cane against the table. "As I said, George was seven years old, maybe almost eight. Mr. Howard was running the mercantile at that time…just before I took over for a few years. We'd had some heavy rain that fall, and he was up repairing the roof before the next round." Annabella nodded toward George. "He managed to pull the ladder away from the back of the mercantile and left it in some tall weeds."

George shook his head and raised a hand. "I was going to move it closer to the other end so he wouldn't have to crawl as far when he was ready to get down. The ladder was much heavier than I expected and when it started to fall, I just dropped it and ran."

Annabella stared at her grandson. "Then you should have informed someone of those circumstances." Annabella exchanged glances with the group gathered. "Instead, George went home and poor Mr. Howard was on the roof when the next round of storms hit."

Molly gaped. "How did Mr. Howard get down?"

Annabella harrumphed. "Thankfully, someone coming from the depot heard him yelling up there over the commotion of the storm. Mrs. Howard had gone out to look for him when he hadn't returned, but when she didn't see the ladder at the side of the building, she thought he had finished. The ladder was found in the weeds, finally, and the poor man was helped down."

Molly looked up at her father. "That really wasn't very nice, Papa. Did you get a spanking for doing something so terrible?"

George nodded. "As a matter of fact, I did, and then I washed windows at the mercantile every day after school until the weather turned cold."

Annabella gave a curt nod. "Just as you should have, my boy. Mr. Howard caught a chill and was very sick for a couple weeks after that."

Helen took another sip of lemonade. "Well, I was in New York by the time that happened. I just remember all the little things like him jumping out of bushes to scare people, or catching snakes and bringing them to school." She shivered. "Ellen can't reach into a canister to this day without checking first, thanks to Georgie."

George patted the top of Helen's head. "Well, this walk down memory lane has been special, but Ellen needs some help getting the tables and chairs back to the hotel. So I'll leave you women to your fun and games at my expense." He crooked a finger at Molly. "But you need to help me. You shouldn't be hearing such things about your father."

Molly stood. "Yes, sir." She waved as she followed her father over to the group of men gathering chairs for the hotel.

Evelyn smiled. "Was he really as bad as all that? He seems so nice now. Everyone in town likes him."

Annabella nodded. "Yes, he was a trial. There were days I wondered if he would grow to adulthood. But even back then, people loved him. Why, Mrs. Howard made him cookies every day when he reported for window washing duties." She laughed. "There was just something about him that you couldn't help loving—"

"Even when he put water on your seat at school and you walked around with a wet skirt." Helen smiled. "I could have strangled him more than a few times."

Annabella sighed and struggled to her feet. "Well, I really need to get home now, or I won't be up in time for church in the morning. Pastor Drummond is having that special service for our graduates and I don't want to miss it."

Helen stood. "I'll walk you home, Mama."

Annabella waved her away. "I'll be just fine. I've been walking home from this park for over eighty years. I can find my way."

Helen looped her arm through her mother's. "I have no doubt about that. But you do look a little weary. I'd never forgive myself if something happened to you and I wasn't there."

Annabella patted her daughter's hand. "Well, I would enjoy the company. And if you have a minute or two, I have a couple things I need some help with."

Helen looked over at Evelyn. "I have the entire evening. I'm sure Evelyn would like some time to be with her friends. Graduation day can be a little sad in some ways."

Evelyn stretched her back and rose from the chair. "I'm going to help clean up and then I'll probably walk down by the river for a little while."

"Just be careful and try to be home before dark. You know I worry when you are by the water after the sun goes down." Helen turned to her mother. "Ready?"

Chapter Eight

EVELYN RECLINED AGAINST THE tall cottonwood, her long, blue jean-clad legs crossed at the ankles. She wiggled her toes and looked up at the fluttering white puffs drifting on the breeze. Sunlight sifted through the canopy of leaves.

It's so pretty and peaceful here, my own little retreat. Her gaze shifted to the water lying along the banks, dark shadows shifting with the movement of the trees. *Maybe I will have another dip of the toes before I head home. The water is so nice and cool this time of year...plenty of it from the spring rains and not too green yet from the heat of summer. Just perfect!*

She closed her eyes and thought back over the events of the day. *I've graduated from high school! No more days of sitting in class and nights at home doing endless homework. I'm free to do what I want with my life and live it how I feel is best.* She scowled. *And no more Cynthia Rowe making my life miserable because she thinks I'm keeping Aaron from her.*

Evelyn opened her eyes and pictured Aaron. He had sat next to her mother in the crowd of people gathered to watch the graduates receive their diplomas. He had not smiled or looked at her...just given her a word of congratulations after the ceremony, as he had with all the other graduates. He had not even stayed for the festivities in the park, even though the mercantile had been closed for the afternoon in honor of the day.

Evelyn frowned. *I'm so very sorry, Aaron. I feel terrible that you are so miserable right now. I don't want you to be hurting. But it feels so wrong to just marry you so you will be happy. Maybe I am selfish, just as Mama has said. Maybe I want too much out of life, feel that I am owed certain things. Maybe it is best that I just stay in Rubyville, marry you and be content with the life you provide. You* would *care for me and our children…we would probably be happy…eventually.*

Slate-blue eyes floated through her thoughts, causing her to catch her breath and grow warm all over. They looked deep into her soul and wrapped around her heart. *I could do all those things…if I hadn't met Richard King.*

Evelyn covered her face with her hands. *Oh Father, what am I to do? Mama won't be a part of me marrying Mr. King. I will have to leave Rubyville, and we would have to start a life somewhere else, with no family for love and support. Is that better than marrying Aaron and being secured a future of my mother's making?* The tears slid down her face, dropping upon her blue jeans, leaving dark splotches. *Why does this have to be so difficult? Why can't Aaron just fall in love with Cynthia? Why can't Mama accept Mr. King…or anything that I want for my life? You have all the answers, Father. Please share them with me. I want to know what to do with my future.*

The sound of an automobile approaching silenced her thoughts. She looked up the slight embankment, trying to see through the trees to the road beyond. All she could make out was a black vehicle. The automobile stopped and was turned off.

Evelyn sighed. *Bother…I should have walked further upstream. Probably someone wanting to fish. There goes my chance for dipping my toes again.* She reached for her socks and penny loafers at the sound of a door slamming. *Maybe they'll see me here and go somewhere else. That's what I would do if I saw someone enjoying a nice evening breeze beside the water all by themselves.* She pulled on her socks, cuffing them down, and then slid on her brown shoes. She turned at the sound of footsteps coming down the gradual slope to the water and gasped.

"Mr. King, what are you doing here?" She jumped to her feet, brushing the dirt and leaves from her pants. She patted her hair, smoothing strands away from her face.

"I've been looking for you. You are a difficult person to track down." He stopped before her and gave her a smile as he narrowed his eyes. "Have you been crying?"

Evelyn brushed at her cheeks and blushed. "Only for a minute…it was just one of those days. I guess my emotions got the better of me. I'm fine…really."

"So, are congratulations in order? Have you graduated?" His blue eyes twinkled as he asked the question.

She nodded. "Yes, I did. And you?"

He grinned. "An important-looking diploma and all...so I'm officially ready to tackle the real world." He winked at her. "At least that's what they keep telling me."

She smiled and looked down at her feet. "How long have you been looking for me?"

He shoved his hands into his pockets, his eyes twinkling. "I would say my entire life, but that would sound cliché." His eyes swept over her face. "But it would be very true."

Her eyes met his and she gulped.

He scuffed his shoe upon the dirt. "I drove into town about an hour ago. There looked like there had been some sort of celebration in the park that people were finishing up with."

"Yes, my grandmother had a big party for all the graduates and their families. I was supposed to help clean up, but I was told to go and enjoy the rest of my day." She shrugged. "So here I am...one of my favorite places in Rubyville."

His eyes scanned the river and drifted to the trees overhead. "It sure is pretty and peaceful. I can understand why you like it here." His eyes caught hers. "I went by your house after I checked in at the hotel. There was no one home. So I thought I would see the river while I was so close...and here you are."

She frowned. "You checked into the hotel?"

He smiled. "If you don't mind, I would like to attend services at your church in the morning. I really appreciated what your pastor said when I visited a couple weeks ago."

Evelyn smiled. "That...that would be fine...but Pastor Drummond is having a special service tomorrow for the graduates."

"Even better, since I'm one as well." He looked down at her. "Will it cause problems with your mother if I stay in town and go to church in the morning? I don't need to stay all afternoon like I did the last time. I got a room at the hotel so I wouldn't have to leave from Emporia so early in the morning...and..." he tapped her chin up, "I was hoping to see you tonight."

Evelyn looked up the embankment. "My mother can't say who is allowed to go to church. And don't be silly. If you're in town, you need to eat Sunday dinner with us. Ellen will have a nice breakfast for you at the hotel."

He raised a brow. "Ellen?"

"Ellen Johnson, my cousin. She runs the hotel now that her father has retired from it. She is a wonderful cook."

"Is she a rather stern-looking woman, around forty with graying blonde hair?" Richard winced.

Evelyn laughed. "That would be her. She *is* a bit cranky, I'm afraid, but she does an excellent job running the hotel. People return year after year to stay there and eat her cooking."

"So, in a roundabout way, you just skipped over my question about your mother." He scrunched down and looked at her eye to eye. "Your mother is not happy about me coming into your life, is she?"

Evelyn took a deep breath. "No, she is not."

He straightened and pressed his lips together. "Is it because of Mr. Darby, or something else?"

Evelyn shrugged. "She's not happy that I won't marry Aaron. She has made *that* very clear. But she also doesn't think you are appropriate for me."

"How so?"

"She said you don't have any way to take care of me." She stared up at him, her eyes wide. "I tried to tell her that I thought you were a hard worker and a man of integrity and honor. She thinks you're just after my money."

He threw back his head and laughed. A squirrel in the tree above chattered at the intrusion. "*Do* you have money, Miss Hanover?" His eyes grew dark as his lips became a firm line. "That would probably be the one thing that would make me run."

Evelyn's eyes became as saucers. "*If* I have money, you won't be interested in me anymore?"

He nodded, staring over her head. "That about sums it up. The pursuit of money always seems to lead to much unhappiness in this world. I don't want to be part of it." He looked down at her. "Is that why everyone in town seems to be related to you?"

She frowned. "I *am* related to almost everyone in town in some way or another...but not because I have money. That's because my great-grandfather, William Barton founded Rubyville back in the 1800's...around the Civil War time."

"The same man that donated land for the church you attend?"

"Yes...but how did you know that?"

He shrugged. "Miss Rowe offered some information to my friend Bill Caruthers. He shared it with me the night we came out here to take Miss Rowe home after the prom."

She pointed to him. "You were out here that night?"

He smiled. "Miss Rowe told Bill where your house was, so we drove by."

Evelyn crossed her arms. "Well, that explains it. My mother wasn't too thrilled that people were driving by out here so late, or should I say, so early in the morning. She thought I had something to do with it."

"You?" He laughed and shook his head. "Have you been such a difficult child that your mother is suspicious?"

She raised her hands. "I didn't think so. But she seems to believe I'm up to no good most of the time these days."

"Ever since you told her you wouldn't marry Mr. Darby." Richard reached out and stroked her cheek. "You are as soft as a rose petal."

Evelyn's eyes slid up the hill once more. "We shouldn't be down here...alone. It wouldn't be good if someone saw us."

He nodded. "I'm thinking that information would travel fairly quickly to your mother."

She gave a half-smile. "Tongues would be wagging, for sure, and Miss Rowe would be the most eager." She shook her head. "I'm sorry, I shouldn't have added that last part. I seem to just say whatever pops into my head most of the time."

He touched her cheek, sliding his finger to the corner of her mouth. His eyes focused on that spot. "What would pop into your head about me?"

She stared up at him. "That...that I have been waiting for you all my life, as well."

He grinned, running his thumb along her full bottom lip. "That's just what I wanted to hear." He lowered his head.

The sudden slamming of a car door filtered through the trees to where the young couple stood.

"Wait!" Evelyn stopped him with hands upon his chest. "Someone's coming! I can't be seen here alone with you."

Richard straightened as he put one finger to his lips. He turned and looked through the trees. "Well, whoever it is has already seen my automobile," he whispered. "I agree… it's best that we aren't seen here." He looked down the river.

Evelyn placed a hand upon his arm. "I'm going to walk downstream and then I'll circle back around to my house."

The sound of whistling and moving brush came to them.

Richard grabbed her arm as she swung away. "Will you be alright?"

She gave him a smile. "I've walked these woods and fields my entire life. I'll be fine." She waved as she hurried away.

RICHARD SAT DOWN UPON a large rock and braced his elbows on his knees.

"I thought that looked like your Ford parked up there." Aaron set his tackle box upon the ground and leaned his fishing rod against the cottonwood tree. He glanced up and down the river. "I thought for sure I heard voices down here."

Forgive me, Father, for what I'm about to say. Richard shrugged. "Just me down here right now, must have been some raccoon chattering in the woods."

There was a loud crash down the river.

"That's some raccoon." Aaron walked to the edge of the water and scanned downstream.

Richard gripped his hands together, cracking his knuckles. "Do you see anything? Maybe a cow stumbled in from the field."

Aaron shook his head. "There are no cows in that field. They planted corn there just a few weeks ago. You should have been able to see it when you parked your automobile."

Richard shook his head. "Well, I'm no farmer, so if there was corn there, I didn't pay attention."

"Typical city dweller…wouldn't know what a pitchfork looked like if it hit you over the head." Aaron scanned the river once more and walked back to the cottonwood tree.

Richard tilted his head, narrowing one eye. "You run a store. Have you sold a pitchfork or two so you know what one looks like?"

Aaron crossed his arms, his brown hair dropping over his eyes. He brushed it back and returned to his stance. "Actually, I grew up on a farm, as well as helping in the *mercantile*. I spent a fair share of my younger years pitching hay."

Richard switched his stare back to the river. "I did too, my friend." He tossed a rock into the water. "My parents' favorite past time for their children was sending them out to their large garden. We grew just about every vegetable you could imagine. Then they gave most of it away to our church."

Aaron grunted. "You didn't want to share with your church, help people that were more in need?"

Richard pursed his lips and threw another stone. "I didn't mind sharing at all. I believe that you *should* give to those in need…but you don't sacrifice your own children to do it." Richard squinted. "My mother would open up a can of beans for the three of us to enjoy for dinner as she walked baskets of produce to our church."

"You sound rather bitter." Aaron uncrossed his arms and leaned one hand against the bark of the cottonwood.

Richard shook his head. "I pray that I'm not. I just can't abide hypocrisy."

"Well, I can't either, so why don't we get to the real reason you're down here at the river. You're a long way from Emporia." Aaron stared down at the seated form.

"I'm not trying to be anything other than what you're seeing, Mr. Darby." He squinted up at his older peer. "I'm here in Rubyville to see Miss Hanover. But you already knew that."

"What I can't understand is why you keep pursuing a young woman that is already spoken for. It's in very bad taste." Aaron drummed his long fingers on the trunk of the tree.

"Well…" Richard stared up at Aaron, "if she had told me she *was* spoken for, I would have gone away."

Aaron kneeled down, his eyes flashing. "No, you wouldn't have, *Mr. King*. You wouldn't stay away from her the night of the prom…and you knew she was with me, and that we were planning to be married."

Richard raised a hand. "Hold on there. I didn't know Miss Hanover was engaged. And you're right, one dance with her and I was a goner." He pointed a finger at Aaron. "But, if at any time she had said that she *was* in love with you and that she was marrying you, I would have walked away. I would have respected that." He dropped his hand and shrugged. "But if it was only a date for the prom, I figure I had as much of a chance as you at winning her heart."

"Why you lousy…" Aaron stood, shoving his hands into his pockets. "You come along and ruin my life and you say something as smug as that."

"There's nothing smug about it…just the truth." Richard stood, straightening his long form. "I care about Miss Hanover…a lot."

Aaron eyed Richard, curling his lip as he attacked. "I'm sure you think you do after seeing her…what? A measly couple of times? I've known her my entire life. You don't have a clue about her or what she needs." He nodded toward the black Ford, parked at the top of the embankment. "You drive around in that jalopy, wearing clothes that have seen better days. You can't even take care of yourself. Why you just graduated high school today, I'm thinking, and probably barely made it through that."

Richard smiled. "Just valedictorian of my class…thanks for your sentiments. And no, I don't have a lot, but I know how to work hard and I can care for a wife."

"Oh…oh…" Aaron's face reddened to the top of his collar. "So now she's going to be your wife. Who do you think you are…*dancing* into *my* town, taking *my* fiancé right out from under my nose?"

Richard gave a slight smile. "Mr. Darby, if Miss Hanover *really* had loved you, and if she *really* had wanted to marry you…" He shook his head. "Well, wild horses wouldn't have pulled her away. I know that much about her."

Aaron pulled his hands from his pockets, fisting them at his sides.

"I've never been a fighting man, but I could sure flatten your nose right about now."

Rustling of brush jerked two heads in the direction of the sound. The two men paused.

I sure hope Evelyn is home by now. Richard sighed. "Well, I don't see anything down there to be concerned with. But you spend more time here than I do." He turned toward the slight hill. "I'm going to head on out before you follow through on that offer." He brushed his nose. "I kind of like the one I've got."

Aaron flexed his hands at his side. "Maybe this should be your last night here in Rubyville."

Richard paused in his ascent. "Well, I'm going to see if Miss Hanover is home and accepting visitors. No one answered when I stopped by earlier. If she would like for me to leave, I will." He continued up the hill and called back, "But I'm sure praying she would like me to stay, and I hope to be at church in the morning. See you then."

Aaron ran his hand through his hair, pomaded strands standing on end. "If I wasn't a gentleman…"

Richard opened the door to his automobile and slid in, pulling the door shut as he braced his elbow on the open window. He leaned his forehead on the steering wheel. *Father, give me Your love and patience for that man. I wanted to flatten his nose, as well.* He raised his head and started the Ford, turning around on the narrow dirt road. He followed it back to the stone house, turning into the driveway.

Chapter Nine

EVELYN LIMPED TO THE kitchen door, the blue jean material stuck to her bloodied knee. She grimaced as she looked down at the trickle of blood seeping from under her pant leg, pooling in the wide cuff of her white sock. *Mama is going to snap her cap when she sees me.* She eyed the closed garage door. *This would have been a lovely evening for you to take one of your drives, Mama.* She sighed. *Better get it over with before I bleed to death out here on the terrace. Mama would have a terrible time getting all that blood out of the stones.* She smiled. *That's a pretty gruesome thought! Why do you think of these things, Evelyn Hanover?*

She pushed open the door and limped into the kitchen, taking a seat upon a chair.

Helen called from the front room. "Evelyn, is that you?" She walked into the kitchen and gasped. "Whatever happened?" Her eyes followed the drops of blood dotting the floor.

"I'm fine, Mama. I fell and scraped my knee, that's all. I was hoping it would stop bleeding so I could get cleaned up and get it bandaged." Evelyn sat with her leg stuck out straight.

Helen leaned down and looked at the wound through the torn material. "Well, I can't see a thing as long as you have those awful pants on." She took a towel from the drawer and pressed it to the ragged skin. "You're going to have to go upstairs and wash up and put on a dress so I can see how badly you're hurt. We might have to take you over to Dr. Rundell's office if it's serious."

"I don't need to bother Dr. Rundell. It's a Saturday and he deserves a bit of time off, just like the rest of us." Evelyn pulled the towel away.

"See, it's already not bleeding as much as it was before."

The wound seeped again.

Helen put her hand over Evelyn's and pressed the cloth to Evelyn's knee. "We are going to Dr. Rundell's. This is bleeding more than I like." She looked up at her daughter. "I'm going to get the Chrysler out. Do you think you can make it to the driveway?"

Evelyn winced as her mother pressed on the towel, already covered with blood. "Of course, Mama…it's just a skinned knee after all." She pushed to her feet and grabbed the table. *Why is the kitchen going in circles?* "Oh my, I'm feeling a bit dizzy."

Helen sat her back in the chair. "I want you to stay right here." She shook her finger at Evelyn. "Do you hear me? No trying to walk until I get back. I'll help you out. I don't need you falling and hitting your head, on top of all of this."

Evelyn looked toward the front room. "I think someone is knocking on the door, Mama."

Helen straightened and started from the room. "Who could that be at a time like this?"

Evelyn tilted her head, listening as her mother opened the door.

"Good evening, Mrs. Hanover. I was wondering if Miss Hanover would be free to visit with me for a bit." Richard's low, warm voice floated into the kitchen.

Evelyn sighed and closed her eyes. *Thank you, God, for sending just the right person in my time of need.* She opened her eyes and struggled to stand. *Surely if I danced the Lindy Hop, I can walk across a swaying kitchen.*

"No, I'm afraid that Miss Hanover is not accepting any visitors at this time. She fell and hurt herself and I was just about to take her to see the doctor. I'm sorry for any inconvenience to you. Good evening."

"Mama!" Evelyn swayed in the door frame of the kitchen as her eyes met Richard's from across the room. "I would love to visit with Mr. King." She gripped the molding, biting her lower lip.

Richard rushed passed Helen, scooping Evelyn into his arms just as she started to crumple to the floor. He looked at the blonde-haired woman, his dark eyes searching her face. "What happened?"

Helen grabbed the towel from the floor and pressed it to Evelyn's leg. "I don't know. She just returned home and said she fell and skinned her knee." She lifted the towel and examined the knee once again. "But it's obviously much worse than that. I was just about to take her to Dr. Rundell's office when you arrived."

Richard walked to the front door, Evelyn's head resting against the flap of his plaid shirt pocket. "I can drive you over, just tell me the way."

Helen pressed her hand to her chest. "Thank you, Mr. King. I would appreciate that." She followed him out the door, slamming it behind her.

Evelyn looked up at the strong, chiseled chin and gave a half-smile. "I'm so glad you stopped by. It hardly even hurts now...I just feel a bit woozy, is all. Can you make the room stop spinning?"

He smiled down at her as he nodded toward her knee. "Just keep pressing on that towel." He gave her a wink. "I'm glad I stopped by, too." He waited as Helen opened the Ford door. He placed Evelyn upon the seat and waited for Helen to get in. "It will be a bit cozy, but far better than getting blood in a nice vehicle."

Helen patted the dashboard as Richard got in. "It may be old and rusty, but very clean. I must say, I'm rather impressed, Mr. King." Helen gestured. "Just follow this road past the depot. Dr. Rundell's office is two more blocks west of the school."

Richard and Evelyn shared a smile as he put the Ford in gear and started down the road.

RICHARD SET EVELYN UPON the examining table. *Dear Father, please take care of her. She's as white as my mother's sheets on a sunny day!* He walked to the doorway of the large room and shoved his hands into his pockets.

Dr. Rundell patted his patient's arm. "Now I want you to lie back so I may see what you did. There's a nice, comfy pillow there." He took a pair of scissors from the top of the cabinet. "I'm going to have to cut away the material from the area so I may see it better."

"That is quite alright, Dr. Rundell. She will have one less pair of those blue jeans to wear." Helen smoothed the hair back from Evelyn's face. "I wonder what your grandfather would have thought about young ladies wearing blue jeans."

Dr. Rundell chuckled. "I'm sure we doctors aren't as concerned about the clothes our patients wear, as we are the patients themselves."

Evelyn glared up at her mother. "It will be no problem to repair the damage done, Dr. Rundell."

The doctor glanced back at the young man standing in the doorway. "And who might you be? You seem familiar to me."

Helen pulled her gaze from Evelyn's leg and looked at Richard. "This is Mr. King, a...a friend of Evelyn's. He happened by at just the right time."

Evelyn raised her head off the pillow. "You may remember him from church. He attended services just a couple of weeks ago."

Dr. Rundell snapped his finger and pointed at Richard. "*That's* where I remember you from. You were seated next to Miss Barton...I mean, Mrs. Langworthy." He looked at Helen. "I will never get used to calling your mother by her married name. She was always Miss Barton to me."

Helen smiled at the doctor. "That is quite alright. I think the entire town thinks the same thing. After all, she was only married a couple of years."

The young doctor nodded his dark head. "Yes, and that was a very sad state of affairs. They deserved a longer happy life than what they had." He looked at Evelyn. "Now, how did you manage this?"

Evelyn looked at the ceiling. "I was down at the river, walking along the bank, when a snake startled me. He was just kind of curled up in the brush." She raised her head and looked at Richard.

Helen watched the young couple exchange looks. "Would you like Mr. King to go into the other room, my dear? You may not be comfortable with him in here."

Evelyn lowered her head to the pillow. "No, I would like him to remain here, if that is alright with Dr. Rundell."

The doctor shrugged. "Makes no difference to me, just keep out of the way is all I ask." He began cutting a slit up the leg of the blue jeans. "So you saw a snake?"

Evelyn winced as he pulled the heavy material from the wound. "Yes, and when I jumped back, I stumbled and fell onto a piece of flint rock."

Richard took a deep breath. *So that was the crash we heard! I should have investigated the sound rather than being so afraid for Evelyn being seen with me.*

Dr. Rundell looked up at Evelyn. "Yes, I can see that. You have a large piece of that rock still lodged in your knee, which is part of the reason it is bleeding so badly. You are going to need some stitches. It's a big gash."

Helen patted her daughter's arm. "You must be in a lot of pain, my dear." She glanced back at the doctor, her eyes wide and unblinking.

Dr. Rundell smiled. "Yes, I am sure she is, Mrs. Hanover, but she is doing very well. You, on the other hand, are going to need to leave. You are turning a lovely shade of green and I don't need two patients on my hands." He turned to Richard. "Please help Mrs. Hanover from the room and then return." He looked at his patient. "Your..." his gaze shifted from Evelyn to Richard, "presence may be appreciated."

Richard offered his arm to Helen. "May I walk you out, Mrs. Hanover?"

Helen's eyes lowered to the arm. "I will do just fine on my own. I seem to be a bit queasy, but I'm alright. It's difficult to watch your only child in pain and bleeding so much."

Richard dropped his arm. "Yes, I'm sure it is, Mrs. Hanover."

She turned to the doctor. "Please let me know if there are any complications."

Dr. Rundell smiled. "Of course, now just go in and sit down. I will be done in just a few minutes." He watched the older woman walk from the room, then closed the door and returned to the table. "Now, I'm going to pour some iodine over the area to clean it and then I'm going to take that last bit of rock out and clean it again." He gave her a wink. "It's going to hurt like nothing you've ever experienced before, but..." he nodded at Richard, "that's why this strong, young man is here. Hang on to him and don't let go."

Evelyn's eyes widened as she gripped Richard's hand. She gasped when Dr. Rundell poured the iodine over the wound, and bit her bottom lip when he pulled the rock from the gash. Her eyes drifted closed, her face whiter than before.

Dr. Rundell's eyes flitted over Evelyn's face. "You're doing just fine...just fine. I'll be done in a minute."

Richard kept his eyes on Evelyn's face, squeezing her hand within his own. "You're doing a great job, Miss Hanover."

She offered a small laugh, opening her eyes as tears trickled down her face. "I think you can call me Evelyn." She moved her head back and forth over the pillow. "It really hurts and I'd just like to scream."

"Then go ahead, if it makes you feel better." Richard laid a hand across her forehead.

She shook her head vehemently. "No, Mama would come running in here." Her eyes swept over his face. "And I really need *you* right now."

He gave her a smile, leaning over to press a kiss against her temple. "I'm here for you, my dear."

Dr. Rundell straightened and looked at his patient. "You're doing very well, Evelyn. I have it cleaned and now I'm going to put a few stitches in to hold it closed."

She nodded. "I'm ready…I think."

Richard smoothed his fingers across her brow as she closed her eyes, squinting with the pain. "It's okay… it's almost over. This can't be any worse than you walking all the way home on that leg."

Evelyn chuckled again, wincing with each poke of the needle. "I was so afraid someone was going to see me that I didn't even think about the pain until I reached the kitchen door."

Richard stroked her cheek. "Aaron and I heard the crash when you fell. Just how long *did* you listen to our conversation?" He spoke the words softly, for her ears only.

Evelyn's eyes drifted open, caressing his face. "Long enough to be compared to a cow…and know that you care about me…a lot." She offered a weak smile. "I was hoping that the wife you were talking about might be me." Her gaze shifted to the ceiling and she groaned. "I left when Aaron offered to punch your nose."

"Almost done, Evelyn…you're doing a great job." Dr. Rundell pulled the black braided nylon suture and knotted it.

Richard turned his gaze from where Dr. Rundell worked, and gave her a wink. "Well, he didn't flatten it, as you can see. You are a very brave woman, in my opinion." He leaned down close and whispered against her ear. "The fact that I can be in here with you...well, it's like a gift from Heaven."

Dr. Rundell cleared his throat. "If you two lovebirds care, I'm through." He grinned as Evelyn's eyes flew open.

"You won't say anything about us to Mama, will you?" Evelyn stared at the doctor.

He shook his head as he went to the sink and washed his hands. "No, I won't, but she has to see that you both are smitten with one another. If you are trying to keep it a secret, it won't be one for long. There are sparks flying around the two of you."

Evelyn blushed, trying to sit up.

Richard leaned over, one arm behind her back as he helped her into a sitting position, her legs stuck out straight in front of her.

Dr. Rundell dried his hands and sat down at his desk. "Are you both ready for me to call in Mrs. Hanover?"

Richard looked down at Evelyn as he caressed her shoulder.

Dr. Rundell chuckled and stood up. "I'll give Mrs. Hanover the instructions in the other room." He pointed his finger at Evelyn. "No wandering down by the river for a few days. I want you to keep that leg elevated, whenever possible, for about a week to reduce the swelling. I had to put in twelve stitches to close it and I want them to hold. Change the bandages twice a day, and you may take an aspirin if you are uncomfortable. Do you have any at home?"

Evelyn nodded. "I think so."

Dr. Rundell unfolded the rolled-up sleeves of his striped shirt. "Well, if not, Aaron has it at the mercantile. Just follow the directions on the bottle." He pointed to her leg. "I want to look at it again in about a week and see how it's doing, but it should heal quickly. You're young and in good health. I'll tell you then when the stitches should come out." He buttoned the cuff of his shirt, his gaze shifting between them. "Any questions?"

Evelyn shook her head. "Thank you, Dr. Rundell."

He gave her a smile. "Your mother won't be thanking me when she gets the bill...after office hours and all." He waved a hand at them. "I'm going to give you both a few minutes, and then you can carry her out to your automobile. I'll keep Mrs. Hanover entertained for awhile." He nodded his head. "I'm young and in love, as well, and I cherish those few stolen moments."

Evelyn gasped. "I had no idea! Is she someone in town?"

He chuckled. "No, she lives in Manhattan. I met her up there while I was attending a conference."

"I'm so happy for you!" Evelyn laughed. "The mothers in town with marriageable daughters will be sorely disappointed, I'm sure."

He shrugged. "Such is life." He opened the door, walking through and closing it part way behind him.

Richard cupped her face and lowered his lips to hers, moving slowly over her mouth. He groaned and pulled away, pressing her cheek against his chest. "I'm sorry, you may not have been up for that, but having you so close has just about ruined my self-control."

Evelyn smiled against his shirt. "That was the best pain-reliever of all. I didn't even think about my leg for a few seconds."

He ran his hand over her hair and down her back. "This means you won't be able to go to church in the morning."

She leaned back and stared up at his blue eyes. "Probably not, but *you* can still attend services. My grandmother would appreciate a ride over to our house for Sunday dinner. I will let Mama know and I will call Grandmama with the plans."

He raised a brow. "You have this all worked out, don't you?"

She shrugged. "If you can drive over from Emporia to see me, then I can certainly help from my end." She glanced down at her bandaged leg. "I'm just going to be a little slower with it, that's all."

He put a finger beneath her chin and tilted it up. "You should have called out when you saw that snake and fell. It didn't matter what Aaron Darby thought at that point. Your safety was far more important."

She took a deep breath. "It all worked out just fine. Now…please kiss me one more time before you carry me outside."

He grinned, his eyes darkening as he lowered his head once more. His lips covered hers, taking all thoughts from her mind.

She sighed, closing her eyes, and the beat of her heart seemed to pound in her head, coursing through her veins. She felt the sensation of his lips moving against her ear.

I love you, Evelyn Hanover, and you're going to be my bride very soon, if I have anything to say about it!

Startled, she opened her eyes. "Did you say something?"

He gave her a wink. "Who, me? What do you think you heard?"

"That…that…you love me." Evelyn's eyes sparkled.

He chuckled, sweeping her up in his arms. "Your mother's waiting."

Evelyn gave a sigh, then settled into his embrace, replaying the words she had thought she had heard.

HELEN TUCKED THE COVERS under Evelyn's chin and sat down on the side of the bed. She crossed her leg and folded her hands in her lap. "I suppose it was very helpful to have Mr. King here to carry you up the stairs. You wouldn't have been very comfortable on the davenport."

Evelyn pulled her arms from under the covers and clasped her hands over her tummy. "No, I wouldn't have been. And it's wonderful that he will be here tomorrow to help me down the stairs and share Sunday dinner with us."

Helen sighed. "If that makes you feel better, then it's good. I want you to heal quickly." She wrinkled her brow. "I had better add another small roast to what I had planned for tomorrow. Mr. Darby will be here as well."

Evelyn struggled into a sitting position. "Mama! Why did you ask Aaron to dinner?"

Helen turned her blue eyes on her daughter. "Because it was the neighborly thing to do and my prerogative as the head of this house. Mr. Darby had just given me a ride home a few minutes before you arrived bleeding all over my clean kitchen floor. I had asked him then. I know he has been out of sorts since you told him you wouldn't follow through with your plans. I can barely go into the mercantile and see his sad face." She shrugged. "Besides, I had no idea that Mr. King was in town and planning on staying for the weekend. I just don't know if that is appropriate."

"Mama, he's not staying here in my bedroom." Evelyn winced as she leaned back against her padded headboard.

Helen gasped, one hand to her forehead. She closed her eyes. "I would think not! You say the most...the most embarrassing things at times." She opened her eyes. "I just don't see the point of him staying at the hotel. He could have driven over in the morning, just as he did when he came the last time."

Evelyn lowered her eyes, running one finger over her nail. "He was hoping to spend a bit more time with me."

Helen raised her chin. "Well, he accomplished that. I cannot even imagine Dr. Rundell allowing him to stay in the examining room with you while I waited out front. I'm your mother, after all."

Evelyn crossed her arms. "He didn't want you conking your head on the floor. You didn't look very good." She shrugged. "Anyway, it all worked out for the best. Now, what am I to do with Aaron *and* Mr. King here? They can barely tolerate being polite to one another."

Helen stood, smoothing the bright floral pattern of her dress over her hips. "Well, my dear, that is going to be up to you and your grandmother. I'm going to be far too busy trying to figure out how to have enough food for that hulk of a young man to worry about whether he and Mr. Darby are having polite conversation."

Evelyn glared up at her mother. "It didn't need to be so complicated. It would have been just fine having only Mr. King here for dinner."

Helen raised her hands in the air. "Well, maybe another young man will show up at church in the morning and your grandmother will be sure to invite him over, too. We'll just have one big party."

Evelyn raised her brow and smiled. "Or maybe just *one* handsome gentleman, say around fifty or so, will visit...looking for an attractive woman."

Helen leaned down and kissed the top of Evelyn's head. "You say the most ridiculous things, my girl. What would I do with a man around here? I like my life just the way it is...doing just as I please."

"It would keep you from being too lonely when I'm gone." Evelyn's words followed her mother to the door.

Helen braced her red-nailed fingers against the door frame. "I've been lonely since March of 1931, my dear. We've become good friends, and I don't see any need to change it now. Sleep well. Call me if you need anything during the night." She continued from the room, her heels loud upon the wood floor.

Chapter Ten

EVELYN SAT AT HER bedroom window, scowling at the beautiful scenery spread before her. *What a way to begin my first summer of freedom…trapped on a chair with my leg stiff as a board. Mr. King is just blocks away from me and I'm not even close enough to smell his aftershave. Father, I know You have a plan in this, but I honestly don't see it right now.*

She sighed and stared out the window. The mown grass was thick and green around the terrace. In the distance, the cornfield she had limped through just the day before moved gently with the slight breeze, the short shoots quivering. The trees along the river were full and shimmering in the wind. *And here I sit, listening to everyone downstairs. You would think that* someone *would remember me.*

She adjusted the puffed sleeve of her black-and-white-checked dress and then retied the large bow at the collar. *If only Mama had agreed to let me wear her wedge sandals, rather than these black ballet slippers. But I suppose they are better for limping around in.* She covered the white bandage with her skirt and looked at the door once more. *Surely Mama remembers that someone needs to help me down the stairs. If Richard doesn't come soon, I'm just going to try it myself.*

There was a timid knock on the door.

Evelyn smiled. "Come in," she sang out, staring at the door.

Aaron's head peeked around the door. "Your mother sent me up to carry you down. She said to apologize for the wait, but she wanted to have dinner on the table so you could go right to your chair."

Evelyn rolled her eyes. "She did, did she? I was wondering if everyone had forgotten about me. You all have been home from church for about an hour now."

Aaron looked at his wrist watch. "Actually, we've been here about twenty minutes. Mr. King offered to come up several times, but your mother asked him to wait." He gave her a smile. "Are you ready?"

"Of course I'm ready, and I'm starving. I've had about enough of this sitting around." Evelyn frowned and adjusted her position on the chair.

"Your mother said you had to stay off your leg for a week."

"Yes, I know!" Evelyn held out her hand. "Please help me stand up and then I think I can make it down the stairs."

Aaron shook his head. "Your mother said to carry you down and that's what I'm going to do."

Evelyn's eyes swept over his slight frame. "Aaron, *are* you able to carry me, or am I going to be dropped about halfway down and have a broken leg or arm, as well?"

Aaron strode over and bent down, scooping her from the chair. He stood, his legs braced gallantly. "I may be thin, but I'm strong. Who do you think unloads the stock for the mercantile?"

Evelyn shrugged and gestured toward the door. "I've never thought about it before and I don't care to now. Just get me downstairs as quickly as possible without dropping me." She wiggled. "And don't hold me so close. You're squeezing the air right out of me."

He grasped her tighter. "I probably won't get this opportunity again, and I'm going to take advantage of it." He leaned close and sniffed. "You smell like roses...very nice."

Evelyn scowled at him. "Aaron!" She pointed to the door.

He grinned and sauntered over. "Who knew that you getting injured yesterday would be such a blessing for me?"

"Well, I certainly didn't plan it that way, I can tell you that for sure." Evelyn reclined stiffly.

"If you just relax and put your arm around my neck, it will be much easier to go down the stairs." His green eyes traveled the length of her. "I feel like I'm carrying a board."

"If you aren't up to the task, I'm sure Mr. King would take over for you. After all, he carried me up last night and he didn't seem to have a problem with it at all." She sat there, her hands clasped across her hips.

Aaron reached the top of the stairs and popped her up, adjusting his hands to the back of her knees.

Evelyn let out a squeal, grabbing him around the neck. "Don't you dare drop me, Aaron Darby." She said the words through gritted teeth.

He chuckled. "Just getting a better grip." He continued down the stairs and walked through the front room to the dining room beyond.

"There she is." Annabella clasped her hands together from her seat at the foot of the table. "Mr. King was just telling me of your ordeal yesterday."

Richard stood from his place at the center of the long table. "I was just filling your grandmother in on all the details…telling her how very brave you were." His eyes darkened as they met Evelyn's. He gave her a wide smile. "You're looking very well this afternoon…much better than last night."

Evelyn pulled her arm from around Aaron's neck. She lowered her voice. "You can put me down now."

Annabella cleared her throat and patted the table to her right. "I think this is Evelyn's place right here, Mr. Darby. Mr. King already pulled out her chair so it would be ready."

Aaron sauntered around the table, depositing Evelyn on the chair. He scooted it in and placed her napkin in her lap.

"*I* can do that!" She snatched the napkin from him. "Please just sit down." Evelyn scowled up at him.

Aaron shrugged. "Just trying to help." He took the seat next to her as Helen came in from the kitchen, carrying a large platter of meat.

"I'm so sorry to keep you waiting upstairs, Evelyn, but I didn't want you sitting too long at the table with your leg down. You know Dr. Rundell said you should keep it elevated."

She set the platter in front of her mother. "Would you mind serving, Mama?"

"I would be delighted, my dear." Annabella smiled up at her daughter and then patted Evelyn's hand, which was lying on the table. "I'm sure Evelyn will be just fine through dinner, and Mr. King can help her get situated in the sitting room when we're finished. The davenport might be the best place for her to spend the afternoon so she may visit."

Evelyn gripped her grandmother's hand and mouthed, "Thank you."

Helen took her seat at the head of the table and looked at Richard, seated to her right. "Mr. King, would you please pray for our meal?"

Richard smiled at Helen. "Certainly, Mrs. Hanover, it would be my pleasure."

Everyone bowed their head as Richard's low voice began. "Dear gracious Heavenly Father, we thank You for this bountiful meal that has been prepared. I also thank You for the message that Pastor Drummond gave this morning, challenging the class of 1948 to be diligent in their study of Your Word, and to make wise decisions with their futures, always putting You first in all that they do. I ask that You work in my life to apply this message. I also ask that You watch over Miss Hanover, healing her injury quickly and efficiently, while giving her the patience to endure what You have given her to handle these next couple of weeks. Have her to know that You have a plan in all of this. Lastly, let our speech and conversation around this table and this afternoon honor and glorify You. In Jesus name, amen."

Evelyn opened her eyes to see Annabella gazing at Helen.

Annabella raised her white brow and picked up her water glass, lifting it slightly. She smiled and said, "Amen."

RICHARD SAT WITH ONE elbow resting on the arm of his chair, his thumb under his chin and his index finger against his temple. From his comfortable chair in the corner of the room, he had been able to observe Evelyn. He had smiled at her comments, interjected when needed or asked to in the conversation, and had fallen deeper in love with the redheaded girl.

She's all I've ever wanted, Father. She has a love for You, respects her mother and grandmother, and is kind to Mr. Darby...well most of the time. He smiled with the last thought. His eyes caressed her from afar, sweeping over her lips, her long, pale neck and across the sweet slope of her shoulders. His hands fairly ached with the need to touch the smooth arms, letting his hands glide over the petal-soft skin.

He let his eyelids droop, feeling the pressure of her lips against his.

What I would give for just a few hours with you dear, sweet Evelyn. Hours with just the two of us, snuggled close, inhaling your rose scent.

"Mr. King, are you alright over there?" Annabella called. "Your face is a bit pink and I thought maybe you needed some fresh air."

Richard dropped his hand and sat straighter in his chair. "I probably started to nod off with the pleasant conversation around me."

Annabella chuckled. "Yes, it is rather boring listening to two women talk, I'm sure." The elderly woman fanned herself with her gloves. "Summer is definitely on its way." She turned to Helen, seated in the chair across from hers. "Maybe you should open a couple windows. I would think there would be a cool breeze starting with the evening hours."

Aaron jumped up from his place at the end of the long sofa. "I can do that, Mrs. Hanover. No need for you to get up." He rushed to the window and pushed up, straining until his face glowed red.

Helen twisted to look behind her, watching his progress. "Did you unlock the sash, Mr. Darby? I know it's probably silly to keep the windows and doors locked here in Rubyville, but you can never be too safe when it's two women living alone."

Richard's lips twitched as he turned his gaze back on Evelyn. She smiled at him over her shoulder.

"Yes, yes, of course…how stupid of me to forget." Aaron turned the brass lock and then pushed up once again, sending the lower part of the window to the top of the frame with a loud bang.

"Oh my!" Annabella gripped the arms of her chair. "I thought we'd all been shot."

"I'm sorry, Miss Barton. The windows at the mercantile always stick and you have to put some force behind them." Aaron ran his hand through his slick hair.

"How well I remember." Annabella smiled at the young man. "Please continue with your task. The breeze has already cooled down this stuffy room. I daresay I will recover from the fright."

Evelyn placed her hand over the lower portion of her face, her shoulders shaking.

Helen wrinkled her brow at her daughter and shook her head.

Aaron opened the last window and took his place at Evelyn's feet once more. He turned to her. "May I get you some more water?"

"If I have any more to drink I'm going to float right out of this room." Evelyn glanced at her mother. "But thank you anyway for thinking of me. You've been very *helpful* this afternoon."

Aaron patted her shawl-covered leg and three pairs of eyes focused on him. He pulled his hand away and clenched it at his side. "I'm sorry, I don't know what I was thinking."

Helen gave him a reassuring smile. "It's alright, Mr. Darby. I know you've been very concerned about Evelyn. It's very difficult to not show affection for someone you've known your entire life. It's only natural for you to demonstrate that with a pat."

Annabella grasped the cane at the side of her chair. "It has been a lovely afternoon, but time for me to go home. I tire easily these days. Heaven only knows why, since I don't accomplish much."

"Mama, you are always doing too much for someone your age, and you know it." Helen shook her head. "Why, your house is cleaner than mine, and it's twice the size."

Annabella laughed. "That's because I only live in a couple of rooms." Her eyes shifted to Evelyn. "It should have a nice young family living in it, filling it with children. That's what that old house has always needed. That's why my father built it."

Aaron cleared his throat and stood, checking his wrist watch once again. "I will drive you home, Miss Barton. I have my automobile right out front."

Helen glanced at Richard and raised her chin. "I was just going to suggest Mr. King. That way Mr. Darby can get Evelyn settled upstairs for the evening."

Evelyn looked at the grandfather clock by the stairs and gaped at her mother. "It's barely six, Mama. I don't want to go upstairs for a couple more hours yet."

Annabella smiled and smacked her hand upon her leg. "Well that works out perfectly, then. Mr. Darby and Helen may drive me home." She turned to her daughter. "There were a couple more items I needed to show you. I'm sure Mr. Darby won't mind waiting for a few minutes, and then he may drive you back home. After all, his house is just down the road from here."

Aaron turned wide eyes to Helen. "That...that would be fine with me, Mrs. Hanover. I was just going to go home and read for awhile."

Helen flashed her mother a stern look. "Really, Mama, I can walk home from your place. I do it all the time."

Aaron cleared his throat, adjusting the wide tie at his neck. "I don't mind, Mrs. Hanover. I hate to think of you walking around Rubyville after dark."

Helen pushed regally to her feet and took a deep breath. She tightened the fabric belt at her waist. "I don't plan on being as late as that. Surely my mother understands that I need to be here for our *company*." Helen stared at her mother, her blue eyes cold and unblinking.

Annabella smiled, struggling to her feet. "Yes, I do understand my dear, more than you know." She glanced at her granddaughter and Richard, both of them watching the exchange with wide eyes. She raised a hand. "I just thought of a wonderful idea. That new café has advertised ice cream and they will be serving it every night during the summer months. I think that would be a very delicious treat for the three of us."

Helen shook her head. "I really don't think Evelyn should leave the house right now."

"That's why I suggested the three of us." Annabella pointed to Aaron, Helen, and herself. She held out her hand. "Come, Aaron, help an old woman out to your automobile."

"Of course, Miss Barton." Aaron took his straw boater and placed it on his head. He gave a nod to Richard and addressed Evelyn. "I will stop by tomorrow to see how you're doing. Let me know if you need anything at all. I will be over as quickly as I can."

Annabella grasped Aaron's arm and gave it a pat. "I'm sure you will be, Mr. Darby. Evelyn has had a good friend in you since you were both in grade school." She opened her eyes wide, stretching the wrinkles at the corners. "I just remembered that Miss Rowe was going to be at the café tonight. She's helping the owners until they have a full-time waitress. I'm sure she would love to see some of her set come in and brighten up the place."

Evelyn gave Aaron a smile. "Yes, I'm sure Cynthia would appreciate that. I will see you tomorrow, Aaron."

Helen walked over to her daughter and leaned down, kissing the top of her head. "Don't wear yourself out. You are to remain here," she pointed to the davenport, "until I return home." She glanced at Richard. "Do I make myself clear?" She pinned her hat to her blonde hair. "I won't be very long, contrary to what my mother said."

Annabella smiled and blew Evelyn a kiss from the front door. "You are always contrary to what I say, my dear. Some things never change."

Helen hung her purse on her arm and ushered her mother out the door, the screen door banging closed behind them. Bickering female voices floated in through the open windows of the stone house.

Evelyn laughed. "For once I feel sorry for Aaron. I sure hope Cynthia is at the café. She'll keep him busy for awhile."

Richard rose from the armchair tucked in the corner of the room and gestured toward the dining room. "May I bring in one of those chairs so I can set it beside you? You've been much too far away all day. I didn't get the honored seat at your feet like Mr. Darby did."

Evelyn blushed and nodded. "Of course. And I apologize for the seating arrangements today. I think my mother was working overtime to make sure we kept our distance."

Richard chuckled as he went into the dining room and emerged with a mahogany chair. He set it next to Evelyn. "May I get you something? A glass of water?" He grinned.

Evelyn rolled her eyes and shook her head. "I'm fine…just happy for a little bit of time with you."

Richard sat down. "I'll remember to thank your grandmother someday for helping us out. If your mother was working overtime to keep us apart, your grandmother was doing the same to get us together. I appreciate that." His blue eyes slid to her hand upon the cushion, lying next to her hip. "May I hold your hand?"

Evelyn nodded, reaching out to him. She sighed as he grasped it.

"Are you alright? Do you need an aspirin, your pillow—"

"No, I'm fine...really." She smiled at him, her green eyes warm and welcoming. "When you took my hand, it was so warm, and it made me feel shivery all over. It just felt good...and right, somehow."

He rubbed his thumb over hers. "I understand just what you're saying." He nodded to the corner where he had spent his afternoon. "I've sat there and watched you and it was all I could do to not touch you. It just feels right when I'm with you."

She ducked her head. "I feel the same about you."

He leaned his elbows on his knees, placing her hand between both of his. He stroked from her wrist to the tip of her fingers, running his fingertips over the back and the palm of her hand. He watched her tremble and he smiled. "Am I tickling you?" He spoke the words soft and low.

"No...not really." Evelyn gulped. "I just feel warm and tingly all over, and I'm finding it very hard to breathe."

"Is your head spinning in a crazy way and you feel like you're going to melt, but not from the heat?" His eyes swept over her. He reached out and touched one red strand of hair curled against her neck.

She nodded and gulped again. "How did you know?" She turned big, green eyes to him.

His finger stroked her neck, moving slowly up and then down to her white collar then back to her jaw. "Because I feel the exact same way." He leaned his forehead against hers and grinned. "It feels great, doesn't it?"

Evelyn laughed and then closed her eyes, breathing deeply of his Old Spice. "You smell wonderful."

He kissed the top of her nose. "So do you...just like roses in springtime." He slid his hand away from hers and cupped her cheek, his lips caressing her temple. "So good." He found her ear lobe and nibbled gently.

"Please..." She gripped his upper arm and pulled away, her eyes meeting his. "What does this all mean? What are we going to do?"

He took a deep breath and stood. He walked to the window and set his hands upon his hips, trying to calm the frantic beating of his heart and the warmth spreading throughout his body.

He closed his eyes. *Father, give me the words to say. This all seems so fast and crazy. We've only known one another a few weeks. You've designed this desire we have and You've given it as a gift to be enjoyed in marriage. Help me to know if I want more than just her physical body…as gorgeous as it is…I want to care for her soul as well. Please guide and direct me, just as You always do.*

Chapter Eleven

WHAT HAVE I DONE, Father? Have I pushed him away? Is he feeling all the same things I am? I want to be so close to him, a part of him. I know You've given me these emotions…only You could have designed something so intimate and enjoyable to be shared between two people. But I want it to be used to honor and glorify You, Father. I want to know and understand his soul…appreciate everything that makes him who he is. And I want to spend years doing it, Father.

She stared at Richard's back, his bowed head. She wanted to rush to him and put her arms around him. She looked down at her legs, covered by the brightly-patterned shawl. *After lying here all afternoon, it's going to be pretty difficult to move with any kind of gracefulness. I'd probably end up sprawled on the floor.* "Richard, what are we going to do?" She asked the question again.

He raised his head and she watched as he squared his shoulders and turned back around. He smiled, his blue eyes twinkling. "I know you're going to say I'm rushing, that I just want to spend a night with you," He threw one hand up. "That it's not possible to know if I love you already, and that it's too soon to think about marriage."

Evelyn frowned. "Richard?"

He hastened to her, pushing the chair aside as he kneeled on the floor beside her. He took both of her hands in his. "And all of those statements would be true. I *am* rushing you, and I want to be with you in the worst way, Evelyn." He closed his eyes and wrinkled his brow. He opened them, capturing hers. "But I *do* love you, Evelyn Hanover, and I want you to marry me as soon as possible. I want to spend the rest of my life with you…getting to know you, talking about God's Word, and making a family with you."

He touched her lips with his finger. "That last part is probably at the top of my list right now," he grinned, "but I think that is fairly normal for a young man of my age."

Evelyn's face blushed beet red and she put a hand to her cheek, looking down at the shawl. "I never noticed this had so many colors."

Richard followed her gaze and then looked back at her. He pressed a hand to the red cheek and turned her to face him. "I've embarrassed you, haven't I?"

She nodded. "Just a little bit." She gave him a smile. "But I love feeling this way…so alive, compared to the way I've felt with Aaron for so many years."

Richard stared at her, his eyes unblinking. "Is there a chance that you could love me too, Evelyn? I mean, I've loved you since the first time we danced." He shook his head. "No, I've loved you since the first time our eyes met across that dance floor. I went out and told my friend Bill that I was going to marry you."

Evelyn opened her eyes wide. "You what?"

Richard laughed. "I know, I said it was crazy. But I knew that night at the prom that I wanted to marry you. That's why I rode out to Rubyville with Bill and Miss Rowe and why I returned the next morning. I wanted to see if it was an option, or if I needed to get away before I got too involved with someone I shouldn't marry."

Evelyn slumped against the pillow behind her back. "Oh my!" She put one hand to her chest. "I knew you were the one for me that same night at the prom…or I at least hoped you were."

He played with one long tendril of hair. "So am I still the one you want to marry? Is there a chance that you could grow to love me?"

She focused on him, her heart racing. "It makes no sense to me, but I know I love you. I know without a shadow of a doubt that you are the one I am to spend the rest of my life with."

He grinned, his blue eyes sparkling like sun on water. "Well then, will you marry me? Will you become my wife and share this life with me?"

Evelyn gasped and nodded. "Yes, yes to everything!" She flung her arms around his neck, pressing her lips to his.

He slid an arm around her waist and one under her knees, scooping her into his arms. He walked to the center of the room and spun in a grand swirl, the shawl taking flight and floating to the floor in a kaleidoscope of colors. He laughed as she clung to him, giggling with delight.

HELEN WAVED AS AARON'S Plymouth drove down the street. She turned toward the house and paused at the sound of excited young voices. One hand went to her chest. *Surely not. No Evelyn, don't do it. Please, God, please don't let me be too late.*

She rushed to the screen door, placing a hand on each side as she stared in at the young couple spinning in the center of the room. The shawl fell from Evelyn's legs to the floor, Evelyn giggling with happiness.

Helen opened the screen door.

"Stop that this instant!" She let the screen door slam shut. "Put my daughter down immediately and leave my house!"

Richard skidded to a stop, gripping Evelyn against his chest.

Evelyn smiled at her mother. "Mama, Richard just proposed! We're going to be married!" She looked up at Richard as he stared at her mother.

No. Helen met Richard's eyes, leveling her gaze at him. "I told you to put her down and leave my house. You are not welcome here, *Mr. King.*"

"Mama…did you hear what I said? We're going to be married…just as soon as possible." Evelyn frowned, gripping Richard's shoulder.

"I heard you." Helen dropped her purse upon the table by the door and tightened the belt at her waist. *I knew I shouldn't have gone with Mother.*

She turned back to the couple in the middle of the room. Her eyes sparked as she stared at her daughter. "Do you recall our conversation of a couple weeks ago? That Sunday night? I told you that you would not have my blessing or be married in the church here in Rubyville if you proceeded with this ridiculous idea."

She switched her gaze to Richard and pointed to the davenport. "I told you to put her down. You don't need to be pawing her like some cheap date."

"Mother!" Evelyn gasped. "That's a very unfair thing to say. You don't know Mr. King at all."

Richard deposited her on the cushions.

Helen crossed her arms. "Exactly, my dear…and you don't either."

"I know that he is kind and loving and that he works very hard! I know that he loves the Lord as I do…and that he loves me!" Evelyn leaned forward, gripping the back of the long sofa. "I don't know why you are so cruel and hateful, Mama. All I've ever tried to do is love you enough for Papa and me." Tears slipped from her eyes.

Helen raised one finger at her daughter. "*Do not* bring your father into this conversation."

Richard gathered the shawl from the floor and draped it across the wood chair he had carried in. "I will respect your wishes and leave, Mrs. Hanover. But you need to understand that I *do* love your daughter and I want her to be my wife. I pray that we can come to some sort of mutual respect out of our love for Evelyn and have a wedding here at the church she grew up in. I have no desire to cause a rift in your family."

Helen sneered at him, giving a low laugh. "Well, you *have* caused problems. More than I can count, young man." She looked at Evelyn, who was sobbing, her shoulders shaking with the effort. "Evelyn had a very nice life planned out before you came along and ruined it with your grandiose ideas and schemes. Mr. Darby loves her and can provide very well for her."

"I don't have a store or a business, but I can and will provide for her. I will take good care of her, Mrs. Hanover." Richard stuffed his hands into his pockets and looked over at Evelyn.

Helen ran her hand up and down and snorted. "You can't even care for yourself. You've had that same old suit every time you've been here. Your shirts are shabby and frayed at the cuffs, your shoes thin with holes through the sole." She gestured to Evelyn. "And you tell me that you will provide for my daughter? That's ludicrous!"

Richard looked around the room. "No, I can't begin to give Evelyn all that she has grown up with in the way of material comforts. But she will have clothing and a roof over her head and food to eat." He glanced at Evelyn once again. "God will provide those items that He promises to us and He will provide work for me."

"It seems like you are dumping an awful lot upon God to handle." Helen shook her head.

"With all due respect, Mrs. Hanover, I trust what God says to us in His Word. He *will* take care of us." Richard pulled his hands from his pockets. He walked to the hook by the door and took his fedora by the crown. He met Helen's eyes and squared his chin. "God *can* and *will* handle it."

"Richard?" Evelyn sniffed loudly and brushed at her cheek. "Please don't leave like this. We all need to discuss this and work something out."

Richard looked at Helen. "I love your daughter, Mrs. Hanover, and I want to marry her. It's up to you to take the next step." He angled the fedora upon his head and walked quietly out the door.

Evelyn scooted from her seat and limped to the door, grabbing the frame. "Richard! Richard, please don't go like this!"

Helen turned and placed her hands upon Evelyn's shoulders. "You are making a scene."

Evelyn turned to her mother and narrowed her eyes. "They're called emotions, Mama. Haven't you ever had any?" She shrugged her mother away and limped to the stairs.

"Evelyn, you're making it bleed again." Helen gestured at the red bandage covering her knee. "You can't be walking on it."

Evelyn looked down and shrugged. "I don't care. Dr. Rundell can just cut it off. If I don't have Richard in my life, I don't have a life." She pulled herself up the stairs.

Helen rushed to the bottom of the stairs and gripped the newel post. "Don't be so dramatic. If you take care of it, your knee will be healed in no time and you will be back to normal."

Evelyn paused, looking down at her mother. "*Nothing* will ever be normal again! Good night!"

Helen sank to the bottom step, covering her face with her hands and sobbing quietly. *You're right, my dear. Nothing will be normal again. You have no idea the emotions that I've gone through in my lifetime. The love and hurt that I've experienced. You don't understand how much I want you by my side, and how hard it is to let go. I'm your mother, after all. And it's been you and me all these years. I know what's best for you.*

THE THUMPING CAUSED EVELYN to turn toward her bedroom door. She watched through blurry eyes as her grandmother pushed the door open with her cane.

"May I come in and visit with my granddaughter?" Annabella smiled, turning to shut the door. "Your mother said you haven't been accepting any visitors this week. It must be very lonely up here in your self-imposed seclusion."

Evelyn leaned her head against the upholstered headboard and crossed her arms. "I welcome visits from you, Grandmama. I denied Aaron and Cynthia the privilege to gloat."

Annabella took the chair from the corner and dragged it across the floor. She sat with a sigh, leaning her cane against the side of the bed. "Mr. Darby and Miss Rowe came together to visit you?" She wrinkled her brow.

"No, Mr. Darby has stopped by every day this week, twice some days. Cynthia came once, doing her civic duty, I imagine." Evelyn plucked at the skirt of her flowered dress.

"Would you deny Mr. King access to your honored presence?" Annabella asked the question with a twitch of her lips.

"Is he here in Rubyville?" Evelyn leaned forward, her eyes wide.

Annabella shook her white head. "Not yet. I wanted to speak with you first. I've heard your mother's side of the story, and now I want to hear yours. I fear they are very different."

Evelyn scowled. "I'm sure she reported lies about Richard." She looked at her grandmother. "Mama hates him, you know. She completely detests him...for no reason."

Annabella patted Evelyn's arm. "Your mother does not like Mr. King because he has changed what she had planned for you. He has given you options she didn't want you to have." She smiled. "And at the very least, he has stolen your heart, and that is very difficult for any mother, no matter how wonderful a young man is."

Tears slid down the pale cheeks. "Mama comes in here every night and lectures me on all the reasons I shouldn't love him or marry him. The things she says just aren't true. I want to respect her, but I don't believe her...and I don't trust her anymore."

Annabella took a tissue from the box on the small table beside the bed. "Here, my dear. Blow your nose. It's as red as a cherry and your eyes are as puffy as Martha's dinner rolls used to be. You need to stop feeling sorry for yourself and think about what you're going to do. You have a young man waiting for your decision."

Evelyn snorted into the tissue and rubbed at her nose. "What's that supposed to mean? Richard is gone forever. No man would want to come back after the way Mama acted…the things she said to him."

Annabella looked at the white bandage upon Evelyn's knee. "Mr. King came to my house after leaving here last Sunday."

"He did? What did he say?" Evelyn's eyes sparked.

Annabella rested her elbows upon the rolled arms of the chair and tented her fingers. "If you would let me speak without being interrupted, I will explain everything." She smiled at her granddaughter and continued. "He said he remained here until you went up the stairs on your own. I suppose he was watching from the front porch. He said your leg was bleeding again and he was very worried about you. He wanted me to send over Dr. Rundell."

"No need to worry about that." Evelyn rolled her eyes and stared out the window. "Mama called him and he came over. I had ripped out two stitches and it had started bleeding again. Dr. Rundell replaced them and gave me a stern warning about giving the wound time to heal. He said it was in an awkward location, with the skin badly torn and bruised. That's why he didn't want me moving it too much."

Annabella nodded. "I figured as much, and I said the same to Mr. King. He agreed to return to Emporia that night if I would telephone him of any changes."

Evelyn stared at her grandmother. "But that was almost a week ago."

"Yes, it was. But I wanted to give you and your mother a chance to simmer down and talk if necessary. I also wanted Mr. King to be very sure of his decision before I offered my help in this situation. I will suffer grave consequences for this, my dear. I have to be sure I'm doing the correct thing." Annabella sighed. "Your mother has always been hot-tempered, jumping before thinking. It has caused so much misery in her life."

Evelyn looked down at her hands, shredding the tissue. "I couldn't believe she was so rude to Richard. I thought we could sit down and talk when she returned, just the three of us, but she would have none of that." Evelyn turned red eyes to her grandmother. "She told me that she would not support me if I married Richard, and there would be no wedding here at the church."

Annabella pursed her lips and looked out the window. "I know, my dear. She is very angry about you not marrying Mr. Darby. I fear she will not forgive that and you need to understand those conditions. Are you willing to marry Mr. King without your mother's approval?"

Tears coursed down Evelyn's cheeks. "I love Mama, and I want her to like Richard and be happy for me, but…" She sniffed loudly. "I love him and I know I am to marry him and spend my life with him. I don't even understand why or how, but I know that's what I am to do."

"That's all I needed to hear, my dear." Annabella reached forward and took Evelyn's hand. "I believe Mr. King to be a man of integrity and honor. He loves the Lord and understands more about His Word than I do. That will stand you in good stead for all the years ahead. He is a hard worker, and I know he loves you." Annabella smiled. "The love is immature and full of physical emotions right now…for the both of you…but it will grow deeper. I am sure of it."

Evelyn clenched her grandmother's hand within her own. "Thank you for understanding, Grandmama. You don't know how much that means to me."

Tears slipped from the wise, green eyes. "I *do* understand my dear. More than you will know this side of Heaven. I want you to experience all that I did not because of my pride and arrogance. I want you and Mr. King to be with the love of your youth. I'm sure there is nothing like it." She gave a smile and released Evelyn's hand. "Don't ever regret or abuse this gift God has given you. It's most precious."

Evelyn blew her nose, her hands shaking. "What do I do now? Should I remain here with Mama? I don't have a way to contact Richard. I don't have his address and Mama would *never* let me telephone him…for so many reasons."

Annabella took a deep breath. "I've wanted to talk with you to proceed with the plans. I will telephone Mr. King when I go home. He has been waiting to hear from me. Mr. King will then stay with me until you both can be married." She gave a light chuckle. "It seems that Pastor Drummond has taken a liking to the young man, as well, and he has agreed to marry you as soon as you are ready."

"Pastor Drummond will marry us there in the church?" Evelyn's eyes jumped with excitement.

Annabella shook her head. "I think that would be rubbing salt in your mother's wounds. There are some sacrifices you're going to need to make, my dear. I hope you understand that."

Evelyn nodded. "I do."

"I think it best that you are married at my house. Pastor Drummond will perform the ceremony and Mrs. Drummond will be there. I will be a witness and Mr. King said his friend Bill Caruthers," she watched for Evelyn's acknowledgment of the young man, "will stand up with Mr. King as another witness."

Evelyn laughed. "It seems you *do* have this all planned out."

"I apologize for that, my dear. You should have had the privilege to plan your wedding and wear a beautiful dress. Your mother had that, as did I," she smiled, "for a few minutes." She shook her head. "But I didn't see any other way. Your mother will continue to lecture you and try to wear you down to her way of thinking. It will make you both miserable, and neither of you are going to change your mind. You are Barton women." She rubbed her brow. "In time, there is a chance that your mother will change her opinion of Mr. King. But it won't be today, or even next year. So you and Mr. King need to get on with your lives…together."

Evelyn bowed her head and spoke softly. "Should this all be kept secret from Mama? It seems devious and unfair to her."

"I see no need to tell her that Mr. King is staying with me. He has agreed to do some chores around the house to pay for his room and board. I offered the same for after you are married, just until you both know what you want to do next." She rubbed her temple. "I will invite her to the wedding, when you decide what day it will be. You want to be sure that you were not the one that pushed her away. Her option to stay or leave the relationship she has with her daughter is her own."

"She will never come to our wedding!"

"Probably not, my dear. But Helen needs to be given the opportunity to refuse." Annabella looked away. "The only other people at the wedding will be the ones I've already mentioned. I think that's for the best. Anyone attending will be taken as an enemy by your mother."

"What about Pastor and Mrs. Drummond? Mama has been friends with them for years."

"I realize that and we talked about that very thing. They both agreed to take part and deal with the consequences. I don't want to involve Daniel and Beth, or any of my grandchildren." Annabella sighed. "My life here in Rubyville will be difficult concerning your mother, but what I'm doing is correct and good. God will see me through. I won't ask that of anyone else, though."

Evelyn closed her eyes and pressed her hands to her face. "Why does life have to be so difficult at times? Why can't people just love one another and get along?"

Annabella smiled. "Those are age-old questions that we won't have the answers to here on this earth. Each of us was born with a sin nature. We are human. We cause much trouble because of that."

Chapter Twelve

Rubyville, Kansas
August 5, 1948

THE THURSDAY MORNING DAWNED overcast and sultry. The lavender voile curtains at the open window hung limply, seeming to be tired of the long summer. Evelyn rolled to her back and stretched her long legs and arms. Her cotton shorties clung to her damp skin.

She smiled. *I can't wait to see what Richard thinks of my white silk nightgown.* The smile receded, and Evelyn rolled to her side, one hand tucked under her chin, her knees drawn to her chest. *Our wedding day...and Mama still refuses to attend the ceremony this morning. Oh Father, why does it have to be this way? Mama knows how important it is to me to have her there, and yet she won't come.*

She jumped from the bed, wincing as the skin stretched over her knee. She propped one foot upon the mattress and examined the long, jagged scar traversing her knee cap. *At least it's healed and I'm back to normal for the wedding. I thought I would be limping down the aisle when it took so long to heal. I know Dr. Rundell thought I was the problem because I kept tearing it open. But how could he expect me to remain in my bedroom the entire summer? Especially when the love of my life was just across town?*

She made her bed in record time and then stood with her hands on her hips, staring at the pretty lavender flowers that had decorated her bedroom since she was a small child. *Maybe I should have taken the sheets off. After all, last night was my last night in this room...maybe for the rest of my life.* Her heart seemed to sink to her feet and she gasped with the stab of pain. *Mama, this could all be so very different if you weren't so stubborn! Even Aaron has moved on to Cynthia, just as I had hoped. He still stares at me with that vacant look whenever I go into the mercantile, but at least he is trying to move on with his life.*

She collapsed to the edge of the bed and buried her face in her hands, the sobs shaking her long frame. *I'm so angry with you, Mama! So hurt that you would send me off for the rest of my life and not even care to be there and try to be happy for me. I'm so disappointed in you and your treatment of Pastor Drummond and his wife. You will be a recluse here in your town. You won't attend church services, or speak to the people you think did you wrong, because they wanted to support Richard and me. How could you, Mama?*

BILL PUSHED BACK HIS white cuff and looked at his watch. "Are you about ready? I think I'm more nervous than you and I'm not even the groom. How can you be so calm?"

Richard grinned as he formed the knot on his brightly-patterned tie. He looked at Bill's reflection standing to his side in the long mirror. "Just about, old pal. I'll need my suit coat over there." He nodded to the chair in the corner of the hotel room.

Bill collected the brown coat and carried it back to Richard. "I'm happy that you finally purchased a new suit, but I still think you should have gone with the double-breasted one, and the cuffed trousers."

Richard shrugged into the suit coat. "I'll let you be the flamboyant one. I just wanted a suit I could wear for a long time and that was tailored for me." He gave a side-grin. "Believe me, I've appreciated your old clothes over the years…they were far nicer than what I could have afforded. But it's still real nice to have something that was made to fit me." He stepped back, buttoning the jacket and standing tall. "How do I look?"

Bill shook his head. "You forgot your pocket square again." His eyes traveled to the top of the bureau. He slid the small, folded material off the bureau and tucked it into the suit chest pocket. He gave it a pat. "At least it matches your tie." He eyed his handiwork. "Well, I guess you look pretty handsome. But you'll have to ask your bride for sure."

"She *is* going to be my bride, isn't she?" Richard flashed a smile. "I can't believe this day is finally here. I thought the summer would take forever…and now it's gone."

Bill rolled his eyes. "Believe me, it's not gone. It has to be about one hundred and ten degrees out there. I thought we were going to have some rain this morning, but no, the sun is sizzling. Remind me to get married around November…you know, when it's cool outside and you want to cuddle."

Richard winked. "It's going to have to get to more than one hundred and ten for me to stay away from Evelyn. I've only seen her occasionally over the summer even though she was right across town. Between her mother being fit to be tied and me working at Miss Barton's, there just wasn't much courting time left. I'm going to make up for it this next week." He took his brown fedora off the bed. "I'm going to enjoy that nice, long drive to Topeka this afternoon and then a whole week with Evelyn, all to myself." He placed the hat on his head at a rakish angle. "I worked hard to be able to take this little trip and I'm going to have one humdinger of a time."

Bill laughed. "Yes, just as long as you don't get stranded on the way there. That old Ford of yours will probably overheat on the way. I hope you thought to bring a tent and some blankets for the ground. Because that's where you will be tonight, snuggling under the stars and sweating like a stuck pig."

"But I'll be a very happy, sweating, stuck pig." He shrugged. "Besides, it won't be the first time I've done repairs along the road. It just comes with the territory."

"Well, at least you'll have a gorgeous tool assistant." Bill walked to the door and opened it. "Come on, you're going to miss your own wedding."

"Not on your life!"

EVELYN SAT IN THE middle of her grandmother's bedroom, clad in a light robe while Beth worked on arranging the sides of her red hair and fastening a coronet of wild roses.

"Mama Bella, these are beautiful with Evelyn's hair. They are just a light enough pink to almost look white. I'm so glad they were still blooming." Beth added the finishing touches on the upswept hair. It was rolled elegantly, with large pin curls entwined with the roses.

Annabella smiled from her seat on the bench at the end of the bed. "I was afraid they would all be gone with this heat, but the Good Lord must have known we needed them for today."

Beth set her hands upon her hips. "Well, I think we are ready for a dress." She exchanged looks with her mother and smiled.

Evelyn pointed to the blue dress with the gold circles lying across the bottom of the bed. "There it is. It's one I usually wear for church, and I thought it would be comfortable enough to travel in this afternoon. I couldn't bear the thought of wearing a skirt and jacket today with it being so hot." Evelyn narrowed her eyes at the hand mirror she held. "My hair is lovely, but I think it's a bit fancy for the dress."

Beth smiled at her mother. "It *is* your wedding day. You want to be beautiful, don't you?"

Evelyn nodded as she looked at her grandmother. "Of course I do, but you have to admit this is not your ordinary wedding. It's not in a church and there are no guests and...and my mother won't be there." Evelyn's bottom lip trembled as she looked up at her aunt. "I'm thrilled that you're here, but it won't bode well for you later on."

Beth waved a hand at her niece. "When Helen told me you were getting married," she nodded toward her mother, "at Mama Bella's house, nothing was going to stop me from watching my only niece say her vows, and your mother knew that. I'm not pleased with Helen's attitude toward this whole affair, but that is *her* decision. You are marrying a wonderful young man, and you should be celebrating, not hiding away like you are doing something shameful."

Evelyn held out her hand for Beth. "Thank you for being here. It means so much to me."

"I think it's time to put on your dress, my dear. You don't want to keep your groom waiting." Annabella nodded and Beth walked from the room, returning with an ivory satin confection draped over her arm.

Evelyn gasped. "What is that?"

"I hope you won't mind, my dear," Annabella began. "I know you said you wanted to keep the clothing simple since you weren't going to be in a church, but I discussed this with Beth and we both thought it would be a lovely idea...as long as you want to do it." Annabella smiled at her daughter, and then her granddaughter. "If not, then you can wear the blue dress and nothing is changed."

Beth laid the ivory satin skirt across the bed, the yards of satin billowing over the coverlet. She held up the bodice, pleated to a deep 'v' over the waist and up to the short cap sleeves. "This is Mama Bella's wedding dress, packed away since May of 1886."

"It was also *my* mother's dress, and it seemed very fitting to have you wear it. It's high time it was worn through another wedding ceremony." Annabella's green eyes sparkled with unshed tears. "I would be honored if you would agree to wear it, my dear. I know it's old and probably not in fashion. But I had Mrs. Rowe do some slight alterations on it according to your measurements, and we cleaned it so it wouldn't smell too musty. I didn't think you would want to wear hoops, but you are a bit taller than me, and I think the length will be fine."

Evelyn rushed to her grandmother and fell at her feet, laying her head on her lap. "Oh Grandmama, it's absolutely perfect. I would be honored to wear it." She looked up, tears flowing down her face. "I will actually *look* like a bride!" She brushed at her cheek. "I just hope it fits."

"It will." Annabella smiled. "You are very close to my size and you won't have to wear that silly corset either. I really didn't need it, but my mother insisted that a proper young lady *always* wore one. I think your undergarments will do just fine."

Beth gestured at Evelyn. "Hurry, we don't have much time left." She raised a finger at her. "And no more crying. Your face is going to be all red and blotchy."

Evelyn smoothed the tears from her cheeks. "I'll try not to." She slipped the robe from her shoulders and stepped into the voluminous skirt. Beth helped her into the bodice and then laced up the back.

"There you go!" Beth took a step back and smiled. "It's as if it was made for you."

Annabella put her hands to her wrinkled cheeks, her eyes overflowing. "You are beautiful, my dear...just beautiful."

Evelyn held out the skirt, the aged satin shimmering in the morning sunlight. She spun around, the skirt lifting like an opening flower, closing again as she swirled to a stop. She looked in the mirror over the fireplace mantel and sighed. "I *am* beautiful! More than I ever thought I would be on this day." She touched the flowers in her hair, turning her head to see the side view. She ran her hands over the pleats on the bodice. "I will be very careful with this."

"I know you will be, my dear. But I wouldn't worry about it. It will just go back into the trunk for another eighty years." Annabella stood, leaning heavily on her cane.

Evelyn's eyes widened as she lifted the skirt and showed her foot. "I don't have any shoes to wear. Those blue pumps won't do at all under this dress."

Beth laughed and went to the edge of the bed. She pulled a pair of white pumps from under it. "I already thought of that. These that you wore for the prom should work very well."

Evelyn placed a hand at her chest. "Yes, they'll be fine. You both have thought of everything."

Annabella chuckled. "It has been rather fun." She raised her cane and pointed at the small secretary. "Now don't forget your bouquet. Mr. King spent several hours gathering all those roses. Beth did a wonderful job of putting it all together. Those yellow chrysanthemums that she added are just lovely."

Beth carried the small bouquet to Evelyn, adjusting the flowers here and there. "I thought the yellow added just enough cheer. You've always had a bright and sunny disposition, and yellow just seems to fit you somehow." She placed the bouquet in Evelyn's hand and stepped back, the long, multi-colored ribbons slipping from her fingers. "You are a vision."

"If I'm not allowed to cry, you two can't either." Evelyn's gaze went from Beth to Annabella. "I love you both so much. Thank you for making this day so special for me." Her eyes sought the bouquet and she held it to the side, her eyes sweeping over her attire. "I'm actually a bride…and I look and feel so beautiful because of both of you."

"No, the credit for that goes to God and the relationship you have with Him, my dear." Annabella placed a kiss upon Evelyn's cheek. "The love you have for Him reflects in your life, just as it does in Mr. King's life. You have the most important ingredient for a long and happy marriage right there. Cherish it."

Beth looped her arm through Annabella's. "Let's go. I'm sure Mr. King is very anxious to see his bride." She blew Evelyn a kiss as they left the room.

Evelyn brought the bouquet to her nose, sniffing the gentle rose fragrance. Her green eyes traveled to her image in the mirror and she closed her eyes. *Thank You, Father, for this day. Thank You for my grandmother and aunt, for their willingness to help and make this day a blessing for me. Thank You for their love and support, no matter the cost to them. Thank You, Father, for the man that You sent me. Help me to be a godly woman and helpmate for him. I ask that You give us many years together. My heart is overflowing with the love I have for him. And Father...please watch over Mama. Heal her broken heart and bitter spirit so that we may have the kind of relationship we should have. I love her so.*

She opened her eyes and smiled at her reflection. "I'm ready!"

RICHARD STOOD TO THE left of Pastor Drummond, with Bill on his left. The trio stood in the half-circle of turreted windows in the parlor, the morning sun dimmed by the heavy, rose-colored velvet swags. Richard's gaze was glued to the large doorway and the foyer beyond, the bottom steps of the black walnut staircase just visible through the crowd of people gathered. *Evelyn will be so surprised to see everyone that insisted on being part of this wedding. Even though we tried to keep it a secret for Mrs. Hanover's sake, we didn't succeed.*

His eyes found Miss Barton, seated on the rose-colored velvet sofa and she gave him a wink and smile. He returned the smile and raised a brow. She nodded. *So maybe it wasn't such a secret after all?*

He searched the crowd filling the parlor and foyer and spilling onto the front porch. He noted Beth's husband, Daniel, and their son Charles and his family. The rather stern woman from the hotel, Ellen, stood next to George and his family. Others from Rubyville were also there, Miss Rowe and her mother, along with several other families from the church that he had enjoyed fellowshipping with over the summer. Even Aaron

Darby stood to the side, tucked away near the door leading to the dining room. *That took more backbone than I have.* He watched as Miss Rowe turned to Aaron and flashed a brilliant smile. *There's hope there yet.*

But no Mrs. Hanover. The otherwise bright and happy day took on a momentary veil of gray and sadness. *Please watch over her, Father. Help her to understand that her daughter needs her. I don't want to be the reason for their split.*

The people gathered in the foyer turned and lifted their eyes. He watched as billowing, ivory skirts were followed by the form of his radiant bride. He took a quick breath as her glowing face came into view, her sparkling eyes taking in the crowd of people. She smiled, brushing at her cheeks, as she thanked them for coming as she neared the bottom of the staircase...and then she turned to him.

He swallowed, his head spinning. *She is so beautiful! How did I ever deserve such a gift? Please help me to be worthy of her, to care for her and love her all the days of our lives.* She walked toward him, stepping slowly, her eyes captured by his. She reached out and he went to her, grasping her warm hand within his. He bent his head to her ear and whispered, "You take my breath away." He kissed her temple and led her to Pastor Drummond.

THE CLAPPING SUBSIDED AS Annabella struggled to her feet. She leaned on her cane and raised a hand. "I would like to thank all of you for coming and sharing in this moment with our family and this new union of Mr. and Mrs. King." She gestured to Ellen. "My granddaughter, with the help of many of you, has prepared a light meal over at the hotel to be shared by everyone before the bride and groom leave Rubyville. Please come and express your good wishes for this *very* special couple." She continued, her eyes sparkling as she turned to each guest. "Ellen has also made a gorgeous cake for the newlyweds, so be sure to see it. And as you know, it will be just as delicious as it is pretty."

A round of laughter followed the last statement as people headed out the double doors at the front of the foyer.

Evelyn leaned her head upon Richard's chest, smiling at her grandmother. Her eyes slid up to her new husband's face. "Did you know about this…all the people, the meal, the cake?"

He shook his head. "This was all just as much as a surprise to me. I arrived with Bill and the house just started filling up." He placed a hand upon her shoulder. "This town loves your family. They are here for your grandmother and what she stands for here in Rubyville and all that she's done." His eyes slid to where the elderly woman stood, chatting with Mrs. Rowe and Mrs. Drummond. "She *is* Rubyville, just as her father was before her. She is an amazing woman."

Evelyn stood on tiptoe, pressing a kiss to Richard's lips. "I couldn't agree more. She has always been there for me."

His arm slid around the back of her waist. "You are so beautiful. I didn't realize you were going to wear a bridal gown. I feel underdressed for the occasion."

"I didn't think I would be." She fingered a pleat near her waist. "This gown was my grandmother's and my great-grandmother's. I'm honored that Grandmama thought to have me wear it."

His eyes slid over her. "It looks as though it was made for you. You are a beautiful bride…*my* bride." He captured her chin and tilted her head, caressing her lips with his own.

"I'm sorry to interrupt," Bill said with a clearing of the throat, "but you will have plenty of time for all that later. I didn't have much of a breakfast this morning…you know, rushing around and taking care of the groom and all. Can we head over to the hotel? I think you would be more comfortable in my automobile."

Annabella waved the last of the guests through the parlor door. She turned to Evelyn and Richard. "Beth is waiting for you upstairs, my dear. She thought you might like to change before going to the hotel. That way you both can leave as soon as you like."

Richard smiled down at his bride. "That sounds good to me. I'm hungry as well and I want to see that cake…but I'd also like to get on the road to Topeka as soon as possible."

Evelyn blushed as she exchanged looks with Richard and Annabella. "I'll be back. I left my luggage by the kitchen door. It needs to be put in the trunk of your automobile, Richard."

Annabella smiled at her granddaughter. "I have just one more surprise. Your luggage has been placed in the trunk of *my* automobile."

Evelyn frowned. "*Your* automobile?"

"Yes, my dear. I am giving you both my Plymouth."

Bill coughed. "That '47 Special Deluxe Sedan parked at the side of the house…the burgundy-colored one?"

"That's the one, Mr. Caruthers. I purchased it because I liked the thought of the ignition key and I thought the color was very pretty for an automobile. It's actually maroon, not burgundy." She shrugged. "But I've only driven it a handful of times over the past year or so. I think Mr. King and Evelyn could put it to much better use."

Richard's mouth gaped. "You're giving us your Plymouth?"

"Don't you like it?" Annabella smiled.

Richard rubbed the back of his neck. "I've admired that automobile all summer, but you've done so much for me," he looked at Evelyn, "for *us*, that it just seems like too much. I don't know what to say."

Annabella patted his arm. "Mr. King, you have been a very big help to me this summer. And I'm very relieved that the both of you have agreed to stay here in Rubyville through the winter. It will be lovely to have someone sharing that old house with me. Giving you that automobile is a pleasure to me…pure pleasure."

Bill chuckled. "Well, I'm going to put the luggage in the trunk and take a look at that Plymouth if you don't mind, Miss Barton."

"You'll have to ask Mr. King about that." Annabella turned and started walking toward the parlor doorway. She turned back. "But I will need a ride over to the hotel, Mr. Caruthers, and my daughter Beth will, as well. It's much too hot to walk in fancy clothes today."

"Sure thing, Miss Barton." Bill turned to Richard. "Come on, let's check out your *new* jalopy."

Richard kissed Evelyn. "I'll be outside waiting for you."

"I'll be back in a few minutes…and remember dear…we're supposed to drive to Topeka today." She gave Bill a stern look.

He raised his hands and shook his head. "Don't worry, Mrs. King, I'll keep him on schedule."

HELEN STOOD HIDDEN IN the grouping of trees and shrubs beside the gazebo, her cover for the last couple of hours. Her feet ached and her heart clenched tightly with the pain of regret and remorse. She had watched as Richard and Evelyn left her mother's house, driving her mother's Plymouth. Evelyn had been seated close to her new husband, grins upon their glowing faces. An hour later she had observed Evelyn throwing the bouquet, Cynthia Rowe catching it with a shrill squeal. The happy couple had run to the automobile amidst handfuls of rice showering over them. He had kissed her daughter, far longer than needed, beside the door and then helped her in.

And then they were gone.

Helen clenched the material across her chest, her nails digging into the soft flesh beneath. She leaned her forehead against the harsh bark of an oak tree and sobbed. *How could he just take her away from me? She's all I have left. My mother, Beth, my nieces and nephews, and everyone in this horrid little town has turned against me. They have supported my daughter running off with that man...that man no one knows a thing about. Even Pastor Drummond and his wife turned against me...he married my precious daughter to that...that tramp!*

She pushed away from the tree and stepped out of her hiding place. She brushed her hands upon her skirt and started the long walk home...alone.

Chapter Thirteen

Rubyville, Kansas
Christmas Day, 1948

EVELYN STOPPED THE PLYMOUTH in front of the stone house and turned off the engine. Her view out the passenger window showed the row of lilac bushes quivering in the cold wind, their naked branches thin and forlorn. Her eyes traveled up the sidewalk to the long front porch, not a Christmas decoration to be seen.

She flexed her fingers incased in the leather gloves and opened the heavy door, slamming it shut behind her. She walked around the automobile and passed through the gap in the hedge, striding up the sidewalk. Inhaling a deep breath, she climbed the stairs and crossed the porch, stopping in front of the door. *Please, Father, don't let her turn me away again. It's Christmas Day, after all.*

Her knuckles tapped on the door, and there was no answer. She knocked louder and the door opened, with Helen standing there, just as beautiful as she had always been. The older woman stood straight and tall, her hair coiffed, every strand where it should be. Her mother's eyes stared at her, the blue orbs dark and unwelcoming.

"Good morning, Mama! I wanted to wish you a Merry Christmas and give you this." Evelyn held out a small package.

Helen glanced at it and turned her gaze back to Evelyn.

Evelyn pulled it back. "It's nothing that special. Just something I made to show you I was thinking of you and hoping you had a good Christmas."

The red lips spoke. "You should be home with your *husband* and grandmother. It's much too cold to be out running around town." She crossed her arms and gave a shiver.

"Mama, may I come in and visit for a little while? There are so many things I would like to tell you." Evelyn bit her bottom lip. "Please, I promise not to stay long."

"I don't see the point. I have nothing to share with you." Helen stared past the line of trees edging the opposite side of the road.

Evelyn smiled, her bottom lip quivering. "I…I wanted to let you know that Richard and I are expecting a baby sometime in July. I just found out the other day. I wanted to let you know quickly this time. I…I lost a baby back in September. I didn't even know I was going to have a baby. Dr. Rundell said I wasn't very far along and that was normal." Evelyn looked away, fingering the small package. "I wanted to talk with you about it because…because I know you lost a baby too. I thought you might understand how I was feeling."

"I understand nothing about you, Evelyn. You'll just have to get through it, the same as I did." She put her hand on the door. "Now if you'll excuse me."

One tear slipped from the green eyes. "Alright, Mama…I won't keep you. I just wanted you to know I was thinking about you. I didn't want you to spend the day alone."

"Beth has invited me over for dinner."

Evelyn used her tongue to dab at the tear at the corner of her mouth. "That's…that's very nice. I'm happy that you will be going over. I remember how much Christmas meant to you…how much you enjoyed decorating and wrapping presents."

Helen raised her chin. "Well, I have no need to do those things any longer. With just me here, it seems rather a waste of my time."

"Well, Merry Christmas, Mama. I love you! I'll stop by again, after the new year."

The door closed with a soft click. Evelyn stared at the grain of the wood, tears running in rivulets down her face. She set the package on the porch and rushed away.

The interior of the Plymouth was cold and unwelcoming as she turned the key, the engine roaring to life.

She turned around on the narrow road and stopped just before the mercantile. Laying her head upon the steering wheel, she sobbed.

Mama, how long are you going to hate me?

HELEN WATCHED FROM THE cover of the drapes as Evelyn drove away, then she retrieved the small package from the porch. She walked back to the kitchen, setting the package upon the table. Staring at the brightly-wrapped gift, she slid her hands into her apron pockets.

A baby? I'm going to be a grandmother next summer. For a moment, her heart leapt for joy and she thought of all the memories she had of Evelyn as a baby. *But she's chosen that Mr. King over me. She doesn't really want me in her life. She came today out of duty...something my mother probably told her she should do.*

A swallow of her lukewarm tea caused her to wince as she sat down at the table. She picked up the package and opened it, a square of linen falling to the tabletop. Tears gathered and overflowed as she unfolded the embroidered material, her hand going to her mouth. *I love you, Grandma* was stitched in flowing letters across the handkerchief, purple flowers entwined. The stitches were neat and perfect, just as they should be.

Helen closed her eyes. *All those years of teaching you how to sew. You loved it, and were so talented, but embroidery was never your forte. How very special, Evelyn, just as you said.* She opened her eyes, folding the handkerchief neatly. She pressed it to her nose, the faint fragrance of roses drifting through her senses. *Roses always remind me of you, my dear daughter.*

She clutched the linen to her chest and cried, large tears splashing upon the table.

EVELYN JERKED HER HEAD up at the sound of someone tapping on the window.

"Are you alright?" Aaron called through the blurry glass.

Evelyn hurriedly wiped her eyes and rolled down the window. She gave her childhood friend a smile. "I'm fine. I...I just came from Mama's house, wishing her a Merry Christmas."

"Did she speak with you?" Aaron shoved his hands into his pockets.

She shook her head. "Not really. She did say she was going over to Aunt Beth's for dinner, so at least she is getting out of the house once in a while."

"If it makes you feel any better, she still comes into the mercantile a couple of times a week. I know she has quit going to church and you don't see her out and about like she use to be, but she does get out."

Evelyn smiled up at him, her eyes drifting to the small house beside the mercantile. Mrs. Rowe and Cynthia stood at the front window, watching their exchange. "You had better go. You're making someone nervous."

Aaron turned and waved at the duo. The lace curtain dropped back into place. "Since you are here, I'll share the news with you first. It seems only right since you were the one that threw us together."

"Did she accept?" Evelyn tilted her head and looked up at her friend.

Aaron grinned. "I asked her just this morning and gave her the ring. She would like to have the wedding on Valentine's Day. I tried to explain to her that it was a Monday and probably not the best day for a wedding, but she insists on it." He blushed, his brown hair falling in front of his eyes. "You know how persuasive Miss Rowe can be."

Evelyn laughed. "Yes, I do!" She looked at the twinkle in his green eyes. "I'm so happy for you, Aaron. She adores the ground you walk on, and has for years. I think she will make you a wonderful wife."

He nodded. "I think so too. I was so infatuated with you and not wanting to change, that I couldn't see what was right in front of me." He leaned a hand on the window frame. "You know what?"

"What?"

"It's really nice to have someone that adores you. She makes me feel special and loved. She's always doing little things for me, making me treats so I won't be hungry." He patted his lean tummy. "It might not be good for my physique."

"Cynthia likes your physique just the way it is, I can assure you. I've caught her staring more than once."

Aaron straightened and looked away, his face red. "You shouldn't talk about such things."

Evelyn shrugged. "I'm an old married woman now. I understand these things."

His gaze caught hers. "I wanted to thank you, Evelyn. I know I told you back in May that I would never say those words to you, but I *am* thankful. I love Miss Rowe in a way I never did with you. I'm really excited about our future…and it's all because of you."

"No, it's because of God and His plans for our lives. All we need to do is listen to Him and then obey." Evelyn shook her head. "If only my mother would come to understand that."

"Just give her some time. I think she does understand. After all, she probably taught you that. But you've been her whole life, and she thinks it's all been ripped away from her. It didn't help that the entire town showed up for your wedding. She wanted them all to see the error of your ways and stand behind her."

"Your lips are turning blue, Aaron Darby. It's too cold to be out here without a coat. Cynthia would never forgive me if you died of pneumonia. She is so close to achieving her goal." She gave him a smile as she began rolling up her window. "Congratulations to both of you, and I hope we get an invitation to the wedding, even if it is on a Monday. Merry Christmas!"

"Merry Christmas!" He stepped away from the Plymouth and jogged back to the little house.

EVELYN SHUT THE KITCHEN door and shrugged out of her coat as Richard entered the warm room. The smells of Christmas dinner permeated the air. Ham roasting in the oven, mashed potatoes on the warming shelf of the large range. A cherry pie, red fruit bubbling through the lattice top, sat upon the table.

Annabella looked up from her task of slicing fruitcake and smiled at her granddaughter. She laid the knife upon the table. "From the look on your face, your visit didn't go well."

Evelyn shook her head and reached for Richard, burying her head in his neck. "She wouldn't even let me in. I just stood on the porch, just like every other time I've been there. I thought with it being Christmas Day, she might be different. But she wasn't." She sniffed as she raised her knuckles to her red nose. "I don't know what else to do. I even told her about the baby…and she didn't even seem to care."

Annabella wrinkled her brow. "Maybe it's time for me to have a talk with her. This can't continue."

"I don't think she'll talk to you either, Grandmama. She hates us all." Evelyn sobbed into her husband's neck.

Richard smoothed his large hand over her back. "Your mother is angry and hurt…mostly hurt. She'll come around in time. Just wait and see."

Annabella gave a long sigh.

Evelyn lifted her head. "I'm not going to go over there anymore and stand there, begging like some kind of waif for a bit of her attention and love." A loud sniff shook her body. "She has had her last chance."

"Those are lovely Christmas sentiments for the woman that birthed you and raised you." Richard took Evelyn by the shoulders and gently pushed her back. He bent his knees, lowering himself to look into his wife's eyes. "'A *new commandment I give unto you, that ye love one another; as I have loved you, that ye also love one another.'* John 13:34." Richard wrinkled his brow. "Christ gave His *life* for us…we cannot love others?"

Evelyn lowered her eyes. "When you put it that way, I feel awful." She wiped the tears from her cheeks. "I know. I'm a terrible daughter."

Annabella walked over and laid a hand upon Evelyn's arm. "You're not a terrible daughter. You've done what you had to do under the circumstances. All Richard is saying is to not become bitter like your mother. Just keep loving her and trying to have a relationship with her, just as Christ does with us when we fail."

Evelyn gave a half-smile along with another sniff. "The problem is that He is God, and I'm certainly not."

Richard and Annabella laughed.

"None of us are, dear heart." Richard placed a kiss on Evelyn's cheek. He clasped his hands together and then rubbed them back and forth. "So, are we ready for gifts?" His blue eyes sparkled as his gaze flitted back and forth between the two women.

Evelyn patted her husband's cheek. "You are more excited for this day than any adult should be."

"You bet I am. The past few months have been the absolute best of my life, and this is the best Christmas ever." He grinned and winked at Annabella and Evelyn. "I get to spend it with my two favorite people."

Annabella linked her arm through Richard's. "You've become a very special part of our lives as well. I don't know how we ever got along without you. Now, please escort me to the parlor and I won't have to thump along with that old cane. It can be cumbersome at times, I must say."

Richard held out his left arm for his wife. "Two beautiful women to look at all day long. How'd I get so lucky?"

Annabella smiled, the skin wrinkling around her lips. "Just keep up that kind of talk. We don't mind a bit, do we Evelyn?"

Evelyn looked up at her husband, her eyes melting into pools. "No, we don't. I feel like the most loved and beautiful woman in the world."

Richard nodded his head curtly. "Good, that's just how it should be." He grinned. "Now what did you get me for Christmas?"

Evelyn laughed. "You have to wait and see like a good little boy."

THE MOONLIGHT STREAMED THROUGH the long, turreted windows of the bedroom, the silvery-blue light illuminating the heavy furniture. Evelyn rolled over and placed her head on her husband's chest, one arm wrapped around his waist. She breathed deeply. "You smell wonderful."

"It must be my new Christmas pajamas." The low voice was soft and sleepy. "You did a great job sewing them and the robe. I've never had pajamas made just for me and I've never worn a robe before. It's rather nice to lounge in at the end of the day."

"Well, it could be your pajamas, but I think it's that Old Spice. Whenever I smell it, I think of you." She took another sniff. "Wonderful, happy thoughts."

He chuckled. "And whenever I smell roses, I think of you. Old Spice and roses…it's a strange combination."

"Sounds lovely, though." Evelyn squeezed her husband. "I hope our baby likes the smell." She sighed. "Just think, this summer we will have a baby. Is everything happening too fast for you?"

He rolled his head back and forth. "Not at all, since I felt like I'd waited my whole life to start living…and then I met you. It just feels right and good." He rubbed her arm. "You're going to be a great mother. Our children are going to be very blessed to have you."

"I hope that's true and they feel that way twenty years from now."

"Don't be thinking about your mother again. She has made her decision concerning this whole situation." He pulled her close. "Plus, I think you felt blessed most of the time with how your mother raised you."

"Yes, I did, even though we disagreed on many things. I always knew she loved me and wanted what was best for me. I just wanted her to be happy and relaxed, not so concerned with having everything the *right* way."

"Her way?" He gave a chuckle.

Evelyn smiled. "Yes, that was usually the problem."

She was quiet for a minute as her gaze flitted around the room. "I always wondered why my grandmother didn't keep this room for herself after Orin died. It's much bigger and nicer than the room she had as a girl."

"She told me that she always thought of it as her parent's bedroom. She said she stayed in here while she and Orin were married, but when he was gone, it just seemed better to move back to her old bedroom." Richard placed his left hand under his neck. "I had asked her the same thing one day when she had me repairing a window in here."

"It *is* a beautiful room. My great-grandmother had wonderful taste in furnishings. Most of them have been in this house for almost a hundred years."

"They've held up fairly well, I'd say."

"My mother said that Martha took great care of this place. She felt it was her personal assignment to see to the Barton family and this house."

"I've heard that name a few times over the past few months. Exactly who *was* Martha?"

"I was only ten years old when she died, but I remember an old lady with white hair that had more energy and stubbornness than was healthy."

Evelyn laughed. "I think she was around ninety-five years old when she died. She was a young Irish girl that came to the Saunders family…that was my great-grandmother Lavinia's maiden name…when she was new to this country. The Saunders family lives near Albany, New York. My mother still keeps in touch with her cousin, Laurel Wyatt." Evelyn sighed. "When my great-grandmother, Lavinia, married William Barton, Martha moved to Kansas with her to care for her. She was a very important part of our family. I know Grandmama misses her very much."

"She must, because she often speaks of her with love."

Evelyn adjusted her head upon Richard's chest. "I know. It must be very difficult to live so long and lose so many people in your life. When the weather is warmer, maybe in the spring, I can take you to the cemetery. I love to walk through there and think of all the people that have gone before us."

Richard kissed the top of her head. "I know you could chatter all night, but it's after midnight and we've had a long day. Church services early this morning were great, but now I'm kind of tired. And I'm sure you are, too."

"I guess I am. But if we go to sleep, it's no longer Christmas, and that makes me sad."

Richard chuckled. "It's no longer Christmas day *anyway*. It's Monday morning, and I have a couple projects I want to complete for your grandmother before the New Year."

Evelyn rose up on her elbow and looked at her husband in the moonlight. "I do love you, Richard King." She kissed him and flopped to her right side, pulling the covers against her ear. "Even if you don't like to listen to me chatter all night."

"That is *not* what I said, dear heart."

Chapter Fourteen

February 1949

THE CEMETERY LAY BROWN and dry, the headstones jagged intrusions upon the earth. Evelyn lifted her face to the scudding clouds overhead, the cold wind whipping at her hair. She watched as the gray, billowy masses tumbled over one another, the taste of snow on her tongue. She placed her hand over her abdomen. *You were too little to take your place here among our family and loved ones. Seems unfair somehow, but I know you are safe, and we'll meet again someday.*

She swallowed deeply and looked up at the heavens. *Why Father? I've lost two babies in such a short time. I don't understand. It's almost as if we Barton women were not meant to bear children.*

Her eyes swept over the headstones. William and Lavinia Barton resting close together, baby James next to Lavinia. The inscription read:

James Barton
Born March 1900, Died December 1900
You shared our lives for eight months;
rejoice with the angels, our sweet boy.

Her grandmother had spoken of the baby she had adopted, telling Evelyn of the love her mother, Lavinia, had had for the small boy. It had broken Lavinia's heart when he had died so young. Agnes Saunders came next in the row, Martha to the back of the sisters, watching over them just as she did in life.

And where is Orin's stone?

The members of the Barton family were grouped in a small area near the west side of the church, toward the back of the once empty meadow. Now, it lay dotted with many crosses, headstones, and markers. *The legacy of Rubyville.* Her eyes scanned the expanse, and there, just before the line of trees, a large stone jutted from the grassy mound, graceful carvings across the top. She walked to it and knelt down to read the flowing lines.

Song of Solomon 6:3, "I am my beloved's, and my beloved is mine"
Orin Langworthy
Born February 15, 1856, Died May 8, 1928
Beloved husband to Sarah Langworthy
Beloved husband to Annabella Barton Langworthy
Father to Beatrice and Mark

Evelyn's eyes were drawn to the smaller, identical stone to the right.

Song of Solomon 6:3, "I am my beloved's, and my beloved is mine" Annabella
Barton Langworthy
Born April 17, 1863, Died —

Evelyn gasped, her eyes reading the words once more. *Grandmama, I don't want to think of you leaving this world yet. I need you so right now.* She pushed herself to her feet and wrapped her arms about her waist, staring down at the headstone. *Please, Father, I know my grandmother is no longer young, but surely she can remain here for just a few more years. What would Richard and I do without her...what would Rubyville do?*

Soft, fluffy snowflakes drifted down, sticking to the tall blades of grass near the stones. Evelyn bent down and grasped the tufts, pulling them from the cold ground. She threw them to the side. *This will stay neat and tidy for many years to come, if I have anything to say about it.* She straightened and surveyed the cemetery. *This whole place could use some care. Why, you can't even see some of the headstones because of the tall weeds around them.* Dead flowers adorned some of the grave sites, their brittle petals breaking in the wind. Most of the cemetery was overgrown and obviously had not been mown the previous summer.

Evelyn walked from the cemetery with long strides, taking the shortcut around the back of the stone church. She crossed the dirt road and walked up the long driveway to her grandmother's house. She entered the warm kitchen with a bang of the screen door.

Annabella turned from the large range, one hand to her chest. Fried chicken sizzled in the pan. "My dear, you just about stopped my heart."

"Don't even talk like that, Grandmama!" Evelyn pulled off her coat and hung it on the hook. "I just came from the cemetery and you have a headstone out there with your name on it!" She strode to the range and put one hand on her hip, staring at her grandmother.

Annabella widened her eyes. "Really? Now who would have gone and done such a thing?"

"Why would you put a headstone out there? You're not dead yet." Evelyn took the long fork from her grandmother and moved the chicken around in the pan. "Do you know how surprised I was to see that?"

Annabella moved slowly over to the table and sat down with a sigh. "I am eighty-six years old. It could be any time now."

Evelyn raised her hand. "It could be any time for any one of us."

"That is true. But my odds of being here for very much longer have significantly lessened." Annabella took a sip of her tea and grimaced. "Be a dear and pour some more hot water in here. Lukewarm tea is not very appetizing."

Evelyn took the kettle of hot water to the table and poured some in her grandmother's cup. "I understand what you're saying, but I think you may be taking *planning for the future* to an extreme."

Annabella laughed. "When I purchased Orin's headstone, I took the opportunity to get mine, as well, and have it inscribed. It will be much less for everyone to worry about when I'm gone. And with the way things are going with Helen and me, it was a good thing I did. I'll be surprised if she even attends my services." The wrinkles around Annabella's vibrant green eyes deepened. "Why, I could die in my sleep and not be found for weeks, just withering away in my old bedroom."

Evelyn gaped at her grandmother. "Please don't say such things! It sounds horrible! I'll be at your funeral, and I'm pretty sure Beth will be, too." Evelyn took the pan of chicken from the burner and set it to the back of the stove. "But we won't talk of you going anywhere for many years yet. You have to meet my first child. Why, you could be a great-grandmother to one of my children if you live into your hundreds."

Annabella laughed, her face flushing red. "Why on God's green earth would I want to live that long, my dear?" She took a sip of her tea. "I'm ready whenever He calls me home. My work here is done."

"No, it's not. I *need* you. Besides, Mama and you have to work out things between you." Evelyn scowled. "I just won't hear of you dying right now."

"So shove it under the bed and let the dust bunnies play on it. But I guarantee you it won't be long until you're going to have to pull it out and face it, my dear. That's just the way life goes."

"I'm going to think about all that later." Evelyn took a deep breath. "I also noticed that the cemetery was rather unkempt. I thought a young man was supposed to be mowing it and taking care of the weeds and such around the headstones."

"The *young* man my father hired all those years ago has taken care of it until recently. He became ill and just couldn't put in the hours to do it anymore. He had been training his grandson to take over." Annabella shook her head. "That boy doesn't seem to have the work ethic his grandfather had. It is very sad to see. The young people of today always seem to find something more important to do. The filling station is always looking for a good attendant and mechanic. Every time Mr. Pertz finds a hard-working young man, he goes away for college or gets married and leaves town. If all the young people continue to do that, Rubyville will be a ghost town before long."

Richard walked into the kitchen, whistling a little tune. He grabbed Evelyn around the waist and kissed her. "Are you two ladies talking about me again?"

Annabella chuckled. "No, you aren't like most of the young people of today. I think they all have cotton for brains."

Evelyn ran her hands up and down Richard's forearms. "I was just telling Grandmama that I had been to the cemetery and it's a mess. No one has mown it or pulled the weeds around the headstones. It really looks terrible."

Richard wrinkled his forehead, looking down at his wife. "I thought you were going to give me the grand tour of the place this spring."

"I will, I was just passing by and thinking of our baby. Just seems unfair somehow to not have something marking his or her presence in our lives." Evelyn placed her hand at her waist.

Richard took her cheeks and kissed the top of her head. "God knows and we know, and we will remember. That's what is important."

Evelyn turned toward her grandmother and gestured at her. "And then I see *her* headstone, already filled out and just waiting for the date of her passing."

Richard looked at Annabella and smiled, giving her a wink. "Well that sounds like a good idea to me. You can never be too prepared."

Evelyn jabbed her hands on her hips. "You agree with that?"

"Well of course. Why not?" Richard snatched a piece of crispy chicken skin and popped it in his mouth. His eyes watered. "Wow, that's hot!" He went to the cupboard and took a glass, filling it at the sink.

Evelyn shook her head. "Of course it is. I just took it off the burner."

Annabella pushed to her feet. "Let's get the table set, my dear. I'm sure Richard is hungry. He's been working all morning clearing that brush north of the house."

Richard drained the glass. "I *am* starved, but I guess that's what I get for stealing." He stuck his tongue out at Evelyn. "Do I have blisters? It sure feels like I do."

Evelyn stood on tiptoe and examined his tongue. "No, you don't, but I don't think they would appear already anyway."

He swooped in for a kiss.

She giggled as she swatted him on the arm and darted away. "Are you hungry, or not?"

"I guess hunger wins." He set his glass on the table. "What can I do to help?"

Annabella pointed to his chair. "You can sit down and just relax. We'll have dinner on the table in just a minute."

"Sounds good to me." Richard slid the chair out and sat down, stretching his long legs under the table. He crossed his hands behind his head and stared at his wife. "Now I have the best view in town."

Evelyn shut the oven door with a bang and carried the biscuits to the counter. "You can be pretty fresh at times." She set the tray upon the hard surface and transferred the golden stacks to a linen-lined basket. She folded the napkin over the top and walked to the table.

Richard grabbed her around the waist and pulled her to his lap.

Evelyn laughed. "You are going to make me drop these, and Grandmama worked so hard on them."

"And I'll eat every one of them. I won't let a good biscuit go to waste." Richard nuzzled his wife's neck.

Annabella rescued the biscuits and set them on the table next to the fried chicken. She sat down and looked at the couple snuggled on the chair. "Evelyn, are you sitting there or at your normal place?"

Evelyn blushed. "At my regular spot." She turned to her husband and laughed as he wiggled his eyebrows at her.

"I think it's pretty cozy with you right here." Richard hiked her up on his lap, one hand gripping her waist.

Evelyn sighed and shook her head. "My grandmother is going to get pretty tired of all your shenanigans. There is never a dull moment with you around."

Annabella smiled as she scooped mashed potatoes onto Richard's plate. "And that's just the way I like it. It's been much too boring around here for too many years. I needed some young people in my life."

Richard dropped his hand from around Evelyn's waist. "You may go. You're very distracting and I *am* really hungry." His eyes slid over her as she stood and adjusted the waistband of her plaid skirt.

"So now I'm dismissed, like a sack of potatoes." Evelyn sauntered to her chair and sat down, raising one brow at her husband.

"Until later." His lazy grin spread across his face. He held out his hands. "Let's thank the Lord for this delicious-smelling meal."

Annabella and Evelyn exchanged smiles as they bowed their heads. Evelyn looked up through narrowed eyes, observing her handsome husband as he prayed. *I'm sorry, Father. I am thankful for the food, but right now I'm even more thankful for my husband. Thank You for bringing him into my life and for making me so very happy. Amen.*

RICHARD SWALLOWED THE LAST bite of his pie and placed the plate on the marble-topped table.

Annabella set her knitting on her lap. "Would you like another piece? I think there's one more left. I can make another pie in the morning." She frowned. "It might have to be peach, though. I think I'm out of cherry pie filling."

Richard groaned. "I think two pieces had better be it for tonight." He sat back in his chair. "Any kind of pie suits me just fine. I love them all."

"It's too bad you never had the chance to meet Martha. She would have loved to bake for you." Annabella shook her head. "I'm afraid I just wasn't up to eating as much as she wanted to make."

Richard eyed the black walnut staircase. "I didn't want to say anything in front of Evelyn. Now that she's gone up to bed, I wanted to talk to you."

"It sounds serious." Annabella wrinkled her brow.

Richard sighed, bracing his elbows on the armrests of the chair. "Not really serious, just sad, I guess. I don't understand why Mrs. Hanover is holding such a grudge against me, and taking it out on her daughter especially. I really thought she would get over it by now." He shrugged. "We've been married almost seven months."

Annabella rubbed her brow. "Helen has always struggled with that. I've prayed and hoped that she would learn that it is not a good way to spend your days on this earth…but I'm afraid she has not."

Richard tented his fingers before his chin. "I was over at the mercantile this morning. Aaron was telling me all about his honeymoon." He chuckled. "I was really happy to see him so enthralled with marriage to Miss Rowe…" he rolled his eyes, "Or, Mrs. Darby, rather. I never thought I'd see the day. I think he could actually turn out to be a pretty good friend."

Annabella nodded. "Mr. Darby has always been a very nice young man. He and Evelyn were such good friends for so many years. He was probably the one person Evelyn felt the most comfortable around."

"Anyway, Mrs. Hanover came into the mercantile. For a moment, I thought she was going to turn around and leave when she saw me, but she didn't."

Annabella raised a white brow. "Maybe there *is* hope after all."

Richard pursed his lips, tapping his fingers against his chin. "I don't think so. When Aaron went into the back room to get something Mrs. Hanover had ordered, she approached me. She just stood there and asked when we'd be leaving town."

"Helen asked when you and Evelyn would be leaving Rubyville?" Annabella widened her eyes.

Richard nodded. "I told her that we had no plans to leave as of yet. She said I was taking advantage of you, just using you, and the entire town knew it."

Annabella gasped. "Why, I could just paddle that girl! To say such a thing about her own son-in-law. You have earned your room and board, and then some."

"I sure hope so. If you feel like Evelyn and I are taking advantage of you, we *do* need to leave…and quickly." His gaze met hers. "I've never been treated so well in all my life as I have been with you. You've been my grandmother as well as Evelyn's…and I've appreciated how loved and welcome you've made me feel."

Annabella covered her mouth with her thin, wrinkled hand. "I'm so ashamed of that girl. I just don't know what to do about it. I thought she would eventually see the error of her ways. But she just refuses to." She looked at Richard. "Does she know that Evelyn lost the baby?"

"She does now." Richard leaned forward, setting his elbows on his knees. He clasped his hands. "She told me you didn't need another mouth to feed and we should be gone before the baby was born. So I told her there wouldn't be a baby this summer after all..." He cleared his throat. "And she said that was for the best."

Annabella gasped once more. "Well, of course Evelyn doesn't need to hear that. It would just break her heart, as if that daughter of mine hasn't already destroyed it." Her eyes filled with tears. "I am so sorry, Richard. Those comments were uncalled for, and very untrue."

"I've been praying about it all day, but maybe it would be best if Evelyn and I left Rubyville for a time. Maybe then this whole thing will calm down. It would give you a chance to repair the damage in your relationship with your daughter."

Annabella pointed her finger at Richard and shook it. "I don't want to hear any of that. If you and Evelyn decide to go because it is the best for your relationship, I will be sad, but you need to do what is right for your family. But *don't* leave so that you can appease Helen."

Richard took a deep breath. "I've been thinking of those first John chapter four passages of Scripture all day. There are so many things I don't understand in the Bible, but those verses seem pretty clear. We are to love one another, just as Christ has given His life for us and loved us."

Annabella nodded, closing her eyes. "Verses ten and eleven say, *'Herein is love, not that we loved God, but that he loved us, and sent his Son to be the propitiation for our sins. Beloved, if God so loved us, we ought also to love one another.'*" She opened her eyes and looked at the young man seated across the room. "I believe that Helen has accepted Christ as her Savior, but she has become so bitter and hard-hearted over the years. That is not the way we should live our Christian life. Helen needs much prayer."

"I would agree with that...and Evelyn and I *have* been praying for her. But it's very difficult to see Evelyn have her hopes dashed where her mother is concerned. I want to protect her and love her, and sometimes I feel that I can do that much better away from here. But I know she loves you dearly, and I don't want to take her away."

The green eyes filled with tears. "I appreciate that, but I want you to do whatever God leads you to do. Sometimes He takes us on a journey for the purpose of teaching us to rely on Him, not other people. Trust and obey Him and you can never go wrong."

Richard swallowed. "Well, I wanted you to know. I don't think I will tell Evelyn about the conversation I had with her mother. She has been hurt enough." He stood straight and tall and gave Annabella a smile. "I can't thank you enough for all that you have done for me. You've shown me a side of life that I had always hoped existed, but had not seen. I count it as a privilege and a blessing that we've had these months with you."

"I feel the same about you, Richard. You and Evelyn have made these past few months very pleasant for me."

He walked over to her and kissed her wrinkled cheek. "I'd also like to take care of the cemetery. It shouldn't be left in such a state."

Annabella smiled. "I do appreciate that, but when I talked with my grandson, George, earlier this evening, he said he would like to do it, and he wants his son, Henry, to take over for him." She took her knitting from her lap. "I just didn't want you to have anything holding you here in Rubyville if you and Evelyn felt you should go for a time."

He nodded. "It's probably for the best." He patted her shoulder. "I'm heading upstairs. Do you need anything else before I go?"

She shook her head. "I'm just going to finish this row, and then I'll be up as well."

"Good night, see you in the morning." Richard walked from the parlor and ascended the stairs, his heart beating faster. *This is my favorite time of the day…cuddling with my beautiful wife before falling into a blissful sleep. You have given me many blessings, Father. Too many to count.*

EVELYN SNUGGLED UNDER THE covers, pulling them over her ears to guard against the cold room. She heard Richard's footsteps on the stairs and smiled. *It's about time!*

The door opened and closed softly.

"I'm still awake…and freezing. I need you to get under these covers quickly so I can warm up my feet." Evelyn giggled.

Richard groaned and he shed his clothing. "Your icy toes are as about as cozy as a dip in the river in January."

There was another giggle from the bed. "I know. How do you think I feel? I've had to wear them my entire life...with no one to warm them up with." She reached her arms out to him as he climbed into the bed. "That's why I'm so thankful for you."

He pulled her against his side, wrapping an arm around her shoulders. "So you only love me for my warming qualities?"

She kissed his cheek, then his chin, his neck and his shoulder. "That's just one of the reasons I love you. You're also handsome and strong, and you smell delicious."

He chuckled. "Why do I feel like a roast sitting in the middle of the table?"

Evelyn sighed. "You're much better tasting than any old roast."

Richard pulled her close and pressed his lips to hers. "Why don't you show me, dear wife?"

Chapter Fifteen

September 1949

"I DON'T THINK YOU ever get over the loss of a spouse, do you, Mama Bella?" Beth held the chain of the porch swing as she looked out over the front yard.

"Do we ever forget those that have shared our lives, whether they are spouses or children?" Annabella leaned forward in the wicker chair and adjusted the cushion at her back. "It is just difficult to lose anyone. That is why it is so very important that we share the Gospel message with those around us. When I get to Heaven, I am looking forward to the reunion with those that have gone before me." She gave her daughter and granddaughter a smile. "It gives me hope." Her eyes traveled over the mown grass to the field beyond and the row of trees along the river. "There are so many that I am looking forward to seeing again."

"Well, for now, I want you to concentrate on the ones that are right here." Evelyn bit her bottom lip. "I know that sounds very selfish of me, but I don't want to think of you not being here."

Beth patted Evelyn's knee as they kept the swing in motion. "I agree with you there." Beth's eyes filled. "Now that Daniel is gone, I've been wandering around that big, old house for the past month wondering what I should do." She turned to her mother. "It's very lonely, especially at night."

"I know, my dear. You are always welcome here." Annabella sighed. "Have you tried to visit with Helen?"

Beth nodded. "A few days after Daniel's service, I went over to her house. I wanted to thank her for the food she had brought over that last week before he died. I thought that maybe she would be willing to get together more often since we are both widows now." The tears slipped from her eyes. "I don't know what has become of her. She's polite and she'll talk with me, but it's as if she's not really there." Beth swallowed and brushed at the tears with her tissue. "I will try again after a while, but right now, I'm just hurting too much to try and encourage a relationship with her. That sounds awful, doesn't it?" Beth looked at Evelyn and then Annabella.

"You need time to heal, my dear." Annabella clasped her hands in her lap. "You will never stop missing Daniel, but the sharpness of it will ease."

Evelyn covered her face, her shoulders shaking. "I know I'm immature and selfish, but I can't bear the thought of living in this world without Richard. I would never survive if he died before me."

Beth wrapped her arm around Evelyn's shoulder. "Yes, you would. But I pray you have many years together before you have to deal with that." She gave a small laugh. "You've barely celebrated your first wedding anniversary. You'll have time."

Evelyn turned her reddened eyes to her grandmother. "Grandmama didn't have many years with Orin. Life never turns out the way you expect."

Annabella smiled, the wrinkles around her mouth deepening. "Thank the Lord for that! This life would be very boring if we were given an outline of what was to happen. God knew what He was doing."

"I agree, even though I want to climb into bed and sob for days sometimes." Beth leaned her gray head against the chain. "I just don't know what to do with my life now. I'm sixty-five years old…and lost."

Annabella widened her eyes. "Why don't you go to California and spend some time with Spencer and Dottie? I know you were so disappointed when they couldn't be here for the funeral."

Beth nodded. "I was, but I didn't want Dottie traveling, either. I'm so thankful for my newest grandson, but this past year has been a very difficult one for Spencer and Dottie."

"I didn't know women could have babies at forty-five." Evelyn shook her head. "I sure hope Richard and I don't have to wait that long for our first child."

Annabella laughed. "I am sure you won't. But because Dottie was older and had the complications she did, it was better that she did not travel. Not to mention that traveling by train with a four-month-old would have been quite the challenge."

Beth smiled. "Patrick seems to be a bit of a challenge anyway, from what Dottie writes. He isn't much of a sleeper."

Annabella smacked the chair arm. "So that settles it! We will see about getting you a train ticket to California so you can visit your daughter and new grandson. You could stay out there for several months. I have heard the weather is delightful there during the winter, and Dottie will love having your help. You would be able to spend the holidays with them."

Beth smiled. "I think that could be just the answer, Mama Bella. You always know the right thing to do." She stood and stretched. "I feel better than I have for weeks. I'm going to go by the depot on my way home and see what the train schedules are." She gave Evelyn a hug and then walked over to Annabella, stooping to give her a hug and a kiss on the cheek. "I love you!"

Annabella smiled up at her oldest child. "And I love you. Please let me know what you find out."

"I will." Beth waved, taking the stairs down to the expansive lawn. Her step was light, her arms swinging at her sides.

Evelyn gave an exaggerated frown. "I'm happy for her, and I really hope and pray she has a wonderful time...but I'm going to miss her."

Annabella nodded, sniffing delicately. "I am too. But it *is* for the best. Patrick will be the only baby for Spencer and Dottie, and Dottie needs her mother right now."

"The only baby?"

"Yes, because Dottie was older, she had all those complications, and was on bed rest. By God's grace and mercy, Patrick was born healthy, but the doctor told Dottie she should not have any more children. It would be just too difficult on her body."

Evelyn's hand went to her abdomen. "Do you think something like that could happen to Richard and me? I mean, I've already had two miscarriages."

"I don't think you have anything to worry about, my dear. Sometimes it just takes a little longer, that's all."

Evelyn's gaze followed her aunt down the driveway. "I hope you're right."

March 1950

EVELYN FLIPPED THE THREE eggs and turned the sizzling bacon. Her hands smoothed over the gathered apron at her waist as she went to the refrigerator and took out the pitcher of milk. She set it on the wooden table and put her hands on her blue-gingham hips, surveying the set table.

"Don't you look just as pretty as a picture, standing there with the sunlight coming in the window?" Richard came up behind his wife and nuzzled her neck as he slid his arms about her waist. He breathed deeply. "Fresh roses in the morning. You smell better than that coffee."

Evelyn smiled and placed her hands over Richard's at her waist. She tilted her head to the side. "Doesn't it smell divine? I know Grandmama prefers to boil the coffee on the stove, but I really do love that new percolator she ordered for me."

"Speaking of your grandmother, isn't she usually downstairs by now?" Richard bit Evelyn's ear lobe and went to his place at the table. "Her bedroom door was still closed when I came down."

Evelyn went to the stove and wrapped a towel around the handle of the cast iron skillet. She walked it to the table and slid the eggs and bacon onto Richard's plate. "Maybe she just decided to sleep in a little longer today. I know she has to be tired from going with me each day to get Beth's house ready for her return next week. But she wouldn't hear of me going over there alone. You know how she is."

Richard nodded. "I do, and I wouldn't have it any other way. She has been like a grandmother to me...and I know I've told her that so many times, she's probably tired of hearing it. But she has been a real encouragement."

Evelyn set the skillet on the stove and returned to the table, running her hands along Richard's back as she sat down. "She loves you as well. We Barton women have needed a man around here for a long time."

Richard gave her a wink. "You would be hard-put to run me off now, Evelyn King. You're stuck with me forever."

She grabbed his hand. "I'm absolutely thrilled about that." She nodded to his plate. "Now you'd better pray before your food is cold."

He bowed his head. "Dear gracious Heavenly Father, we thank you for another blessed day to live for You and abide in Your Word. We ask that You watch over us and help us to be productive in our work today. We thank You for this food. Amen."

"Amen." Evelyn laid the napkin in her lap and looked out the window. "I think it's going to be a beautiful spring day. I noticed just this morning that the cottonwoods by the river are taking on a light green hue, so the leaves are coming. It will be full-blown spring before we know it."

Richard nodded as he popped a bite of egg into his mouth. "The redbuds are blooming as well."

"Grandmama has been so pleased with the way the yard looks. After all your hard work here, it is really beautiful. She says it hasn't been so pretty since her father was alive and caring for it."

"Well that *is* a compliment." He took another bite. "From what I've heard about William Barton around here, he was a hard act to follow."

She took a bite of her toast and chewed slowly. "I was in the mercantile yesterday. Cynthia said the baby is moving around all the time now."

"When is the baby due?"

"The first part of June." Evelyn set her toast upon her plate. "She and Aaron are so excited about the baby. They make the perfect couple. She has been so good for Aaron."

"She's been good for the store as well. That feminine touch has really made it nice and inviting."

"Cynthia said the women in town are really happy that they are carrying some of her mother's dresses in the mercantile, readymade." Evelyn moved her toast around on her plate. "She said they sell like hot cakes."

"Well, that's good for business. With a baby on the way, business needs to be great." Richard took his last bite of bacon and looked at his wife. "We'll have a baby of our own someday. Just wait and see. We are working on it...and it will happen."

Evelyn blushed. "I know...it's just that we were married before them...and it seems like we should have a baby by now." She picked up her toast. "But I *am* happy for Cynthia and Aaron. It's nice to have Cynthia for a friend now and not have her treating me like the enemy."

Richard gave her a wink. "See, it all works out for the best. And it will for us too." He looked at the clock on the wall. "I think you should check on your grandmother. I'm beginning to worry about her."

Evelyn pushed her chair back just as a loud crash came from above. Her eyes flew to Richard's. "That sounded like it came from Grandmama's bedroom."

He nodded, his face white. He grabbed her hand and pulled her from the kitchen, racing up the stairs. He stopped outside the closed door. "You'd better go in first…just in case…you know…"

Evelyn nodded as she knocked on the black walnut door. She pushed it open. "Grandmama, we heard—" Evelyn rushed to the side of the bed where Annabella lay on the floor in a crumpled heap, the small table beside the bed turned over at her feet. "Grandmama, are you alright?"

Richard peered in and ran over as Evelyn gestured him in.

Evelyn knelt beside her grandmother. "Grandmama, can you hear me? Are you hurt?" She put one hand to her wrinkled cheek. "She's like ice, Richard."

Annabella opened her eyes, the right side of her face drooping. "I…I…co…co…couldn't feel my…my arm…" The green eyes stared wildly as she struggled to speak.

Richard knelt down and picked her up, gently laying her on the bed. He turned to Evelyn. "I'm going to telephone Dr. Rundell. If no one answers, I'll go over to the house. I'll be back with him."

"Please hurry, Richard." Evelyn gripped his wrist and then turned back to Annabella. She straightened her grandmother's long nightgown and pulled the covers over her thin frame. "Richard is going for Dr. Rundell. He'll know what's wrong. He'll have you better in no time."

"I…I …couldn't…fe…feel…my…my…my…" Annabella closed her eyes, tears slipping from beneath her pale lashes. "I…ca…can't…" The words came slow and garbled.

Evelyn sat down at the edge of the bed and took her grandmother's hand. "Don't try to talk, Grandmama. Just rest. Maybe you hit your head when you fell. Dr. Rundell will know what's wrong. He'll make you better." She looked down at the hand hanging limply in hers.

The guttural words struggled out once more. "I…lo…lo…lov…love…you!" Annabella gasped, her chest heaving with the effort.

"I love *you*, Grandmama!" Evelyn gripped the limp hand and stroked her grandmother's long white braid.

"He…Hel…Hel…I…lo…her!" The green eyes searched Evelyn's face.

"I know you do. I know you love Mama, and Beth. Beth will be here next week, remember? She's been gone such a long time visiting Spencer and Dottie and their boy Patrick. Remember?"

Annabella made a movement with her head and closed her eyes.

Evelyn looked up at the ceiling. *Please, Father, let Grandmama be alright. Just let it be a bump on the head. I know she's been working too hard and I shouldn't have let her, but I'll make her rest. I won't let her do any more work. She can just sit in a chair and tell me what needs to be done. But please, Father…don't take her away yet. I need her more than You do. Please!*

DR. RUNDELL ENTERED THE kitchen and clapped one hand upon Richard's shoulder. Richard raised his head from the table and stared up at the doctor.

"How's she doing?"

The doctor gestured to a chair. "May I sit down?"

Richard stood. "Of course, can I get you some coffee? It may still be warm."

He nodded. "That would help. My day started pretty early with a child with a bad case of the chicken pox. The parents and the child haven't slept in a couple of days."

Richard poured the coffee and set the cup in front of the doctor. He took his seat once again and looked at Dr. Rundell.

"Miss Barton had a stroke. She is paralyzed on the right side, which is why her face is sagging. It has also affected her speech, as you've seen." He took a long sip of his coffee.

"Is she going to be alright?"

Dr. Rundell shook his head. "I don't know, to be honest. I've seen people recover, usually younger than Miss Barton, and other times they don't." He rubbed his brow. "I just don't know."

"What can we do for her?"

"I told Evelyn to just keep her comfortable. It would probably be better if you didn't encourage her to talk too much, just because it is so frustrating for her right now. Just let her rest. I'm going to go back to the office and go through some of my medical books." He stared at his cup. "Richard, I would get in contact with Helen. Let her know what has happened. I know things have been difficult between Helen and Evelyn the past couple of years, but she needs to see her mother."

Richard slid his hands through his hair. "Of course. I will go over right away."

Dr. Rundell slid his chair back and stood, placing his hands at his waist. "Miss Barton is a strong woman, and she's pulled through a lot over the years. We'll just have to see." He gave Richard a tired smile and walked from the room.

Richard yanked his coat from the hook by the kitchen door and rushed out, jogging to the old barn where the Plymouth was kept. He jumped in and backed the long automobile from the narrow space, whipping it around in the driveway. He headed down the long, gravel road, driving quickly through town.

Please, Father, give me the words to say to Mrs. Hanover. Help her to understand how important it is for her to return with me and visit her mother.

Turning left, he drove down the road leading to the stone house. He stopped the automobile alongside the lilacs, their tiny green buds dotting the hedge. *Please, Father, guide me through this.* The curtain at the front window caught his eye as it lifted and fell.

The front door opened, Helen framed in her pretty green-striped house dress. Her eyes widened as Richard slammed the Plymouth door shut and strode up the walkway. "I thought it was Evelyn. Is she alright?" The blue eyes searched her son-in-law's face.

Richard gained the porch, one foot on the wide boards, the other on the top step. "Evelyn is fine. Dr. Rundell sent me." He looked up at the porch ceiling and then met Helen's eyes. "It's your mother, Mrs.

Hanover. She's had a stroke. Evelyn and I found her about an hour ago, lying on the floor beside her bed."

Helen's pale face grew white, her red lips a slash upon the marble. One hand went to her throat, gripping tightly. "Is she...is Mama..."

"She's still with us, but Dr. Rundell thought it best if you see her right away." He gestured to the automobile. "I can drive you over."

Helen nodded, starting for the porch steps. She paused and rubbed her brow. "I should probably get a sweater, and my purse. I was just out a little bit ago and left them on the kitchen table, I think." She frowned and looked down at her apron, embroidered apples upon the large pockets. She reached around to untie it and turned toward the house.

Richard held out his hand for the apron. "Please, if you don't mind, I can put your apron on the table, and get your purse and sweater. I'll be back in just a minute."

Helen nodded, laying the apron across his wrist. "Please lock the door. You just never know these days." She stumbled to the stairs.

Chapter Sixteen

EVELYN HELD HER GRANDMOTHER'S hand as she lay next to her on the bed, her voice holding the last word of a hymn drifting through the room. She reached up and dabbed at the tears slipping beneath the pale lashes and trickling down the wrinkled cheek.

"Mo...mo...sing...plea..." The words came forced, a deep breath between each one.

"Of course." Evelyn swallowed, pressing her lips together. *Please give me another hymn, Father. Help me not to cry. Make my voice strong for Grandmama.* Her thoughts swept back to that May Sunday morning just two years before when she had stood at the front of the church, her heart pounding loudly in her ears. Richard had sat beside her grandmother, visiting the church for the first time...and he had smiled at her, calming her anxious thoughts.

She took a deep breath and began singing the familiar song. Her voice broke, then she continued on. She had begun the last verse when she heard footsteps rushing up the stairs.

"Mama!" Helen entered the room, rushing to the bed. Richard followed behind her.

"Hel...He..." Annabella swallowed, staring up at her daughter.

Helen shook her head. "Don't try to talk, Mama. It will just wear you out." Helen's eyes shifted to her daughter, lying next to the withered form. Helen's blue eyes turned to liquid, and she pressed her knuckles to her nose.

Richard set a chair beside the bed. "Here, Mrs. Hanover, there's a place for you to sit."

Helen offered a weak smile to her son-in-law and sat down. She took

Annabella's limp hand in her own and brought it to her cheek. She gazed into the green eyes, staring back at her. "I love you, Mama. Even though I've been so upset with you, I still love you."

"I...know..."

"But you can't leave yet. Beth will be here next week. She'll want to see you." Helen kissed the hand she held. "So you will just have to get better."

Annabella moved her head upon the pillow. "Nooo...go...home." She gasped and closed her eyes, her lips moving. "I...red...eee."

Helen switched her gaze to Evelyn. "We have to encourage her to hang on until Beth arrives home. She will be so disappointed if she misses saying good-bye."

Evelyn brushed at her cheeks. "Beth will understand. She wouldn't want Grandmama to suffer." She placed a kiss on Annabella's cheek. "*I* don't want her to be in pain...or uncomfortable."

"With that statement, you're implying that I *do* want my mother to suffer...which I do not." Helen's shoulders dropped. "I just know how terrible it is to not get the chance to say good-bye."

Evelyn sat up, and moved to the edge of the bed. She turned, and caught Richard's gaze upon her as he stood in the doorway, one shoulder against the frame, hands in the pockets of his blue jeans. He offered her a smile and held out his hand. She went to him and buried her face against the buttons of his coarse work shirt. "I don't know what to say or do. It will all be taken the wrong way."

"Just love them both." Richard put his hand up and smoothed the red hair at her shoulders. He cleared his throat. "Mrs. Hanover, Evelyn and I are going to step out so you may spend some time with your mother. Dr. Rundell just said to keep her calm and let her rest when she wants to."

Helen looked over her shoulder at the pair in the doorway. "Of course. I know what's best for my mother." She turned back to the frail woman lying in the bed.

THEY WALKED HAND-IN-HAND TO the large bedroom at the front of the house. Richard closed the door and took his wife in his arms.

"It was wonderful to hear you singing when we came in. I know your grandmother appreciated that. She loves it when you sing at church."

Evelyn wrapped her arms around Richard's waist, her cheek against his chest. "She isn't going to get better...is she?"

Richard cleared his throat. "Dr. Rundell said he just didn't know what to expect. He's seen younger people recover—"

"But not someone that is eighty-seven years old."

"He didn't say that outright, but that is probably true."

Evelyn pulled away and walked to the turreted windows. "I don't know what I'm going to do without her. She's been here my entire life. Someone to go to when Mama was being, well...Mama. Always a word of encouragement, helping me see the better side of things. Directing me back to what God would want me to do, rather than my own selfish pursuits."

Richard walked up behind Evelyn and put his hands on her shoulders, kneading them gently. "I'm very thankful for the short time I've had with her. She's given me hope in the human race...and the ability to love." He wrapped his arms around her waist, clasping his hands. "Just as you have."

Evelyn leaned back against Richard and closed her eyes. "I'm happy that Mama agreed to come over. I was so afraid she wouldn't."

"That's a strange thing about your mother. I know she loves you and your grandmother. I think she would do anything for either of you. But she keeps her distance when she's been hurt...almost as though she is punishing herself for something."

Evelyn shrugged. "I always thought it was just pride and stubbornness."

"There's a huge chunk of that as well, but I think it's mostly hurt. And that's a very sad way to live your life. She will miss out on so much."

"I know, but I don't know what to do about it. I've tried over and over to reach out to her...and she always turns away."

"All you can do is love her, let her know that you are there. Maybe someday, she will seek you."

Evelyn turned, narrowing her eyes to see the small alarm clock on the table beside the bed. "I need to put the kitchen in order. We just ran out when we heard the crash. If I stay busy, I won't think about Grandmama lying there, struggling so hard to talk, not able to move."

Richard gave her a squeeze. "Hurry back to her. You want to be there for her if she needs anything. It might be a good time for you and your mother to repair some of the damage."

Evelyn nodded. "I'll try, but I think the best thing I can do is sit beside the bed and pray."

HELEN SMOOTHED HAND CREAM over Annabella's limp wrist. "I keep hoping this will help Mama. She hasn't spoken or opened her eyes for three days now. I was so sure she was going to be alright the day I arrived."

Evelyn turned from the lace-covered window to look at her mother seated beside Annabella's high mahogany bed. "I know. I thought her speech would get better and she would be just fine after a while." She wrapped her arms about her waist. Her eyes swept to where her grandmother lay, so still upon the bed, her chest rising and falling. "Maybe she is waiting for Beth, after all."

Helen laid her mother's hand upon the covers and sat back in her chair. Her shoulders drooped. "I probably shouldn't have said that. I just remember how devastating it was for me to never have had the chance to say good-bye to your father. I thought it would help Mama to be near Beth again."

"She'll be here tomorrow, and we'll see what happens." Evelyn rubbed her brow. "I just wish we had more information, some way to help her," she gestured to the still form, "rather than just watch her lie there."

"I know, but Dr. Rundell is doing everything he knows to do, and he's spending every moment he has to read about new treatments." Helen leaned her head back and closed her eyes. "There just isn't much hope, I guess."

Evelyn walked to the bench at the foot of the bed and sat down, facing her mother. "I'm thankful to have you here, Mama. You've made the past few days more bearable."

Helen opened her eyes and gave Evelyn a small smile. "I'm thankful your husband came and got me. I wouldn't have wanted to be anywhere else right now."

Evelyn stared at the hands clasped in her lap. "Mama, can we try to go back to the way things used to be…before I married Richard? I mean…the relationship between you and me."

Helen shook her head. "I don't know how to do that. You chose him and her," she nodded toward her mother, "over me."

"Mama, it doesn't have to be like that. I love all three of you, just as much, but differently. I want all of you in my life. I *need* all of you in my life." Evelyn sought her mother's eyes, her own growing dark as they filled with tears.

"You have your husband now…and I don't see any place for me in your life. That was the decision you made, Evelyn. You didn't want my advice…and you didn't include me." Helen crossed her arms in front of her.

"But I *did* include you, Mama." Evelyn turned, gripping the covers at the foot of the bed. "You were invited to the wedding. No one wanted to leave you out."

Helen raised her chin and took a deep breath. "But I was left out just the same. What Pastor Drummond and Mrs. Drummond did was unconscionable. I thought they were my friends and that they wanted what was best for me and my family."

"They *did*, Mama…they *still* do. You are prayed for and missed each Sunday morning."

Helen stood and paced to the fireplace standing dark and cold. She stood in front of it, staring at the empty cavity. "So now all of Rubyville is gossiping about me as well, with Pastor Drummond's blessing. Maybe it's time for me to attend the Methodist church. It's a bit closer to me anyway."

Evelyn gaped at her mother's back. "But you've attended our church your entire life. It's the Barton family's church."

"I attended a church while I lived in Loudonville and one in Albany. They met my needs just fine. Rubyville doesn't have the only church in the world, my dear."

"Well…of course not…I just assumed you would want to go—"

"You assumed I would do whatever I was supposed to do according to Annabella Barton, just as this entire town has always assumed." Helen gripped the mantle over the fireplace and turned to her daughter. "My mother decreed that you should marry Richard King, and so it was done. Then she said you should live here, and you have, for almost two years.

What are you going to do when she is gone? Who is going to support you then, give you shelter, food to eat, new automobiles to drive?"

"What is the meaning of this?" Dr. Rundell rushed into the bedroom, dropping his black leather bag upon Helen's vacated chair. "I could hear you the moment I walked in the front door." He leaned over his patient, laying a hand upon her chest. "Just as I thought...her heart rate is accelerated." He pointed to the bedroom door. "Both of you...out of this room... immediately." He turned back to Annabella, adjusting the covers across her middle.

Helen strode from the room, Evelyn upon her heels. They turned as Dr. Rundell met them in the wide hall, shutting the door to Annabella's bedroom.

"We're sorry, Dr. Ru—" Evelyn's eyes widened as the doctor stopped her.

"I cannot believe the two of you would carry on in such a manner with Miss Barton just feet away...and in her condition. There is every reason to believe that she can hear you, even if she does not respond with words of her own." He leveled his dark gaze at Evelyn and then Helen. "Her heart is *not* strong. She came to me several months ago with complaints of a racing heart and this stroke has not helped that."

Evelyn lowered her head. "I didn't realize she was having problems with her heart. She never mentioned it."

"And she wouldn't allow me to, either. She wanted to be here for all of you." Dr. Rundell pulled at his tie. "But she isn't strong enough to bear all your burdens any longer. She needs both of you now...your love. She doesn't need to hear you bickering over things that don't really matter, especially now."

"Of course. I do apologize for our behavior." Evelyn glanced at her mother and received a cold stare in return. "I didn't think she would be able to hear us."

Dr. Rundell turned his gaze upon Helen. "Do you understand what I'm saying, Mrs. Hanover? Your mother needs your love and consideration now. Nothing else matters."

"I will be sure to keep my emotions where they should be." Helen took a deep breath and smoothed the front of her house dress. She looked at Evelyn. "I'm going to go down and see about something for supper for everyone. If you would sit with Mama, I would appreciate it."

"I can see to supper, Mama." Evelyn started toward the stairs.

Helen placed a hand on Evelyn's arm. "No, I need some time...alone. I really prefer to be downstairs for awhile." Helen walked to the stairs, her footsteps heard on the wood steps as she descended.

Evelyn pressed her lips together and turned to the doctor. "I *really* am sorry. Mama and I just seem to clash whenever we are together for any length of time. I should be thankful that things have been relatively quiet for the past few days."

Dr. Rundell cleared his throat. "From everything I've been able to read on strokes, I'm afraid your grandmother is not doing well. The fact that she is no longer communicating in any way is not a good sign. I had hoped at first that she would be able to recover to some extent...but now..." He shook his head.

Evelyn swallowed deeply. "I'm going to go in and talk with her, share some Bible verses I know she enjoys...maybe sing to her again. If..." Evelyn brushed at her cheeks. "If these are her last days, I want her to hear only good things."

The doctor nodded. "That is best."

THE FIRST RAYS OF the April morning peeked at Annabella's lace-covered windows, the soft smell of new lilacs drifting in the open sash. Annabella moved her left hand, ever so slightly, touching the granddaughter that rested beside her.

Evelyn opened her eyes at the touch, and sat up. "Grandmama?"

Helen jerked her head from her arms resting atop the covers as Beth struggled to sit up from the bench.

Helen stood and went to the head of the bed, gripping her mother's shoulder as she leaned close. "Mama...are you awake?"

Beth went to Helen's side and took her mother's limp hand in her own. "We are all here, Mama Bella."

Annabella's pale lashes fluttered open and her green eyes took in each face. The left side of her mouth lifted…a crooked smile. "I…love…you…all. I…will…be…wai…waiting."

Her chest heaved one last breath and her face softened in the early morning light. Her eyes drifted closed, a smile upon her lips.

RICHARD TURNED AND WALKED away from the weeping women. He descended the black walnut staircase and strode from the house, his steps long and hurried upon the dewy grass. He brushed at his cheeks, swallowing around the lump that seemed to be lodged in his throat.

Soon, his stride became a jog and he ran across the field, entering the trees along the river. He grabbed an old redbud and buried his face against the rough bark and cried.

Miss Barton, I miss you already. But I pray you are happy, healed from your physical afflictions of this world. You are reunited with your beloved Orin and your parents, and all those that have gone before you. I'm sure you're not even thinking of us down here, wondering what we're going to do now that you're gone.

He raised his head and looked back toward Rubyville, just coming awake in the early morning hour. He could see Pastor Drummond entering the old stone church, beginning his day with his devotions, just as he did every day. He knew Ellen would soon be sweeping off the long front porch of the hotel and checking biscuits in the oven. The Darbys would be sweeping their porch too, Cynthia arranging the stock upon the shelves to attract the customer's attention. Mr. Pertz would be spraying off the cement in front of his gasoline pumps, making sure everything was tidy for his day at the filling station. School children would be pulled from bed, rubbing sleepy eyes and groaning at the thought of another day at the brick building west of town.

Richard's eyes swept over the park, the bright green leaves starting to form their canopy. *Another day in Rubyville, Miss Barton, and you aren't here. How will we ever go on without you?*

Richard put his back to the redbud, and slid down to the base, pulling his knees close to his chest.

He laid his forehead on his knees, his shoulders shaking. *For just a bit, Father, let me feel sorry for myself. Let me feel the pain of losing such a great woman that lived for You and loved those around her. No, she wasn't perfect, and she made many mistakes. But she continued to live and learn what You had for her. She was an example to us all. I pray that I can live my life half as well.*

Chapter Seventeen

Lake George, New York
Late June 1951

LAUREL WYATT STEPPED FROM the last stair carved out of the rock and onto the large boat dock. "I had a feeling I would find you down here. You remind me so much of your mother. She loved being by the water." She gave a laugh as she flung her towel to the chaise lounge beside Evelyn. She pulled her white-flowered bathing cap over her short, curly brown hair, and slid her feet from her sandals. Her toweling dress was tossed upon the lounge. She walked to the edge of the dock and turned back. "I'm going to take a quick swim, and then we can talk while I warm up."

Evelyn laughed. "Yes, the water *is* a bit cold. It takes my breath away each time I get in."

Laurel pulled at the modesty apron of her navy blue suit as she nodded toward the glistening water. "Just think... there was ice here only four months ago." She dove into the clear lake and surfaced a few yards out. She gasped, treading water as she turned to Evelyn.

"Frigid, isn't it?" Evelyn called, her hands wrapped around her mouth.

"Yes!" Laurel shivered. "Your mother was always the first one in, and I liked it that way! I'm getting too old for this!" She struck out with the crawl stroke and swam parallel to the shore.

Evelyn leaned back on the wood chaise lounge, fluffing her cap of red curls. Her eyes drifted closed at the sound of the lapping water against the dock, the breeze sifting through the new leaves on the trees.

Laurel wrapped herself in her towel, taking the bathing cap from her hair. She shook her head vigorously and sat down upon the lounge with a sigh.

Evelyn gave a shiver and opened her eyes. She pulled her towel across her legs as she smiled at her cousin. "That didn't take long."

"I swam several laps...enough to help me remember how out of shape I am every summer when we return here." Laurel sat back, resting her feet upon the wood slats. "You must have fallen asleep. I swam for a good twenty minutes."

"Then I *did* have a good nap." Evelyn took a deep breath. "This Adirondack air just invites great sleeping."

Laurel laid her head back and closed her eyes. "Yes, it does."

Evelyn reached out and gave her cousin a playful slap. "Hey, I thought we were going to talk."

Laurel opened one eye and raised a brow. "I'm an old woman. I need a bit of a rest after exercise like that."

"You aren't an old woman. You haven't reached fifty yet, and you don't have a bit of gray in your hair." Evelyn narrowed an eye, assessing Laurel's brown curls.

Laurel gave a delicate clearing of her throat. "Well, I'm *almost* fifty and there are things that help with that gray hair these days. I'll be able to avoid turning gray for another fifty years."

Evelyn laughed. "Yes, because you'll be bald. Be careful with that hair dye. It would probably burn a hole in this dock."

Laurel chuckled.

Evelyn reached out and laid her hand over Laurel's arm lying on the armrest. "I'm so happy you and Stephen agreed to come before everyone else. It's been so much fun having you both here. Richard really likes your husband."

"Stephen has been fairly impressed with Richard, as well. He doesn't remember anyone being so eager to learn God's Word."

"When we visited your church for Easter services, Richard couldn't stop talking about Stephen's message. He enjoyed it so much he said we should move to Vermont just so we could attend your church on a regular basis." Evelyn laughed. "I don't think I could manage the winters there, though. They sound long and cold."

Laurel shrugged. "They are about the same as here." Her eyes drifted over the lake. "But we don't have this where we are in Vermont." She looked back at Evelyn. "Besides, what would my father do if you and Richard decide to leave here? You have been a wonderful help to him since you arrived last September. Losing both mother and Annabella last year, especially only a few months apart, was very hard on him."

Evelyn nodded. "We do adore living here. Richard loves being outside, working around the yard, and seeing to all the little things that need to be done. Grandmama appreciated him so much for all that he did at her house the two years we lived there."

Laurel opened her towel, stretching out her legs. "Well, I know it was perfect timing. The previous caretaker had been here since I was a little girl. When he telephoned Father about having to retire, Father didn't know what he was going to do. Richard has done a wonderful job with the yard, and the house is just beautiful inside from all your cleaning. Father will be very pleased when he arrives next week." Laurel smiled. "Not that he cares much about the house anymore. It's just a place to sleep. Down on the water is where he wants to be."

Evelyn laughed. "I can understand that. It's gorgeous here." Her eyes scanned the shimmering water. "I'm happy to hear that it's been a help to your family. It just goes to show that God works everything out for the best." Evelyn adjusted the towel over her legs. "After Grandmama passed away, things with Mama just never improved. I was really hoping they would, but she just kind of walled herself away. Then Beth decided to go back to California to be near Dottie, Spencer, and Patrick…" She pressed her lips together. "Well, it just seemed best to leave Rubyville for awhile. George was more than happy to look after things for us."

Laurel laughed. "It's hard for me to picture the *Georgie* your mother always told me about as the responsible man you've said he is now…with almost grown children of his own." She shook her head. "Where in the world does the time go?"

Evelyn stared out over the lake. "I know it travels much too fast. There never seems to be enough occasions to make things right."

Laurel shook her head. "Don't be thinking you haven't done your best by your mother. Helen always was a bit different."

Evelyn frowned. "I thought you said you and my mother did everything together while she lived here."

Laurel nodded. "We did, and I have many very happy memories with her." She gave Evelyn a sweet smile. "I remember the day you were born, right here in Lake George. She was *so* happy to finally meet you."

"Mama showed me the stone house just down the road from here. It looks very much like the house I grew up in."

Laurel chewed on her bottom lip. "Yes, it does. Your mother loved that house…and she loved the lake. It broke her heart when she learned that your father had sold it."

"She never would tell me much about that." Evelyn looked up at the blue sky. "Mama just seems to have so many hurts and disappointments. I know I never could live up to what she wanted me to be. I feel like I just quit trying after a while. It was just too difficult."

"It's too difficult for any person to live up to another's wishes. That's why we strive to adhere to God's standards. We learn how He wants us to live our lives. We abide in Him by reading His Word, praying, and getting encouragement from others doing the same. It's a life-long process. Your mother and I talked about that often." Laurel clasped her hands at her waist. "I only wish she could grasp that, and not be so hard on herself and those around her."

"It would have been wonderful if Mama could have joined us here when everyone arrives next week. I know your parents hadn't been to Rubyville for the reunions in several years." Evelyn's eyes misted over. "It would have been special to have everyone together again…especially since Grandmama is gone."

Laurel held out her hand, giving Evelyn's fingers a squeeze when the hand slid into hers. "I know she meant a lot to you, and I know you miss her. Just remember she is waiting for us, along with my mother, Orin, her parents, and Aunt Agnes."

Evelyn gave a smile. "Don't forget Martha."

Laurel laughed. "No one could ever forget Martha. She kept those Rubyville reunions right on track. And her food…" She sighed. "I could eat her fried chicken right now, with a biscuit and some of her gravy. It's probably better that she decided to head to Kansas with Aunt Lavinia. We would have all been as plump as prairie chickens."

Evelyn laughed, withdrawing her hand. "And how many prairie chickens have you seen in your lifetime?"

Laurel sneaked up two fingers. "And then just while visiting Kansas." She shrugged. "Just seemed like the thing to say."

"Well, I've seen a few over the years. But I don't recall them being that *plump*...mostly just noisy during mating season." Evelyn chuckled. "The males do this little stomping dance with their feet and blow up their necks."

Laurel rolled her eyes. "Well, I never dreamed I would get a lesson about prairie chickens. You Kansans talk about the strangest things." She shook her head.

Evelyn shrugged. "What can I say? I spent a lot of time walking around the fields. I was rather a tomboy, and it gave me a chance to escape Mama and her endless chatter about me being a lady. She hated the blue jeans I wore, and she would have never allowed me to cut my hair this short." Evelyn ruffled the curls at the back of her neck.

Laurel sat forward, one hand upon her hip as she gaped at Evelyn. "Well that's the pot calling the kettle black."

Evelyn frowned. "What do you mean?"

"Your mother was about the first woman around Albany, and definitely in our family, that bobbed her hair." She put one hand to her chest and opened her eyes wide. "That was thought of as scandalous back then." She chuckled as she sat back and laid her head against the slats of the chaise lounge. "Helen, Helen...what are we going to do with you?"

"It would probably be very disrespectful of me to even say it...and I have talked with God about it several times over the years. But I think she needs a good talking to." Evelyn laid back and closed her eyes. "It probably wouldn't be the best thing for me to do."

Laurel shook her head with a smile. "No, probably not."

THE RINGING OF THE telephone caused Helen to lay the wooden spoon on the counter and brush her hands on her apron. She shook her head. "Now who in the world would be calling me at the crack of dawn?" She went to the little table in the hall and picked up the black handset. "Hello?"

"Good morning, Helen! How are you?" The voice greeted, causing Helen to put one hand to her chest.

"Why, good morning, Laurel. This is such a surprise. We haven't talked over the telephone in years." Helen frowned. "Is something wrong?"

The tinkling laugh traveled over the miles. "No, I'm sorry, Helen. I didn't mean to frighten you. Everyone here is doing very well. Father just arrived in Lake George for his month visit. He will be eighty-six this September, you know."

"I remembered that he was close in age to Mama." Helen cleared her throat. "But Uncle Jackson is doing alright?"

"Yes, he is fine. Slower than he used to be, but doing well. Edward drove him up, because father doesn't drive anymore, of course."

Helen shook her head. "No, of course not." Helen pressed the receiver close. "I would assume Evelyn is still there in Lake George?"

"Oh, yes, she and Richard have done a lovely job of caring for the house and grounds these past few months. Father has been just delighted."

Helen rolled her eyes. "Those two always seem to find a hand-out somewhere."

There was a cough on the other end of the line. "Helen, why would you say such a thing about your own daughter and son-in-law? They have been a tremendous help and they haven't taken a penny for all that they've done. That is not a fair statement."

Helen nodded her head and placed one arm around her waist. "So, this is the reason behind a telephone call from my dear cousin that I have not heard from in years. You wish to lecture me."

"Helen Hanover, you know I have written you many times over the years, and you have not returned the favor. I was also the one that always telephoned." There was a sigh. "I did not telephone to argue with you."

"Well then, why did you?" Helen braced her elbow upon her wrist as she leaned into the handset.

"I am worried about you, Helen. I've been praying for you, but I felt the need to hear your voice and try to talk some sense into you about what you're doing with your life."

Helen dropped her arm from around her waist and looked around the small hallway. "I am here in Rubyville, abandoned by my family, and you ask *me* what I'm doing with my life?"

Laurel snorted. "You weren't *abandoned* by your family. You ran them off, pure and simple. You haven't changed a bit over the years, have you? Always taking the victim side of everything and thinking everyone is out to do their worst to you."

"Well, it doesn't sound as though you've changed a bit, either. You are just as bossy as you always were." Helen took a deep breath and let it out slowly.

There was a loud click on the line.

"Does someone want to use the phone?" Laurel asked. "I telephoned early hoping to avoid possible interruptions."

"Probably. It is a party-line after all. Everyone in Rubyville will know that you telephoned, and what we argued about, by noon today." Helen replaced her arm about her waist and leaned against the wall.

Laurel sighed. "I'm sure the good people of Rubyville have better things to do with their time."

Helen shook her head. "It's obvious that you've never lived in a small town. People thrive on what their neighbors are doing."

"Well, I don't want to keep you, Helen. I know you must be very busy plotting your revenge against all that have done you wrong over the years."

Helen's eyes widened. "That's a cruel thing to say, Laurel, even for you."

Laurel laughed. "Helen, I do miss you and our bantering. But I *am* praying for you, hoping you won't let Evelyn just slip away. She loves you very much, you know."

"She has a very strange way of showing it, I must say."

"Well, she does. Evelyn was the one that mentioned you joining us all here for the month. She misses you."

Helen swallowed. "I cannot return to Lake George, Laurel. There are too many memories there for me."

"Why ever not? You visited with Evelyn, just after the war. You seemed to enjoy yourself."

Tears slipped down Helen's cheeks. "I…I did. But now Mama is gone, and I just don't want to travel back east. Not now."

"Well, *that's* why I called. I wanted to invite you up here. Someone would meet you at the train station and then drive you up. We could have such fun talking about old times, swimming in the lake, and showing Evelyn around. Everyone would love to see you again."

Helen pressed her lips together. "I can't Laurel…not now. Evelyn has made her choice to stay away, and I'm going to respect that and stay away."

Laurel sighed. "Still just as stubborn as you ever were. We are to soften as we age, Helen. The trials and tribulations we weather are to mold us into a better, patient person. If we remain bitter, hold grudges, and refuse to learn from our mistakes…" There was another long sigh. "Your life won't be very happy."

Helen brushed at her cheek. "I can assure you, I'm happy. I'm making cookies this morning to take over to Ellen at the hotel. She appreciates that, and it gives her guests a little treat in the afternoon with their tea or coffee. I stay very busy."

"I'm sure you do, Helen. You've always managed to avoid the real issues in life."

The line clicked once more.

"Well, you have made your point abundantly clear, Laurel. You think I'm a bad mother and that I'm wasting my life—"

"Helen, that's not—"

"That's exactly what you said. I hope you all have a wonderful time there in Lake George. I will talk with you another time."

Helen set the handset on the base and wrapped both arms around her waist. She stared out the front windows, the lilac hedge framed in the long drapes. *Why can't I just forget all the wrongs done, and just live my life as Laurel said? I really am only hurting myself. But no one else cares. No one truly understands what I've been through.*

LAUREL REPLACED THE HANDSET, shaking her head. She sat back and turned to Evelyn, seated next to her on the davenport. "I tried."

Evelyn heaved a sigh. "Thank you. I suppose that's all we can do." She laid both hands upon her legs, pulling at the floral pattern of her dress. "Mama is not happy that Richard and I are here, is she?"

Laurel shook her head and put a hand over Evelyn's. "No, but you two have been a gift from God. I know my father feels badly that you won't take any payment for all that you have done here."

"Allowing us to live in his beautiful home has been payment enough." Evelyn's eyes scanned the large, rustic room overlooking the sloping backyard to the lake. "We love it here."

Laurel smiled and patted the hand before standing. "I need to run a few errands before dinner. Would you like to come?"

Evelyn smiled as she stood. "I would love to. With our husbands out fishing with Uncle Jackson, I was wondering what I was going to do for the next few hours."

Laurel rolled her eyes. "You thought our husbands disappeared for hours on that lake. Father is with them now. There's no telling how long they'll be. He lives all year for his time out in that boat."

Chapter Eighteen

Lake George, New York
April 4, 1955

THE SUN'S RAYS FILTERED through the bare trees and shimmered golden hues of pink and lavender across the still waters. The voile curtains at the window lifted gently, the cold air causing the inhabitants of the bed to shiver.

Richard leaned down from his reclining position at the headboard and kissed Evelyn on her temple. One long, tanned finger smoothed the tiny hand that rested beside the petal-soft cheek. "Now that your hard work is over, may I shut the window?" He smiled. "I understand that you were hot earlier, but that air is a bit chilly coming off the lake. We don't want to give her frostbite on her very first day here."

Evelyn smiled up at her husband, her green eyes liquid and soft, eyelids drooping. "I am a bit chilly *now*. I wasn't earlier." She sighed. "I never knew it would be so difficult to bring another life into this world." She pulled the baby closer against her chest. "But she is worth every second of the pain."

Richard slid from the bed and went to the window. He pushed the long curtains aside and closed the sash, staring out at the lake. "We have a daughter, Evelyn. A precious new life to love and train in the way she should go." He turned and walked back to the bed. "That's a pretty daunting task ahead."

Evelyn brushed the sleeping baby's cheek. "I know, but right now, all I can think about is how much I love her and how wonderful it is to have a girl."

He chuckled as he lay down and turned on his side, one hand

supporting his jaw. "You told me she was going to be a boy ever since you found out you were expecting a baby."

"I know." Evelyn laughed and winced. "I'm a bit sore in places I never knew I had." She lifted the little bundle and pressed her nose to the tiny cheek and breathed deeply. "I believe it was wishful thinking on my part. There have been only girls born in our family for so many years. I thought it was time to contribute a boy."

Richard chuckled. "I think the Darbys took care of that in Rubyville. They've supplied boys for the entire town."

Evelyn rolled her eyes as she laid the baby on her lap. "I don't know how Cynthia did it. She delivered four boys in just less than three years."

Richard held up his fingers. "The first one was in June of 1950, right after your grandmother passed away, and the twins were born the last of December of..." Richard frowned and he dropped his hand.

"She had one in February of '52, and then the twins were born in late December that same year."

Richard whistled. "Whoee! That's a lot of something in a short period of time."

Evelyn jabbed him with her elbow. "Is that appropriate?"

He shrugged. "Aaron and Cynthia must have thought so." He shook his head. "And he's still driving that '39 Plymouth. That back seat is big enough to get a couple more in."

Evelyn shook her head. "The last time Cynthia wrote she said there would be no more babies in their house. She seemed pretty adamant."

"Well, at least they moved from that little house beside the mercantile. That old farmhouse Aaron grew up in should be big enough for the crew."

"Yes, and Aaron's mother adores having all those grandchildren right there. Cynthia thought she would be lost without Aaron's father after he died, but she is doing much better. And Cynthia's mother really likes living in their old place. She is close enough to keep an eye on the mercantile and help out when she's not at her dress shop."

Richard's eyes swept over her face. "You miss Rubyville, don't you?"

Evelyn nodded. "I do. I am ready to return...at least for a visit."

Richard nodded toward his sleeping daughter. "Well, just as soon as you think she is ready to travel, we can make a trip back." He adjusted his hips and laid back on the bed, his arms crossed beneath his neck.

"I thought you were hoping to move to Vermont at the end of the summer, so we could be near Stephen and Laurel." Evelyn showed him a puckered brow.

He crossed his ankles. "I've been thinking and praying about it, and if you agree, I think it's time we moved on. We've spent a lot of time in Vermont...and I have enjoyed it. But maybe it's time to see some other places like Minnesota or Montana...that area of the country."

Evelyn's eyes sparkled. "I think that would be wonderful. I've always wanted to travel around and see different places."

He turned his head. "You've never said much about it. I always thought you loved it here and that you would want to return to Rubyville."

She nodded. "I *do* want to return to Rubyville, someday, and raise our children there. But we have a golden opportunity right now. We've saved a bit of money over the years, not to mention what my grandmother left us."

Richard shook his head. "We agreed we were not going to use that unless absolutely necessary."

Evelyn sighed. "I still think that is best, dear husband. My point was that we have it. It's a nice cushion and relieves much of the stress that other people have to deal with."

He nodded.

Evelyn smoothed her hand over the little bundle upon her lap. "Besides, I wanted to stay here after I found out I was going to have a baby. I thought it would be very special to have our baby born here, overlooking the lake, just as I was."

"Well, you got your wish. I know I wasn't very comfortable with you having the baby here at the house." Richard raised a brow at his wife. "All sorts of things could have happened."

Evelyn snorted. "Well, nothing did. Babies have been born at home for centuries."

"And women have died." Richard leveled his eyes at her. "If Laurel hadn't agreed to stay with us this past month, I would have taken you back to civilization. At least there are hospitals within driving distance."

"All that worrying for nothing. The doctor showed up just in time—"

"Evelyn, I practically carried him up the stairs when he arrived. He didn't fill me with confidence in his abilities. He must have been ready to retire even back when he delivered *you*."

Evelyn laughed and then groaned. "I can't do that. It hurts too much right now." She looked down at Richard. "He's only in his late sixties...not that old. A young doctor would have been too busy to take the time to make a house call and deliver a baby."

"That's probably because they have sense."

"Well, it all worked out just fine, and she is here." Evelyn picked up the baby, holding her before her face. "We need to give her a name, Richard. We can't just keep calling her *the baby* for the rest of her life."

Richard chuckled and looked at his wrist watch. "She's seven hours old. That's hardly any time at all in the broad spectrum of things." He turned on his side, supporting his head with the pillow. He crossed his arms. "But we do need to name her. Since you were determined she was going to be a boy, you didn't choose any girl names...remember?"

She nodded. "I know...and now none are coming to mind."

"I have one that I think would fit perfectly." Richard raised a brow when Evelyn looked at him. "What about calling her Annabella, after your grandmother? This *is* the exact day she passed away five years ago."

Evelyn frowned. "It's the fourth?"

He smiled. "Yes, dear heart. It's the fourth of April."

"I've lost a couple of days somewhere." She wrinkled her forehead. "Wasn't it Friday when I started having contractions?"

"Yes, and now it's Monday morning. Our little girl just barely made it to the fourth. She was born just after midnight."

Evelyn smiled. "Well then, I think it's very appropriate to name her after my grandmother."

The baby opened her eyes, tiny dark orbs staring up at her mother. She opened her mouth and yawned.

"What do you think, little one? Can you live up to your great-grandmother's reputation?" Evelyn smoothed the baby's downy head.

"This pink fuzz looks a lot like mine. And I think you're going to be tall, as well."

Richard laughed. "She can't help but be so, with us as her parents."

The baby puckered her lips and wiggled.

Richard sat up, and reached out for his daughter. He took her, one hand behind her little head, the other beneath her diapered bottom. "We name you Annabella Barton King. You have the same middle name as your mother, and it's a good name. There is a whole legacy behind it of fiery, redheaded women. You have a lot to live up to, but with God, nothing is impossible."

"Luke 1:37." Evelyn smiled and closed her eyes.

Richard stood up, adjusting the blue blanket around Annabella's tiny feet. "How about we let your mother sleep for just a bit? She's had a very hard couple of days and she is very deserving of some rest."

Annabella stared at her father, watching his lips move.

Richard walked to the window and held Annabella up. "See that beautiful lake? Soon the trees will be covered with leaves. The mountains will turn from gray and brown to new green. The birds will be singing every morning, just happy to be alive." His eyes misted over. "There are troubles in this old world, Annabella. But God is watching over us, and He wants what is best for His children, just as I do for you. I pray you will accept Him as your Savior someday, and live your life for Him. That is what He has designed us to do."

He tucked his new little daughter against his side and bowed his head. "Thank You, Father, for this new life. Thank You for entrusting her to Evelyn and me. Give us both the ability and confidence to train her in the way she should go. Help us to be patient and loving, always doing what is best for her in the light of eternity. Thank You, Father, for all that You have given Evelyn and me, and I thank You for giving me the love of my life to share this life with. Help Evelyn to heal quickly…and again, thank You, Father, for this new little girl. I am not deserving of such a gift…but with Your help, we can raise her to be a light in this world. Amen."

Early October 1955

LAUREL HUGGED EVELYN, HOLDING her close. "I'm going to miss you." She whispered the words against Evelyn's ear. She pushed back and looked at her younger cousin. "You've become the daughter I never had."

"Thank you. Those words mean a lot to me." Evelyn brushed at her cheeks and looked to where Richard stood holding six-month-old Annabella, shaking Stephen's hand. The white-haired man pulled him into a hug, clapping him loudly on the back.

"You come back and visit often, you hear?" Stephen cleared his throat and touched Annabella's chin.

Richard glanced at his wife. "I think we can manage that."

Evelyn nodded, tears streaming down her face.

Laurel handed her cousin a tissue. "Your eyes are going to be so puffy you won't be able to see the gorgeous color of the leaves as you drive south." She held a finger up to Evelyn. "And remember…you are always welcome to stay here. The new caretaker won't be living on the premises. Father and Mother would have wanted you to feel as though this house is yours."

"I know. Just before Uncle Jackson passed away, he told me he wanted us to know how much we had meant to him. I'm happy that he went to be with the Lord here, at the place he loved so much." Evelyn's eyes traveled over the large yard and she pulled her cousin into another hug. "I don't know what I'm going to do without you to talk to."

"I feel the same way. Just be sure to write often. Your mother hasn't been too good with that over the years, as you know." Laurel patted Evelyn's back and stepped away, giving her a half-smile.

"I will. I'll write so much you're going to be sick of hearing from me." Evelyn gave her a wink.

"I doubt that." Laurel took a tissue from the pocket of her wide, plaid skirt and blew her nose.

"And if I'm able to get some people together for a Rubyville reunion next summer, promise me you'll come. It will give me something to look forward to." Evelyn blinked puppy-dog eyes at her cousin.

Laurel laughed. "That did it. We'll have to come now." She nodded. "We'll be there, unless one of us dies."

Stephen shoved his hands into his pockets. "I'm the oldest one here, and I have no plans of dying before next summer." He shrugged. "If by chance I *am* gone, have some potato salad for me. Ellen always did make delicious potato salad."

The four adults laughed as Annabella stuck her finger in her mouth and drooled, staring at them.

Laurel's eyes scanned the large expanse of lawn, large oaks and maples dotting the landscape. "Even though I've spent every summer of my life here, and occasionally a winter visit, it won't be the same now that you both, and little Annabella," she reached out and tickled the baby's feet, "aren't here. You somehow change the atmosphere when you're around...and when you are gone...it's as if a light has gone out."

Stephen sighed. "I know exactly what you mean, my dear."

Evelyn brushed at her cheek. "What a sweet thing to say. We're going to miss you both so much." Her eyes drifted around the yard. "I'm really going to miss this place. It's been very special to us."

Richard held out his hand to his wife. "It's time, dear heart. We need to get on the road."

Evelyn gave Laurel another quick hug before taking Richard's hand. They walked to their Plymouth, Richard opening the door for his wife. When she was seated, he set Annabella on her lap and closed the door. He waved to the duo standing beside the garage of the stately lake house, their arms wrapped along the back of each other.

"God's traveling mercies with you!" Stephen called.

Richard and Evelyn waved as the automobile disappeared down the long, twisting driveway, flashes of maroon among the trunks of the trees. The last of the brightly-colored leaves drifted through the air, settling to the ground.

Chapter Nineteen

Rubyville, Kansas
October 1955

RICHARD STEPPED ON THE brake, setting the Plymouth in park. He shut off the engine and turned to his wife. "Are you ready?"

Evelyn's eyes scanned the long row of lilacs, badly in need of trimming. The scraggly branches almost covered the view of the long, front porch of the stone house. "The yard is really in need of some care. I'm surprised Mama has let it go so much."

Richard lowered his blond head, narrowing his eyes as he looked through the passenger window. "It was a long, hot summer. It was probably difficult for your mother to be out in the heat long enough to do all that needed to be done." He looked at Evelyn. "She *is* getting older, you know."

"Yes, she is. And I'm sure she didn't ask anyone for help. She's always been that way." Evelyn shook her head and turned toward the back seat. Annabella lay in the travel bed, sleeping soundly. Her pink fuzz had turned to curls of red, clustered over her round head. One finger was stuck in her mouth, sucking motions made every now and then. "She's been such a good baby on this trip."

"She has been." Richard smiled and gave his wife a wink. "But it's not like she's up and about much. Sleeping and eating are pretty much her daily activities and she's been able to do those very well the past two weeks."

Evelyn playfully smacked her husband's shoulder. "You are such a pest at times."

Richard reached out and grabbed Evelyn, pulling her beside him. He nuzzled her ear. "I can be more of a *pest*, if you like."

"Stop that!" Evelyn giggled, pushing at Richard. She glanced at the house. "Mama will be looking out the windows, wondering who's out here."

"She can't see over the shrubs, remember?" Richard chuckled as he slid his hands from Evelyn's waist. "You go on in. I'll wait with Annabella. That will give you some time with your mother."

Evelyn rolled her eyes and took a deep breath. "That's probably best, but I would much rather you were there for protection from her barbs."

Richard kissed her cheek. "You'll be just fine. She knows you're coming, so it won't be too much of a surprise."

"I wrote her when we left New York, Richard." Evelyn chewed on her thumbnail. "Maybe I should wait until tomorrow. I can telephone her and let her know we are back in town."

"We had the telephone disconnected at your grandmother's house, remember?" Richard gave her another kiss. "She's your mother and you lived with her for eighteen years. You'll be fine."

Evelyn raised a brow. "Why aren't you going to see your parents then?"

Richard propped his elbow on the window ledge, leaning his temple against his knuckles. "We've been through this, Evelyn. I didn't have a relationship with the *people* that raised me. I survived there until I met you. They wouldn't care one way or the other if I was back in Kansas."

"Well, I think that is just sad." Evelyn looked at her husband. "If they knew you were married and had a daughter, maybe they would be different."

"I contacted them, at your request, when we were to be married, and they were not interested." Richard dropped his hand and bent his neck to look at the house. "Now you need to stop procrastinating and let your mother know you are back in Rubyville. As soon as Annabella wakes up, I will bring her in, so your mother can meet her granddaughter."

Evelyn sighed, smoothing the gloves upon her hands. She took her purse from the seat and opened her door, swinging her longs legs from the car. Brushing a piece of lint from her tweed skirt, she glanced back. "Promise to come in just as soon as she wakes up."

Richard laughed as he spread his large hand across her back. "I will…now go."

Climbing from the car, she smoothed her skirt. She placed the short handle of her brown purse over her arm and pulled down the edges of her short jacket. *Please, Father, still my racing heart. Richard's right...she is my mother and I've known her all my life. There's nothing to be scared of.*

HELEN STOOD TO THE side of the front window, watching through the lace curtain as her daughter approached the front steps. *Marriage and motherhood have agreed with you, Evelyn. You are beautiful and confident.* Her blue eyes swept over her daughter, lingering on the Italian-cut hairstyle of the red hair, the color so much like her own mother's. *There's that Barton red that completely skipped me. That's alright. I've always been the black sheep of the family, anyway.* Helen walked to the front door as the knock sounded.

Evelyn stood, framed in the doorway, a beautiful smile upon her lips as she looked at her mother. "Hello, Mama, we've returned to Rubyville."

Helen's eyes lingered on Evelyn's face before shifting to the maroon automobile out front. "Are you alone?"

Evelyn gave a weak laugh. "No, we are all here. But...but Annabella was sleeping, so Richard said he would stay with her and give us a chance to visit."

Helen raised her chin. "I was beginning to think you had changed your mind. You had written to me two weeks ago, and Georgie said you hadn't contacted him regarding the day when you would arrive. He wanted Mama's house to be in order for you, but that's difficult to do when you don't have an *exact* date."

Evelyn looked down at her brown shoes. "We were taking our time, not knowing when we would arrive. There are so many states to see and interesting little towns to go through on the way to Kansas. The autumn colors have been so pretty on our trip over."

Helen stepped aside and gestured into the front room. "I'm sure."

Evelyn glanced back at the car, then entered the house.

Helen nodded to the davenport. "You may sit down. I can make some tea or coffee, but I'm afraid I don't have any baked goods. This isn't my baking day, and I take most of everything I do make over to the hotel to help Ellen. She isn't as busy as she used to be. Not as many people come through Rubyville as they once did. But she's older now too, so every little bit helps."

"That's fine, Mama. I would appreciate a glass of water, though." Evelyn went to the davenport and sat down, pulling the gloves from her hands. "We just wanted to stop and let you know we had arrived. I'm sure we will have plenty of time to visit over the next few months."

Helen paused on her way from the room. "I won't be allowed to see my only granddaughter today…my first grandchild?"

Evelyn sighed. "That's not what I said, Mama. Richard will bring her in just as soon as she wakes up. She has been so good on the trip, and I've wanted her to stay as close as possible to her nap and eating times." She slid the purse from her arm and laid the gloves upon it.

Helen observed as her daughter put the accessories into a neat little pile beside her. "I'll be right back with your water." She continued into the kitchen, taking a glass from the cupboard. She turned on the tap, filling the glass. She set it on the counter and looked at the overgrown backyard, the terrace sprouting weeds between the cracks. *I am happy to see you, Evelyn. So happy…but I just don't know how to show it to you anymore. You took your love from me, and I don't know how to fill that gap.*

There was a knock on the front door.

"I'll answer it, Mama! I'm sure it's Richard."

Helen carried the glass to the front room and stopped in the doorway as Richard entered the house, carrying the seven-month-old child. *Annabella.* Her eyes pooled as she looked at the baby. *My granddaughter. So much like my little Evelyn. Oh, Malcolm. I so wish you were here to meet her.*

Helen smiled and stepped forward, blinking back the tears. "Hello. She has your red hair, Evelyn." She walked to the threesome and gave Evelyn her water. She held her hands out to Annabella. "Will she come to me?"

Evelyn's eyes widened as she glanced at her husband. "You can see if she will. She is usually pretty cautious with someone she doesn't know."

"Well, if you had been here, she would know me."

"Mama—"

Richard cleared his throat and held Annabella out toward Helen.

Helen took the baby from Richard, unbuttoning her little sweater. She untied Annabella's bonnet, taking it from the round head. "Your hair is so curly…just beautiful. Just as you are, little one."

Annabella stared at her grandmother, watching her talk. She put one finger in her mouth and sucked on it.

"Is she hungry?" Helen walked with Annabella to the upholstered chair in the corner and sat down. "I have evaporated milk in the kitchen."

"Actually, *I* feed her." Evelyn raised her glass and drank it down.

Helen's eyes shifted from her granddaughter to her daughter's chest. "I didn't realize mothers still did that. Cynthia Darby fed all of her babies with a bottle, and they are doing very well."

Evelyn gripped the glass. "Well, I prefer the way we have been doing it, and the doctor said Annabella was growing and gaining weight just as she should."

Helen shrugged. "I suppose a doctor from the east should know what they are talking about. Dr. Rundell told Cynthia that her boys were doing just fine."

"I'm sure they are, Mama." Evelyn took Richard's hand and led him to the davenport. "The doctor Annabella was seeing in New York was the same one that delivered me."

Helen gasped. "Oh my! I'm surprised he's still alive. He was *ancient* when I had you."

Richard chuckled, scooting close beside Evelyn as they sat down. "See, what did I say?" He turned to Helen. "How have you been, Mrs. Hanover?"

"Just as well as can be expected, I guess. Georgie checks in on me every now and then, but he's not much younger than I am. There seems to be a shortage of strapping young men to take care of things around here." Helen pulled the sweater from Annabella's chubby arms and laid it on the side of the chair. "He has his own home and family to care for, as well as mother's place. He is very busy…" she looked up, shifting her gaze from Richard to Evelyn, "as I'm sure you know."

Richard nodded. "There should be a couple more weeks of good weather. I'll plan on coming over to take care of some of the items needing attention."

Helen lifted her chin. "And what items might those be, Mr. King? Are you saying my yard is a mess?"

"Not at all, Mrs. Hanover. But I did notice the lilacs need trimming, and the grass could use a mowing before winter. I just want to help in whatever way I can."

"If you're expecting to be paid, then don't bother to show up. I live very frugally. You never know when the financial situation in this world can change. You both are too young to remember the hard times of the '30's." Helen looked down at Annabella and gave her a wide smile.

Richard leaned back and put his arm around Evelyn's shoulders. "I do not want to be paid, Mrs. Hanover. That was never an expectation."

"Well, I would think not. You've taken about everything this family has ever had." Helen stared at Richard, her blue eyes growing dark.

Richard met her gaze. "I have not taken anything, Mrs. Hanover. *Everything* I have has been given to me by my Heavenly Father. I take care of it to the best of my abilities. Since you are Evelyn's mother, and she loves you, and now you are the grandmother of my daughter, I care for you as well. For now, that may be only physical needs. Someday, I pray, an emotional bond will be formed as well. It will make life much more pleasant for all of us."

Helen gave a delicate snort. "If that is how you prefer to see it, I can't change your mind."

"That is definitely how I see it." Richard smiled at his mother-in-law. He patted Evelyn's shoulder and stood. "I think it's time we headed home. We need to get unloaded and settled in before it's late. I'm sure George has taken very good care of everything, just as he said in his letters over the years, but there may be something I need to attend to tonight."

Evelyn stood, smoothing her skirt. "I will be over again very soon, Mama, so that you may visit with Annabella more. Her best time of day is in the morning."

"Just as it is with most babies." Helen stood, holding Annabella close. She kissed her chubby cheek. "I'm very happy to have met you." She gave the baby a squeeze and handed her to her mother. She took the little sweater and bonnet from the chair and gave them to Evelyn as well.

"It was nice to see you, Mama." Evelyn pressed her lips together and turned quickly away. She walked to the front door where she struggled to put the sweater on Annabella. Soon, the baby was crying.

Richard swept the purse and gloves from the davenport and walked to Evelyn. He took Annabella, talking softly to her as Evelyn snatched her purse and gloves and rushed out the front door.

"She doesn't seem to have much concern for her child," Helen scoffed, as she tilted her head and crossed her arms.

Richard turned, jostling the crying baby as he slid the sweater over her arms. "Mrs. Hanover, I pray you discover how very blessed you've been before it's too late. God has given you much in your life and you have spent so many years just shoving it away. One day, you will push too hard…and it will be gone." He turned and walked out the front door.

Helen stood in the middle of the room and put one hand over her trembling lips. *He's right, and you know it, you foolish old woman. You need to run after them right now and ask for their forgiveness. You need to love them and cherish them, just as you should have done with your husband all those years ago. You didn't listen then…and you're not listening now.*

Chapter Twenty

Rubyville, Kansas
August 1959

RICHARD PUSHED THE SWING back and forth, his arm around Evelyn as she reclined with her head on his chest, her bare feet tucked beneath the wide skirt of her sundress. "You always become melancholy after the Rubyville reunion is over."

She sighed. "I know. Even when I was a child I felt the same. I was rather lonely growing up, and to have cousins, aunts, and uncles all around was so much fun for me."

"I was missing Stephen and Laurel this year." Richard cleared his throat.

"Me too. Since we haven't returned to New York or Vermont to visit, I always looked forward to the reunion here in Rubyville." Evelyn sat up, dropping her feet to skim along the porch with the movement of the swing. "I pray Stephen is alright and that the doctors find out why he is having the headaches."

"Mama, Papa, look what I found." Annabella came running to the porch, her bare feet dirty and scratched. The four-year-old stopped before her parents, running one toe up and down her leg to scratch a bug bite. She held out grubby hands. "I found a paper bug."

Richard laughed as he leaned forward and gently took the brown, paper-thin creature. "This is the shell from a cicada. The *bug* that lived in it is gone now, and it left this behind."

Annabella frowned as she swiped the red tangle of hair from her face. "It found another home?"

"Well..." Richard looked at Evelyn and shrugged his shoulders. "What do you know about cicadas?"

"Not much." She smiled. "They make a lot of noise in the evening."

Richard set the shell upon the arm of the swing and reached out, grabbing Annabella around the waist. He swung her up and set her on his lap. He pointed to the shell. "That bug used to live under the dirt for a very long time. Then it crawled out. It shed that skin and now it has wings and can fly around Rubyville."

"Just like a bird?" Annabella pointed one grubby finger to the sky.

Richard nodded. "In the evening, you can hear them singing. The papa cicadas sing to the mama cicadas."

Annabella nodded. "The mama ci…ci…" She shook her head. "I can't say that word."

"Cicada," Richard supplied.

"The mama bugs like the singing, 'cause *my* mama likes *your* singing." Annabella grinned as she leaned her head back and looked up at Evelyn.

Evelyn kissed the sweaty forehead. "Yes, Mama loves Papa's singing."

Richard smiled at his wife over his daughter's head, giving her a wink. "I guess I'll have to sing more often."

Annabella scooted from her father's lap and took the shell from the armrest. "I'm going to find more. This one's lonely." She scampered off the porch.

"Please stay in the front yard where we can see you," Evelyn called to the little girl.

"I will!" Annabella skipped across the yard, her long red hair bouncing against her back.

Richard pulled his wife close. "She's such a cutie. We really should have a brother or sister for her. We don't want her to be lonely like her bug." He nibbled on her neck.

Evelyn giggled, pushing him away. "You don't want Annabella seeing that."

"Seeing what? Her father terribly in love with her mother?" He smiled down at Evelyn. "Because I am, you know. Every day I spend with you I'm pulled in deeper and deeper." The blue eyes grew dark as they lingered on her lips.

Evelyn tapped the cleft in his chin. "I feel the same about you. I don't even want to imagine what my life would have been like if I hadn't met you."

Richard laughed as he set the swing in motion once again. "You'd be married to Aaron Darby, living on the farm, running around after a tribe of boys."

"You forgot about the part of me working in the store." Evelyn adjusted the wide strap of her mint-green sundress.

"Well, I'm happy that everything worked out the way it did, and that you're Mrs. Richard King, and not Mrs. Aaron Darby." Richard placed a kiss on her bare shoulder. "Although, Aaron *has* become one of my closest friends here in Rubyville. God works in mysterious ways."

"Yes, He does." Evelyn patted her husband's knee.

A long shrill whistle blew in the distance.

Annabella paused her digging in the dirt long enough to stand and point towards the park. "Here comes the train!"

"Yes, dear, that's the train coming into Rubyville." Evelyn smiled at her daughter. "She gets so excited whenever she hears that whistle. I don't even notice it after all my years here."

Richard looked at his wrist watch. "The last train of the day." He crossed his arms and narrowed his eyes, looking south. "I wonder what it will be like when the trains no longer serve these smaller towns."

Evelyn gasped. "What do you mean? The train will always go through Rubyville. That's why my great-grandfather founded this town. He wanted the train to stop here."

Richard nodded. "I understand that, but Rubyville was always just a whistle-stop on the line. If you notice, not as many trains go through here now as when you were a child."

Evelyn puckered her brow. "Now that you mention it, there aren't as many." She turned to Richard, her eyes wide. "But what does that mean for Rubyville?"

Richard shrugged. "Aaron and I were just talking about that at the picnic yesterday. More people are leaving Rubyville than coming in. That's not good for the community."

"What can we do to stop it?" Evelyn jerked to her bare feet and strode the length of the porch. "Grandmama would be heartbroken to hear that people were leaving Rubyville."

"Most of the old families are still here. But their children are not. They graduate school and go to the bigger cities to further their education and find jobs." Richard shook his head. "They aren't coming back."

"We have to stop it, Richard!" Evelyn stopped in front of her husband, her chest heaving.

He chuckled. "We can't stop it. These smaller towns don't have a lot to offer young people." He pointed at her. "*You* haven't stayed since you were married."

Evelyn sputtered. "I'm here every year for at least a month to plan and get the Rubyville reunion going. We take care of my grandmother's house, my mother's house, and the cemetery when George and Henry can't. We shop at the store, buy gasoline at the filling station, and eat at the café. What more can we do?"

"Live here permanently…make it our home year-round. That's what Rubyville needs. Residents that really care about the town and want to make a commitment to it long-term, just like people used to."

"But I thought you liked moving around and seeing places, just as I do." Evelyn walked to the porch railing and sat down, gripping the white post. "I thought you enjoy living in Texas."

Richard nodded. "I do, but it doesn't help Rubyville maintain what's been here all these years, much less grow."

"So you're saying that unless some new people move here, or young people that have grown up here stay after they graduate, the town is going to fold up?" Evelyn blinked rapidly.

"I think that about sums it up, my dear." Richard sighed. "You probably don't want to hear this right now, but Pastor Drummond is leaving the church at the end of the year."

Evelyn gasped. "Where is *he* going? Doesn't he want to be a pastor anymore? Our church is the only one left in town."

Richard held up a hand. "Slow down. He wants to retire and they are going to move closer to their children and grandchildren."

Evelyn flung her hands in the air. "See, that's the problem. Now we won't even have a pastor for our church. And they never had any children of their own. Their foster children can't be that important. "

"Evelyn, you knew that your grandmother was keeping the church alive financially until she died. Pastor Drummond said they have always struggled in that area. But since the Drummonds cared for foster children off and on over the years, they really didn't need an established salary. Food and clothing for the children was always given to them." Richard ran his hand through his hair. "And that wasn't a very nice thing to say about them. You know that the Drummonds always considered those children part of their lives. They haven't lost that love for them now that they have grown and have families of their own."

Evelyn leaned her temple on the post. "I know...and it was a mean thing to say. I just can't believe that they are going to leave. What will we do without a pastor?"

"Pastor Drummond is going to talk to the congregation about me leading some Bible studies whenever we are in town, but our church attendance is already down. I think people will take it as an opportunity to go elsewhere." Richard put his hands behind his neck, clasping his fingers. "Besides, people don't have the funds to keep the church building up. There are repairs that need to be done, and heating in the winter. It's just too much money."

"We could use what we've saved up over the years," Evelyn spoke softly.

Richard shook his head. "I don't think that would be a good idea. I would love to see the church kept up and the congregation grow...but I think it's a losing battle at this point."

Evelyn sighed and turned to watch Annabella running around the yard. "So our daughter will never know Rubyville as I did? All I'll have is my memories, and the stories my mother and grandmother passed down."

Richard unclasped his hands and set them on his knees. "Unless we decide to make Rubyville our home for more than a month or so each year."

Evelyn faced her husband. "I'm not ready to do that right now. Not with the relationship I have with my mother. I can bear a few weeks of her barbs and pokes, but not day after day. And I don't want Annabella growing up with that either."

Richard sighed. "Alright, then we head back to Texas next week."

Evelyn stood and walked over to her husband. She took both of his hands in hers. "Are we being good parents for Annabella? I mean, is it healthy to move her around so often like we've been doing? Will she hate us for it someday?"

Richard laughed. "We can be sure that there will be something she will be upset about. And when she starts school, I think we need to be settled before the year begins, and stay put until the year is over. We always need to find a good church to attend…one we can be part of and grow spiritually." He gave her a wink. "I don't think it's a bad way to raise a child. We can think of ourselves as missionaries of sorts."

Evelyn tilted her head, looking at her husband. "Annabella will have opportunities we never did. She will get to experience a variety of things, learn about places, and meet different people. I don't believe that is all bad."

"Of course not." Richard pulled her down to his lap, one arm sliding around her waist. "When we have more children, we can return to Rubyville. Traveling with one child is one thing, traveling with a brood is…"

"Complicated."

"Yes, that is one word for it." He took her hand, smoothing his thumb over her knuckles.

"I don't think we are ever going to have to worry about having more than one child. We celebrate our eleventh anniversary in three days. I haven't been pregnant since Annabella was born." Evelyn laid her head on Richard's shoulder.

He stroked her back. "We need to be patient and see what God has planned for us." He nodded to where Annabella stood in the yard, singing her heart out. "For now, we have a precious gift. That's enough for me."

Tucson, Arizona
May 1964

EVELYN SET THE LETTER on the kitchen table and took a tissue from the pocket of her apron. After blowing her nose, she tossed the tissue at the waste can, the crumpled white lump landing on the floor with five others. She set her elbow on the table and her chin in the palm of her hand and stared out the small window above the kitchen sink.

"Why are you so sad, Mama?" Annabella set her school books on the table and reached out, patting Evelyn's shoulder.

Evelyn sniffed. "Why do you think I'm sad? Don't I normally sit here every day and go through a box of tissues?" She smiled, wrapping her arms around Annabella's waist. "How was your day at school?"

Annabella gave her mother a hug and then pushed away, pulling a chair over. Plopping down, she faced her mother. She gripped the front of the chair with both hands and swung her legs back and forth. "It was just the same as always. I'll be glad when it's summer vacation. I miss you and Papa so much when I'm away. We don't do fun things in school like we do here at home."

Evelyn laughed. "That's one for the records. What child prefers to be with their parents over friends at school?"

Annabella rolled her eyes. "That's the problem. I don't have any friends at school."

Evelyn held up one finger. "Not even one?"

Annabella shrugged. "I have people I talk to, but no one really special. I'm not at school long enough to make friends, I guess."

"You've been at this school for two years now."

Annabella nodded. "I know, but I heard you and Papa talking just the other day. Papa said he was thinking of going to Colorado." She shrugged. "There doesn't seem to be much point in making friends if we are leaving soon."

"Yes, we have talked about Colorado." Evelyn took her daughter's hand and looked into her green eyes. "But if you would like to go somewhere else, or just stay here, I'm sure your father would be just fine with that. We really enjoy the church here and…" Evelyn's eyes scanned the tiny kitchen, "even though this house is small, I rather like it. It's very different than what we've lived in before."

Annabella rolled her eyes. "That's for sure. I don't like stucco, and I don't like floors with tiles on them."

Evelyn laughed. "Well, if that's all that is bothering you, I think we are alright. Your father and I wanted a house that was authentic to Arizona so we could really get the feel of living here."

Annabella scrunched up her face. "So you really like it?"

Evelyn wrinkled her nose and laughed. "No, I don't." She sighed and looked around the room once more. "I guess I'm just missing Rubyville. I remember the rustle of the trees in the wind, the fields on a summer morning, and fishing beside the river."

"So why don't we just live in Rubyville? I could go to school there. I could see my grandmother and we could live in that big house. I love that house." Annabella crossed her arms and pushed out her bottom lip.

"I thought you enjoyed traveling around and living in all the different places."

"I do…sometimes. But now we've seen the Grand Canyon, and all the cactus I ever want to see." Annabella looked at her mother. "But the most important thing is that I'm with you and Papa. I just want to be with you both."

Evelyn leaned over and gave her daughter a hug. "Thank you for saying that. You are the very best part of our lives." She sat back. "But we want you to be happy. Your father and I thought it would be a great experience for you, growing up in many different places. Then, when you were older, you could decide where you liked it the most. What about Vermont and New York? Did you like it there when we visited last summer?"

Annabella grinned. "I *loved* the lake. And it was cool to sleep in the same room I was born in." She shook her head. "But I wouldn't want to live there all the time." She sighed. "I suppose it's just like you said. I'm just missing Rubyville."

Richard opened the kitchen door and strode into the room, setting his black lunch box on the counter. He set his hands on his hips and looked at Evelyn and then Annabella. "Well, I've never seen such long faces in all my life."

"Mama was sad when I got home from school." Annabella pointed to the pile of tissues beside the waste can. "I think she misses Rubyville."

Richard's eyes focused on Evelyn. "Is everything alright?"

Evelyn shook her head and picked up the letter, handing it to Richard. "It's a letter from Dottie in California. She said my Aunt Beth passed away last week. They will be taking her back to Rubyville so she may be buried next to Daniel." Evelyn's lips quivered as the tears slid down her face. "I haven't seen her in several years, but it was such a surprise. Dottie said it was stomach cancer."

Richard's eyes scanned the letter and he set it on the table. "She had to have been in her eighties. I remember you telling me she was a bit older than your mother."

"Yes, yes she was. She just turned eighty last month." Evelyn looked up at her husband. "It seems as though everyone that I've ever loved is dying."

"I'm still here, Mama." Annabella looked at her mother, her green eyes blinking back tears.

"Of course you are, my dear. And I pray we have many more years together." Evelyn pulled another tissue from the box and dabbed at her eyes. "I'm just sad, is all." She glanced at Richard again. "I would like to be there for the funeral."

Richard walked over to his wife and stood behind her, rubbing her shoulders. "And you should be. Your mother will need you there as well."

Evelyn sighed. "Probably not. I don't think she's ever needed anyone."

"We all need *someone*, Mama. God gave us people to make life more enjoyable. That's what Papa always says." Annabella looked to her father for confirmation.

Richard nodded. "That's true. Even Jesus Christ had His disciples to pray with and lend Him support."

"And isn't Aunt Beth in Heaven now?" Annabella looked at her mother.

Evelyn smiled. "Yes, she is. She accepted Christ as her Savior when she was a little girl. I'm sure she is very happy to be with Mama Bella and Uncle Daniel."

"Why did Aunt Beth call her mother *Mama Bella*? I don't call you Mama Evelyn." Annabella wrinkled her brow.

"Many, many years ago, my grandmother lived in St. Louis with her Aunt Agnes. They volunteered in the orphanages there and took food to poor people in the city. My Aunt Beth was one of those orphans. She lived with my grandmother and Aunt Agnes for several years before moving to Rubyville. She called my grandmother Mama Bella."

"So Mama Bella wasn't her *real* mother?" Annabella widened her eyes.

Richard cleared his throat. "Mama Bella was her *real* mother in every sense of the word. She took care of Beth and loved her, giving her a home and a family. You don't always need to have a baby to be a mother."

Annabella bit her bottom lip. "I didn't know that. Maybe someday I can have an orphan live with me and I will love them just as much as you love me."

Richard gripped Evelyn's shoulders and looked down at his wife. She glanced up at him. "Then that child will be loved very much."

Chapter Twenty One

Rubyville, Kansas
June 1964

ANNABELLA KICKED AT THE stone in her path. "I don't understand why we can't have the Rubyville reunion this summer. It's the *most* fun thing that *ever* happens and now we aren't going to do it."

Evelyn waved to Mrs. Rowe as they passed the mercantile. "Good morning!"

The plump, older woman paused in her sweeping of the front steps and greeted Evelyn. "Good morning to you, Evelyn, and you too, Miss Annabella. It's a beautiful day in Rubyville, a beautiful early summer day. Not too hot, not too muggy..." She looked up at the sky. "And not a cloud to be seen."

"We thought the very same thing during breakfast this morning." Evelyn nodded to Annabella. "That's why we decided to take a walk."

Mrs. Rowe glanced down the road to where the stone house could be seen amongst the cedars. "I know your mother would appreciate a visit. It's always just terrible to receive news like that from the doctor." She shook her gray head. "And to think it came just before her sister passed." She gave a couple vigorous swipes with the broom. "But our Heavenly Father never gives us more than we can bear."

Evelyn wrinkled her brow. "My mother has been seeing Dr. Rundell?"

Mrs. Rowe stopped sweeping and leaned against the broom handle. "I had been telling her for a few months that she needed to stop in and see him. You don't have pain like that without something being wrong." She continued sweeping. "Cancer is such a terrible thing."

Evelyn pressed a hand against her chest. "Cancer?"

Mrs. Rowe paused and looked at Evelyn. "Well, I thought for sure you already knew. The doctor diagnosed it back in January."

Evelyn closed her eyes and took a deep breath. She opened them and gave Mrs. Rowe a trembling smile. "Well, I had best let you get back to your sweeping, and we'll continue our walk. You have a good day, Mrs. Rowe." Evelyn waved and took Annabella's hand in hers.

Mrs. Rowe shouted after them, "I thought for sure you knew!"

"It's alright…really!" Evelyn threw over her shoulder as she resumed her pace.

Annabella looked up at her mother. "So grandmother is sick?"

Evelyn shook her head. "It sounds as though she is. But she hasn't told me anything. When we arrive, you had best stay out on the terrace for a bit so I can talk with her and find out what is going on. I'll call you in when we're through."

"So I won't get any milk and cookies like I sometimes do, when she's in a good mood?"

"You'll just have to wait and see what happens. I don't know right now." Evelyn smiled down at her daughter. "I know you are disappointed about not having the reunion next month. But it just doesn't seem right to have it with Aunt Beth gone. And now this news about my mother…" She shook her head. "I've debated whether to just stop having them all together. There are less people each year."

Annabella groaned. "Just take away my very most favorite thing in the world."

Evelyn slid her arm around her daughter's shoulder, giving her a pat. "I understand what you're saying, my dear. They were my favorite days as well. But I just don't have the heart for it right now. Maybe next year we can try again."

Annabella scuffed her toe, kicking another rock. "I'm going to remind you all year long."

"I'm sure you will."

They walked along the newly trimmed lilacs, the dark green leaves forming a barrier between the front yard of the stone house and the road.

"I remember when the lilacs bloomed. They smelled so sweet in the springtime. I asked my mother several times if I could move my bedroom to the front of the house so I could smell them at night."

Annabella squinted. "And she wouldn't let you?"

"Nope. She always said it was best that I was at the back of the house and she was at the front." Evelyn's eyes surveyed the large yard and the newly planted fields behind the house. "It was alright with me, though. I loved my view of the trees by the river and the field."

"I thought there were lots of bedrooms upstairs." Annabella stepped through the opening in the hedge and paused.

Evelyn nodded, looking up at the four windows lining the top floor. "There are four bedrooms upstairs, two on each side of the hallway."

Annabella shook her head, her long braid skimming her waist. "That's a lot of bedrooms for only two people. You must have had lots of company."

"No, not really." Evelyn gestured to the side of the house. "Go around back and I'll call when you may come in. Please stay in the yard."

Annabella set her hands on her hips. "Mama, I'm nine years old...not a baby. I know what I'm supposed to do." She dropped her hands and ran around to the back of the house.

Evelyn rolled her eyes. "Well good for you. *I'm* thirty-four years old and *I* don't have a clue as to what I should do." She climbed the steps to the porch and knocked on the door.

The door opened slowly, Helen leaning on the handle. She straightened her back. "I thought I heard voices out here. I've had the windows open to enjoy this lovely morning."

"Yes, it is beautiful. Do you have some time to sit with me on the porch? I would like to talk to you about something."

Helen puckered her brow. "I was doing some ironing while it was cool, but it can wait until later. Did you bring Annabella with you?" Her blue eyes scanned the front yard.

"Yes, I did, but she's out back. I told her I would let her know when I was finished talking with you." Evelyn gestured to the front room. "I can turn off your iron while you sit down. I'll be right back."

Evelyn scooted through the doorway and headed to the back of the house. She entered the kitchen, turning off the iron, and going to the kitchen door. Smiling, she watched Annabella humming a tune on the old metal glider. "We'll be out front if you need anything."

Annabella shaded her eyes and looked back at the house. "Yes, Mama."

Evelyn walked through the kitchen, pausing at the sight of a cane leaning against the small table beside the front door. She picked it up and carried it to the front porch, letting the screen door slam as she exited the house.

"Oh my!" Helen placed a hand on her chest. "You know how much I dislike you doing that."

"I'm sorry, Mama. It just sort of slipped from my hand." She set the cane beside her mother's chair. "Maybe you will need this."

Helen's eyes slid to the wooden hook and they followed Evelyn as she sat down on the wicker chair next to hers. "So who told you...Mrs. Rowe or Dr. Rundell?"

Evelyn crossed her leg and folded her hands in her lap. Her gingham Capri pants hugged her calve as she swung her leg back and forth. "Mrs. Rowe shared the information with me just a few minutes ago as we walked past the store."

"So Annabella knows as well?" Helen sighed.

"I don't think she really understood what Mrs. Rowe said." Evelyn lifted her hand. "*I* don't know what Mrs. Rowe said." Evelyn stared at her mother. "Why didn't you tell me you were sick? Mrs. Rowe said it's cancer."

Helen took a deep breath. "It is very simple, really. I was having some pain in my leg last winter, around Thanksgiving. I had tripped on the stairs and I thought I must have pulled a muscle. When it was still painful after Christmas, I made an appointment to see Dr. Rundell. He had some concerns when I told him my symptoms, so he and his wife escorted me to Kansas City for further tests—"

"Kansas City?" Evelyn gasped, widening her eyes. "You should have told me. I could have gone with you."

"And leave your precious husband?" Helen shook her head. "It worked out very well." She swallowed, her eyes growing dark. "They took x-rays and their diagnosis was a form of cancer I had never heard of before. It was advanced, so they recommended amputation of my leg."

Evelyn bit her bottom lip, her eyes turning to liquid. "But if that treats the cancer, maybe that is the best thing to do."

Helen turned to her daughter. "They said the cancer was what they call stage three. It could be elsewhere in my body. I don't care to live with one leg, nor have parts of me cut off as I slowly die."

Evelyn gulped, uncrossing her legs. She sat forward on her chair, bracing her elbows on her knees as she gripped her hands together. "What did Dr. Rundell recommend?"

Helen harrumphed. "The surgery, of course. *That is the route to take in these cases,* is what he said." She shook her head. "It's not for me."

"So what's for you, Mama? Dying here, alone, probably in pain?" Evelyn brushed at the tears trickling down her cheeks.

"I've been alone for the past sixteen years, Evelyn. What are a couple more years?" Helen lifted her chin.

Evelyn covered her face with her hands. "I can't believe you didn't tell me. I'm your daughter!"

Helen's face softened as the lines relaxed around her mouth. "I appreciate your concern for me. But there is nothing you can do. Beth had telephoned me with the news of her cancer just after I found out about mine. I certainly didn't want to burden her with my troubles. I knew if I told anyone here in Rubyville, the news would spread like a wildfire."

"But you told Mrs. Rowe."

"Not until after Beth's funeral. Mrs. Rowe and I have been having a Bible study of sorts for a few years now. It was only natural to ask for prayer. I also asked her to keep it quiet…" Helen shrugged. "But that was too much for her, I suppose."

Evelyn laid her hands upon her knees and raised her eyes to her mother's face. "Why do you hate me so? Is this all because I married someone you didn't like?"

Helen smiled. "I've come to admire that man you married. He *is* a hard worker and he takes good care of you and little Annabella. I've appreciated all that he does around this house for me." She looked away, pressing her knuckles to her nose. "But there is bitterness in me that I can't seem to get rid of. I've prayed about it, and God just won't take it away."

"*Nothing* is impossible with God." Evelyn stated the words as she gritted her teeth. "You have been given *so* much, Mama."

"And so very much has been taken away." Helen took a deep breath. "I have lived my life in the way I wanted to. But I will never understand why God took my husband, and then my daughter. My mother is gone, and now Beth. I have nothing left."

Evelyn narrowed her eyes. "You've always had a daughter that loved you and wanted your love in return. You have a granddaughter that would welcome a relationship with you, but you just keep pushing us all away. You have to forgive and forget, Mama."

"Do I? What would I gain? It won't bring Malcolm back, and it won't bring back the last sixteen years since you married." Helen shook her head. "What difference does it make now? I'm dying and I will go to Heaven because I've accepted Christ as my Savior. Isn't that all that matters today?"

Evelyn reached out and took her mother's hand. "No Mama, it isn't. God wants us to grow to maturity in our Christian walk with Him. It's not just about salvation…it's about our life, our testimony before Him. He loved us enough to send His only Son to die for us. Is it so very difficult to live for Him, to uphold His values? Someday we will stand before Him, and I want to know that I was a light for Him, a testimony of what He accomplished for me. We will be rewarded for our life here…but I want to grow to be like Him *while* I'm here."

Helen shook her head, tears spilling from her eyes. "I've spent a lifetime searching for the assurance and faith that you have. I don't know if I can get beyond the pain and the hardness in my heart."

Evelyn squeezed her mother's hand. "You can, Mama. Abide in Him, study His Word, and pray without ceasing. He promises to give us peace and understanding. He is there. You just have to seek Him."

Rubyville, Kansas
Early September 1966

THE SETTING SUN GLOWED orange in the west, the tall church

steeple a silhouette against the backdrop. Richard leaned against the white column on the porch, his arms crossed. *She is with You, Father. I pray she has found peace at last.* His thoughts traveled to the graveside service that Helen had requested. It had been simple and to the point, conducted in much the same way that Helen had led her life.

The words from an old hymn pierced his soul as he remembered Evelyn singing it, standing bravely beside the box that held her mother's earthly remains. Her sweet soprano had lifted, clear and true, the words drifting through the throng of people gathered to say good-bye. When she had faltered on the last verse, he had walked to her side, taking her trembling hand in his and joined with her in the triumphant last words.

Thank You, Father, for taking Mrs. Hanover to be with You. She suffered so those last few months. I know those words are true, and love's purest joys have been restored.

Evelyn closed the front door and walked to Richard, sliding her arms about his waist. She laid her head against his chest.

"Is she asleep?"

Evelyn nodded. "She had so many questions about Mama. I feel badly that I didn't allow her more time with my mother, but I didn't want Annabella's last memories of her grandmother to be of her in bed, riddled with pain."

"She's young enough that she may not remember a lot anyway. My visions of being eleven years old are probably far different than what really happened." Richard kissed the top of Evelyn's head. "You did what you could for your mother. It was good that we remained here after you found out about the cancer, even if she didn't allow you to care for her until the very end. She knew you were here."

Evelyn's lips trembled and she buried her face in Richard's chest. "I hope so. I feel as though we missed out on a wonderful life that we could have shared...if only she would have let me."

"She loved you just the same. She was just so afraid of being hurt that she wouldn't allow herself to feel." Richard held his wife close, rubbing his hand up and down her arm.

Evelyn raised her head, looking up at her husband. "She gave the house to Annabella."

Richard frowned. "The stone house?"

Evelyn nodded. "She was talking about her will one day...one of her good days. She said the house and any of her assets would go to Annabella."

"And none to you, her daughter?"

Evelyn smiled. "That is how it should be. Mama said that her mother had taken very good care of us, and she wanted to make sure that her granddaughter was taken care of, as well."

"Annabella will be a very wealthy woman one day. You've already decided to pass this house to her. I wonder what our little girl will do with all this monetary *stuff*." Richard chuckled. "God does have a sense of humor."

Evelyn tilted her head. "Well, I think it's best she doesn't know about any of it until she is much, much older. The things we have are not what are important in this life. It's the relationship we have with God and others. I want Annabella to learn to be content with little, and to share with all. She will have a lifetime to think about money and bills and all the trappings of this life."

Richard pulled his wife close. "I couldn't agree with you more, dear heart." He nodded toward the violet sky to the west. "It's beautiful here, isn't it?"

His eyes scanned the scenery before them. They followed the long drive ending at the road before the stone church, and then traveled to the tall, stately trees in the park. Their entwined branches offered protection from the sun on a hot, summer day. The opposite side of the park was lined with businesses, some closed now, their vacant windows staring out at Rubyville. The remains of the two-storied hotel took up almost a block on the west side of the park, the pile of rubble and the limestone chimney all that remained from the fire that had consumed the building in 1963.

"Yes, it is...and someday, I want to return here and finish out my life." Evelyn took a deep breath. "But right now, there are too many memories here. I can't bear to see all the changes, and most of them not for the good of Rubyville. What will become of it?"

Chapter Twenty Two

Longmont, Colorado
June 1969

LONGS PEAK STOOD MAJESTIC in the distance, white-topped with snow, the long valley carved in the stone showing as a vein on the side of the mountain. The brilliance of the blue sky foretold a beautiful day. The birds agreed, chirping happily outside the open window.

Evelyn rinsed the last plate and set it in the dish drainer. She leaned her wet hands on the side of the sink and smiled at the view. "Those Rocky Mountains always amaze me. I don't think I will ever tire of them."

Annabella picked up the plate and glanced out the window. "Yes, I can appreciate how beautiful they are…from afar. I really don't like our weekly drives into them. And it's just strange to see snow on them now. There wasn't any yesterday…and it's summertime." Annabella scowled. "No snow allowed."

Richard lowered his newspaper to the table. "I think it's pretty exciting to never know when it could snow up there. It's a surprise every morning."

"Surprise!" Annabella flung her hands in the air, the dish towel falling to the floor.

Evelyn shook her head. "It's a good thing you had already put the plate away." She held her hand out for the towel. "Hand it here. I'll put it with the dirty laundry."

"Mama, it was only on the floor for a second. I can just hang it up." Annabella rolled her eyes as she gave her mother the towel. "You wash the kitchen floor every day. It's just as clean as the dishes in the cupboard."

Evelyn walked to the closed in back porch. "It certainly is not." She laid the towel over the basket on the washing machine. "Besides…" she entered the kitchen, taking her apron from around her waist, "*you* washed it yesterday. There's no telling how clean it really is."

Annabella pulled a metal chair from the table and plopped down on the yellow vinyl. "Do you hear what my mother is saying about me?" Annabella poked the paper her father was reading. "She thinks I'm a pig."

Evelyn laughed. "I did not say that! But if I need evidence, I can take you both up to your bedroom and make my point. You're a cute piggy, but a messy one."

Annabella crossed her arms and wrinkled her brow, bottom lip stuck out. "I just don't see the need to pick up everything every day when I'm just going to use it again. I make my bed every morning, and I *know* most kids don't."

Richard folded the paper and laid it on the table. "And how would you know what *most kids* are doing?" He reached out and pulled Evelyn to his side, his hand resting on her hip. He looked up at her and gave her a warm smile.

Annabella rolled her eyes ceiling-ward. "Here we go again. You guys are always doing mushy stuff."

Evelyn raised a brow. "Mushy stuff?"

Richard's eyes sparkled. "You mean stuff like this?" He scooted his chair back and guided Evelyn around to the front, setting her upon his lap. He leaned her back and placed a long kiss upon her lips.

"Yes!" Annabella covered her face with her hands. "All the time…you never stop! Good grief, you've been married how many years—"

"It'll be twenty-one years on August fifth," Richard supplied, helping Evelyn to sit up. He pulled her close, laying his head against her chest.

Evelyn's cheeks blushed pink as she twirled the hair at the back of his neck. "Someday you'll understand."

Annabella uncovered her eyes. "I don't think so. I've never seen people act the way you two do."

Richard gazed up at his wife. "Well, that's too bad. There's nothing wrong with being as much in love when you're…" He narrowed his eyes. "How old are we?"

Evelyn laughed. "We're thirty-nine."

Richard whistled. "We're getting old. It's a good thing we look so young for our age." He gave Annabella a wink. "As I was saying, there's not a thing wrong with being in love just as you were when you were young. As a matter of fact, I love your mother much more than I did when I first saw her at that prom all those years ago."

Annabella shook her head. "I don't understand how you can love someone *more*. Don't you just love them? I've loved you both all my life, ever since I can remember."

Evelyn kissed the top of Richard's head. "Love can deepen over the years as you get to know that person better. You grow to respect them, admire them, and cherish them. That love can take on different aspects over the years, more feelings and emotions." She smiled at her daughter. "And yes, that has probably happened in your love for us…you just aren't aware of it."

Annabella shrugged. "Well, I have lots of time before I think of getting married. I guess I'll just have to watch you two *being in love* until then." She took her long braid and pulled it over her shoulder, smoothing her hand down it. "What are we going to do today?"

Richard put one hand to his chin and stroked it. "Well, since it's Saturday, I thought we could go for a drive in the mountains. I know how much you both love that." His lips twitched.

Annabella hit her forehead. "Oh no! Not again! You know, there's a lot of flat land here in Colorado. Why don't we ever drive through that?"

Evelyn laughed. "You *are* a Kansas girl, aren't you?"

"Actually, I was thinking we could take the Valley Highway through Denver, drive around a bit, have some lunch, and then go to the zoo." Richard looked at his wife and daughter.

"The zoo?" Annabella raised her brows. "Isn't that more for little kids?"

Richard shrugged. "I was reading an article about it a couple weeks ago. It sounds pretty interesting to me. They have giraffes and elephants. There was also something about an animal hospital opening there this year."

Evelyn clasped her hands together. "I think that sounds like a lot of fun. We've never been to a zoo before. I can make us some sandwiches to take with us. I'm sure they have a park or something nearby where we can eat. That way we don't have to find a restaurant."

Richard helped Evelyn to her feet, giving her another long kiss. "That sounds good to me. I'm going to check the car, make sure we have gasoline and oil for the trip." He pushed his chair in and leaned on the back. "I rather liked that old Plymouth your grandmother gave us on our wedding day. It took us a lot of places. This new Ford Galaxie is taking me a bit of getting used to."

"New?" Annabella guffawed. "You've had it almost two years."

"Well, it is pretty new to us considering how long we had the Plymouth." Evelyn opened the bread box.

"At least our old car was a nice color. I don't know why you got a green one." Annabella stood and went over to the kitchen counter. "Can we take some of those chocolate chip cookies you made yesterday?"

Evelyn nodded. "Just bring the whole Tupperware container. I'm sure your father will enjoy snacking on them."

Richard looked at his wrist. "My watch says it's time to get going...not just stand around talking about our plans." He tweaked Annabella's nose. "Can we all be ready in half an hour? I'd like to get on the road."

Evelyn set her hand upon her hip. "You just take care of what you have to do and let me take care of this. I'll be ready."

"Alright, I'll see you girls outside." Richard walked from the kitchen, singing out of tune.

Annabella crossed her arms. "Why does he have to sing like that?"

Evelyn frowned as she took a plate of fried chicken from the refrigerator. "What do you mean?"

"When we're at church singing, his voice isn't too bad. But whenever he sings around the house, which he does all the time...he sounds *really* awful." Annabella took a drumstick from the plate and started eating it.

"You won't be hungry for lunch." Evelyn waved the butter knife at her daughter.

"I'm always hungry. You know that." Annabella nibbled away. "So what's Dad doing with the singing stuff?"

Evelyn laughed. "Actually, your father has a beautiful voice. We sang many times at church when we were younger. I think he just likes to give you a hard time because he can get a reaction out of you."

"Well," Annabella licked her fingers, "isn't that a bad thing to do to your child? Doesn't the Bible say you're supposed to be a good example to your children?"

Evelyn nodded. "Yes, it does, and it also says you're not to provoke them." Evelyn leaned near her daughter and whispered, "But I think he just has a little fun provoking you at times."

"At times? Make that *all* the time." Annabella tossed her chicken bone in the garbage can. "I never know when to take him seriously."

"You'll know, my dear. Your father is a very patient, understanding man. He has a lot of love and forgiveness in him." Evelyn shook her head. "But there have been a couple times over the years that I've seen him pushed beyond his limit."

"Only a couple, in all the years you've known him?" Annabella puckered her brow. "I don't think I'm going to be that way. I get pretty upset when someone does something to me that I don't like."

Evelyn put the tops on the chicken sandwiches. "So do I, my dear. Your father is a rare individual. There's not many like him."

"Great! That means I'll probably get some cranky man when I want to get married." Annabella looked down at her blue jeans. "I'm going to go up and change."

Evelyn's eyes slid over her daughter's attire. "That would be a good idea. That blue bib-front dress would be nice for today. You know the one…with the white collar?"

"Yes, Mom. That's just what I was thinking too." Annabella gave her mother a kiss on the cheek. "I'm fourteen and I've lived with you my entire life. I have a pretty good idea of what you want."

Evelyn smiled. "That's good. So I won't have to tell you to wear the white flats with it?"

"The ones with the buckle on top?"

Evelyn nodded. "Just don't take too long."

Rubyville, Kansas
June 1970

THE GREEN FORD GALAXIE turned onto the road leading into Rubyville. Annabella slid to the front of the bench seat in the back and rested her arms on the long front seat.

Evelyn glanced back and gave her daughter a smile. "We're almost there. Are you excited?"

Annabella closed her fist and set her chin on top. She smiled as she narrowed her eyes and looked out the front window. "I'm always excited each time we return. Rubyville is my heritage. I love that I'm a part of it."

Evelyn slid her tinted sunglasses to the top of her head, leaving them to rest on the wide, brightly-patterned scarf used as a headband. She placed her hand on Richard's knee and gave him a smile. "I am too. Looking back, I thought my mother was always so strict and just needing to have everything her way. I thought life must be better in other places."

Richard raised a brow as he gave his wife a quick look. "You don't think that's true anymore?"

She shook her head. "Not as much. She was a woman, a mother, trying to raise her child alone. I'm very thankful she returned here after my father died. It was the best place for me to grow up. It helped me to put down roots."

Annabella rolled her eyes. "Then my roots are growing all over the place."

Richard and Evelyn exchanged smiles, laughing.

"We will just have to get back here, then." Richard looked at his daughter in the rearview mirror and gave her a wink. "Then your Barton roots can grow long and deep."

Annabella squealed as she pointed out the front window. "There's the gazebo, just ahead…and the church."

Richard turned right, driving past the ruins of the hotel. He stopped, leaning down to look out the passenger window.

"It's so sad." Evelyn leaned her arm on the open window. "I remember when the front porch was bustling with people coming and going all day long. People traveled on the train, stopping for the night and sometimes a few days. Everyone loved Ellen's cooking."

"It sure made up for her crusty attitude." Richard slid his arm along Evelyn's shoulders. "That's where Bill and I got ready for our wedding." He pulled Evelyn close, kissing her temple. "You were beautiful that day, coming down the stairs of your grandmother's house."

"You didn't look so bad yourself, if I remember correctly."

"It would have been nice if someone had taken a picture." Annabella sighed. "You don't have any wedding pictures."

Evelyn shook her head, running one hand over her side-swept bangs. "I'm afraid not. People didn't take as many pictures back then. To be honest, I never even thought about it. I was more concerned with getting everything else ready."

Richard continued down the road, turning left at the mercantile.

The windows were dark, no movement from within. Thick dust and Kansas dirt blanketed the porch, brown leaves from the previous autumn still captured in the corners.

"Rubyville won't be the same without the mercantile." Annabella shook her head.

Evelyn looked at Richard. "When did you say the Darbys left?"

He ran his hand through his hair. "I think two summers ago. Right after Cynthia's mother passed away. Aaron said that Cynthia just couldn't stand coming into town and seeing the little house where she lived just sitting there vacant."

Annabella leaned back against the seat and crossed her arms. "Everything's disappeared. There's a couple children playing in the park, but it looks like a ghost town."

Evelyn brushed at her cheeks. "I don't understand how it could have gone downhill so much since my mother passed away. Everything is boarded up."

"Well, once the train stopped going through here a couple years ago, I knew it would be bad…but I thought people would stick around a little longer." Richard shook his head. "We can drive by the filling station. I know that's still open for business."

Evelyn shook her head. "Please just take me to my grandmother's house. This is making me sad. I need something familiar."

"Alright." Richard continued down the road slowly, turning left at the corner where the Methodist church had once stood. Richard gestured to the vacant lot, covered with brush and new cedar trees. "People dismantled it and built something else with the lumber, from what Aaron said."

Evelyn sighed as she stared out her window. "Well, it was put to good use, then, and not just burned up like the hotel." Evelyn nodded toward the east. "At least this looks the same…the line of trees along the river and the meadow next to the house."

"The church looks just as it always did." Annabella pointed to the left, the imposing stone structure reclining on the corner. Large trees shaded the entrance way and the steps leading to the double wood doors.

"Aaron said there was a group of people still meeting on Sunday mornings. They must be caring for the old place." Richard stopped the car, three pairs of eyes assessing the tall building.

"George has talked about attending services there once in a while, just when he and Katie come to town." Evelyn sighed. "I never thought they would leave, but I guess there wasn't much reason for them to stay in Rubyville if the siblings were living elsewhere." Evelyn gulped and swiped at her cheeks. "I just expected everyone to always be here, but I can't expect others to do what I did not."

Richard drove the Ford up the long driveway to the Barton home. Its white façade glowed in the afternoon sun, the windows reflecting the light. "Your grandmother's house is looking pretty good as well. The caretaker George hired is doing a good job, from what I can see."

Evelyn clasped her hands before her chest. "I hope so. I don't think I could take seeing Grandmama's house in shambles."

Annabella jumped from the car the moment it stopped before the long porch at the side of the house. She opened her mother's door. "I have a great idea! Why don't we invite a few people over and have a party? It won't be like it used to be with several days of activities, but we could have a picnic in the park. George and Katie, Charles and

Madeline, maybe even some of their children would come. The Darbys certainly would…they don't live that far away."

Richard got out of the car and leaned on the roof. He pointed to Annabella. "I could give Dr. Rundell a call, and the Drummonds…they are all in Manhattan. It wouldn't be that far for them to drive."

Annabella clapped her hands. "That would be great. Mom and I could do all the cooking—"

Evelyn stood and raised her hands. "What are you volunteering me for?" Her eyes danced as she smiled at her daughter.

Annabella gave her mother a hug. "Wouldn't it be cool? All those people here again…in our town?"

Evelyn nodded. "I must admit, it would be pretty nice to see everyone again. But we had only planned to stay a couple of weeks, just to check on everything. We can't get all that together in such a short time."

Richard thumped the top of the car. "Sure we can! And who's to say that we can't stay longer? Annabella's off from school and so am I. The other custodian at the school won't mind a few extra hours."

Evelyn chewed on her fingernail. "You have to remember that some of those people you are speaking of aren't exactly young anymore. Charles and Madeline are in their late sixties—"

"That's not old, Mom!" Annabella flung back her long, red hair with one hand. "Besides, it's to spend time with family and friends. We haven't had a Rubyville reunion since before Grandma Helen died."

Richard looked at his wife. "If you're concerned about people traveling, there are more than enough rooms for people to stay a night or two if they want. We have this house," he gestured toward the white edifice, "and there's your mother's house as well."

"That's true, but we haven't been inside yet. Who knows what we'll find." Evelyn glanced up at the two-storied building. "Raccoons may have moved in and taken over."

Annabella shook her head as she looked at her father. "May I take the car over to Grandma Helen's house? I can see what kind of cleaning it will need."

Evelyn crossed her arms. "Certainly not, young lady! Your father may be brave and foolhardy enough to let you drive around the outskirts of Longmont, but we don't need someone in this family being arrested right here in Rubyville for driving without a license."

Richard and Annabella looked at one another.

"How many police have you seen around Rubyville lately, dear heart?" Richard walked over to where his wife stood. "It's far safer for her to practice her driving here than where I've been taking her."

"Knowing you, you've probably let her drive up the side of a mountain." Evelyn looked up at her husband.

Annabella raised her hands and shook her head, her long hair swaying at her hips. "No mountains! *I* don't drive in the mountains...*ever!*"

Richard grabbed his wife around the waist and lifted her off her feet. "You know this is a great idea...and you want to be happy about it. You're just being a stick-in-the-mud." He kissed the top of her nose.

Evelyn laughed, laying her hands on his upper arms. "No, I'm being practical." She glanced at Annabella. "Yes, it's a great idea. I know all those people you mentioned would love to come and visit." She gaped at Richard. "But there is *so* much to do!"

Richard set her on her feet. "The three of us can accomplish great things. And we can have fun doing it." He started making drum motions with his hands, deep *drum* sounds coming from his throat. Then he leaned back and made sliding moves with his right arm, replicating a trombone.

Evelyn covered her face and started laughing. "You are the silliest man alive!"

"And the one in love with you!" He grabbed her hands, pulling her into the Lindy Hop. They began swinging around the short grass, stepping in time to the tune they both remembered so well.

Annabella rolled her eyes and crossed her arms as she smiled at the two people dancing around the yard. "You both have to be about the strangest parents any child could ever have!"

"Yup!" Richard gave his daughter a wink as he swung Evelyn around.

Chapter Twenty Three

Estes Park, Colorado
Mid-October 1972

RICHARD OPENED EVELYN'S DOOR, gesturing grandly for her to step out of the car. "We've arrived at our destination."

Evelyn stood, breathing deeply of the cold mountain air. "Isn't it just beautiful? The aspens still have a bit of color. I was so afraid they would be all gone by the time we made it up here."

Richard shut the door and went to the back of the Ford, opening the trunk. He pulled out two small suitcases and shut the trunk with his elbow. "I really wish we could have gotten away closer to our anniversary in August, but you have to admit," he scanned the valley around them, "this is much better."

Evelyn's eyes lit up as she took in the small cabin that was to be their home for the next week. The logs showed beige chinking between each one, a small window on each side of the heavy plank door. Black hinges stretched across the door to complete the rustic look. The small porch held two wooden rocking chairs, faded calico cushions upon the seats. A tin sign hung crookedly from a nail beside the door, *welcome* etched into the metal.

Behind the small cabin, a stream gurgled by, water tumbling over the rocks. The sides of the mountain rose high behind the cabin, the rocky face sprouting vegetation here and there. Pine trees and aspen dotted the brown grass of the small meadow across from the cabin, mountains climbing high around the flat area. In the distance, elk moved gracefully, lowering their heads to nibble at the grass and lifting them, antlers arched majestically.

Richard flashed a smile. "I could get used to this scenery every day." He gave her a wink as he walked past her to the steps leading to the porch. "You wait right there. I'll be back just as soon as I put these down inside."

Evelyn laughed, setting her hands upon her hips. "So you get the first look, is that it?"

"Of course! I have to make sure everything is just right." He disappeared inside and stuck his head out the door. "It looks pretty comfy in here. Nice fireplace, little kitchen so you can make breakfast."

"Just breakfast? Won't you be hungry the rest of the day?" Evelyn put her hands in the pockets of her coat.

Richard skipped down the stairs. "I thought we might splurge and eat dinner in Estes Park. Then we can walk along the streets checking out some of those great-looking shops we saw on the way in."

Evelyn's eyes sparkled. "Did you see the cotton candy shop? I could smell it from the car. We have to try some…and watch them make it."

Richard bent down and scooped her up.

Evelyn squealed, grabbing him around the neck. "What are you doing? You're going to injure your back and that won't be a fun way to spend our vacation."

"I'll be just fine. I'm in great shape…for my age." He walked over to the stairs and swung her sideways to clear the railing. He jogged up and sauntered across the porch. Stepping into the cabin, he kicked the door shut with his heel.

Evelyn looked around the small space, taking in the stone fireplace and small loveseat in front of it. The kitchenette was at one end, with a table and two chairs in the corner. The opposite side of the room held two doors on the wall. "This is perfectly lovely. A great place to spend a belated anniversary trip." She kissed his cheek, breathing deeply. "You still smell just as good as you always have."

"Old Spice and mountain air mix well together, I guess." He strode to the first door and nudged it open. He peered inside. "Well, that's the bathroom, so…" he thumped the next door with his arm, "this must be the bedroom."

The door opened to a quaint room with a log bed covered in a red patterned quilt. A rocking chair stood in the corner, a pillow with the same pattern situated in the corner. White curtains sprinkled with red flowers hung cheerily at the small window.

Richard walked to the bed and deposited Evelyn. He stretched his back, arching it with one hand at his hip. "I think I'm a bit more out of shape than I had hoped."

Evelyn sat up, unbuttoning her coat. "It's not every day you go around carrying a one hundred and…" Evelyn concentrated on the buttons.

Richard leaned down, nuzzling her cheek. "What were you going to say…one hundred and what?"

Evelyn pursed her lips. "That's just none of your business. I share a lot with you, but not that." She slid from the bed and took off her coat. She started from the bedroom and Richard grabbed her arm.

"Where are you going?" His eyes turned dark, the cleft in his chin deepening as he gave her a sideways grin.

She looked down at the coat across her arm. "I thought I would find a place to hang this and then maybe unpack our suitcases."

Richard took the coat from her arm and tossed it on the rocking chair. He reached up and found the zipper at the back of the high-necked knit top she wore and began sliding it down. "I thought we could start off with something a bit more interesting than nesting. You can fluff your quarters later…much later." His hand went to the back of her head as he took her lips with his own, kissing her, moving gently over her mouth.

EVELYN STUMBLED TO THE heavy door, yawning as she wrapped her robe about her waist. She pulled the door open and looked out. "There you are. I smelled the coffee and then I couldn't find you. I thought you were out hunting down our breakfast so I wouldn't have to fix it."

Richard sat in the rocking chair, one leg crossed over his knee, the ankle resting there. The brown corduroys he wore sat low on his hips, his white undershirt showing beneath the unbuttoned plaid shirt. He balanced the coffee cup on his bent knee, tiny swirls of steam rising from the dark contents. "I've never been hunting before, so it may be a bit dangerous to start now…for me as well as the animals." He took a sip of the coffee and winced. "That sure isn't cooling down very quickly."

Evelyn gathered the neck of the robe about her chin and sat down on the vacant rocking chair. She curled her bare toes against the floor boards. "I should have put on my slippers. I didn't realize you were out greeting the sunrise."

Richard leaned his head back and looked out over the meadow. The sun peaked in the east, a warm orange glow spreading through the blue-violet sky. New-fallen snow scattered the very tops of the rugged mountains. "Beautiful, isn't it? Only God could have created such a sight to behold."

"Whenever I see views such as this, I can't help but think of singing. There are so many old hymns that express God's creation." Evelyn turned to her husband and reached out her hand. "It's been a wonderful week here with you. We've made enough memories to last a lifetime, and then some."

Richard gripped her hand, his thumb caressing her long fingers. "We have had a very special life together so far. I'm looking forward to the next twenty-four years with you."

Evelyn raised her brow. "Only twenty-four? That would put us at forty-eight years. I pray we have more than that. Many couples do, you know."

Richard smiled. "I know, but I like to take it in quarters…I can make it last that way."

Evelyn laughed. "So that's how it works."

Richard's eyes swept over her. "I love you, Evelyn Barton Hanover King. I have since you first looked at me at the prom with those green eyes of yours."

"All the way across the gymnasium?" Evelyn raised a brow.

Richard nodded. "I was ready to marry you that night." He laughed. "Bill thought I had lost my mind." He tilted his head. "Do you remember that song you sang to me?"

Evelyn smiled, rocking her chair. "Most of it, because the words are so very true in relation to how I feel about you. The last part is my favorite." She closed her eyes and sang. "Please follow me dear, to a place that is near.

I'll love you 'til then, until eternity ends. I'm drifting...drifting...drifting away..." " She opened her eyes, meeting his blue ones.

"That's the one. I've heard it on the radio a few times over the years. I've always kind of thought of it as *our* song." He leaned down, bringing her hand to his lips.

Evelyn sighed. "You're going to have to hold that thought for a few minutes."

Richard wrinkled his brow. He drained his coffee cup and set it on the rough railing of the porch. "You sound serious."

Evelyn let go of his hand and stood. She stepped in front of him and gestured for him to uncross his legs. When he had, she sat down on his lap and cuddled close to him, burying her face in his neck. "I have something to tell you."

He leaned back and looked down at her. "You aren't leaving me, are you?"

Evelyn gave him a playful slap on the arm. "Of course not! Would I come up here and spend this kind of glorious week with you if I was leaving?"

Richard pulled her close. "You could want to let me down easy. Give me some happy memories to console myself with as the wind whistled outside my lonely bedroom window on a cold January night."

Evelyn laughed. "I *almost* feel sorry for you."

"I hope so. *I* feel sorry for me." Richard smoothed his hand down her hip and kissed the top of her tousled head. "What do you need to tell me?"

"I'm pregnant."

Richard rocked forward, nearly dumping his wife on the floor boards. He repositioned her on his lap, looking into her eyes. "Pregnant? Annabella is seventeen years old!"

"I know how old our daughter is, Richard." Evelyn stared at her husband. "I am as shocked as you are. I found out just before we came up here, during my routine exam."

"You're sure?"

Evelyn nodded. "Yes, the doctor said I am *pregnant*. We are going to have another baby...after all these years."

"But aren't you too old? I mean there must be risks...problems, that kind of thing." Richard sat back and shook his head. "I can hardly believe it."

Evelyn stared off into the distance. "I know what you mean. I can't either. It's taken me all week to get up the nerve to tell you. I kept thinking the doctor must be wrong, but I'm starting to feel different...the way I felt before when I was pregnant." She turned to him. "And forty-two isn't that old."

Richard held up his fingers, counting off nine months. "Close to forty-three by the time the baby is born." He looked at her. "When *is* the baby due?"

"It's very early yet, but the doctor said around the middle to end of May." Evelyn chewed on her bottom lip. "I've thought about this a lot and I've prayed about it. I don't want to tell anyone about the baby...not yet."

"What about Annabella? She would want to know."

"Yes, she would...and she will be the *first* one to know." Evelyn shrugged. "Since I had those two miscarriages before Annabella was born, and because I *am* older, I just think it best that we wait awhile. I want to make sure everything is going to be alright."

Richard nodded. "You're right, of course." He looked down at her tummy and placed his hand there. "Another life to join our little family. God is so good, Evelyn."

Evelyn lowered her head, looking up at him. "So you're happy about this? You don't think it will change our lives?"

Richard laughed. "Of *course* this baby is going to change our lives...but only for the better. God has given us so much love to share. He's entrusting us with another child. What a privilege!"

Evelyn smiled. "I'm happy that you are taking this so well. I was a little worried about how you would react."

Richard shoved a thumb at his chest. "Me? Why would you think that? You know I've always loved children and hoped we would have more."

"Yes…" Evelyn ran her finger along the neckline of his white undershirt. "But it has been a very long time since we've had a baby in the house. We'll be in our sixties before this child is ready to leave home…and Annabella will be headed toward forty."

Richard chuckled, struggling to stand with her. He rocked forward and stood with a big lunge. He walked her to the door and nudged it open with his foot.

"What are you doing?" Evelyn laughed, wrapping her arms about his neck.

"I'm going to show you just how young I really am." He winced as he neared the bedroom door. "I think I pulled something when I stood up."

Evelyn giggled. "Well, probably! What am I going to do with you?"

Richard wiggled his brows at her.

Chapter Twenty Four

Fort Collins, Colorado
February 8, 1973

"HOW DOES ITALIAN FOOD sound?" Evelyn watched as Annabella dropped her books to the table. She took her coat off and hung it on the back of the kitchen chair.

"We're eating dinner out tonight?" Annabella wrinkled her brow as she pulled the crocheted hat from her head. "But it's a Thursday. I have a ton of homework to get done before the weekend." She pointed to the pile of books and notebooks scattered across the kitchen table.

Evelyn gave her daughter a smile. "You have to eat anyway. It will just take a little longer to drive there and back, and then you'll be home again."

Richard entered the kitchen, buttoning his Sherpa-lined jacket. "Are we ready to go? I'm starved." He gave Annabella a sideways hug and kiss on the top of her head. "Did you have a good day filling your brain with all sorts of knowledge?"

Annabella tilted her head from side to side. "About the same as always. It's school, how exciting can it be?" She glanced down. "Are my clothes alright? I'd rather put on a pair of jeans."

Evelyn shook her head. "You look beautiful. I love that turtleneck and skirt on you, and those boots will be much warmer than jeans anyway."

"Bundle up, you two. We only had a high of twenty-two degrees today. It will be getting even colder as the sun goes down." He kissed Evelyn on the cheek. "I'm going to warm up the car. I'll see you both outside."

Annabella gave a shiver as her father opened the door to the garage. "Why are we going out, on a school night, when it's freezing?"

Evelyn went to the hall closet and took out her coat. "Your father and I have some news to share with you and we wanted to have a special evening with you first." She shrugged into the long, beige coat, tying the belt around her middle. She smiled. "Can't we do something nice for our daughter without getting an interrogation first?"

Annabella lifted her shoulders as she pulled her plaid pea coat from the back of the chair. "It just seems strange to me that we're going out. We never leave the house on a school night unless it's to go to church on Sunday or Wednesday." She slid one arm into the sleeve and stared at her mother. "Are we moving again? Is that the news you have to share?" She continued with the coat and shook her head. "That's not so special anymore. It won't bother me as much now since I'm graduating in a few months."

Evelyn took knitted mittens from her pockets and pulled them on. "No, we aren't moving." She clasped her hands together. "You'll just have to wait and see what it is." Evelyn gave Annabella a wink and walked to the door. "I'll meet you in the car. Make sure you lock the door behind you."

Richard smiled at his wife as she slid into the front seat of the Ford. "Is she coming?" He adjusted the rear view mirror.

Evelyn nodded. "Reluctantly, I'm afraid. She said she has a lot of homework to do before the weekend. Maybe we *should* just stay home." She turned and looked out the back window, the exhaust from the car showing gray in the cold air from the open garage door. "It looks like it's still snowing that icy mix as well. The roads are probably horrendous."

Richard chuckled. "I just drove home from work an hour ago. The roads were alright. I'll be careful." He slid his arm around his wife's shoulders. "I just think you're nervous to tell her about the baby."

Evelyn looked down at her mittened hands. "I am! I'm *so* worried that she's going to be upset." She sighed. "I guess I thought this day wouldn't come, that I would probably lose this baby as well. But the doctor said everything is going along just as it should."

"So, it's time to tell her. First thing we do when we get home. She'll be in a better mood after we eat." Richard kissed her cheek. "I think she's going to be very happy to have a sibling…even if she *is* eighteen years older."

Evelyn shook her head. "If you say so." She looked at her husband. "You're usually right."

"Usually?" Richard raised a brow.

Annabella opened the door and flopped into the back seat. "Sorry I took so long. Carrie just called wanting to know if I could come over later and study for our test tomorrow."

Evelyn frowned as she tilted her head toward the back. "You have a test?" She looked at Richard. "We should just stay home. I have a package of spaghetti noodles in the cupboard. We can have our own Italian dinner right here."

Richard put the Ford in reverse and backed from the garage. "You don't need to fix dinner." He shifted into *park* and jumped from the car, closing the wide steel door. He returned, picking up the conversation where he had left off. "We won't be gone that long, and Annabella can study later." He looked at his daughter in the mirror as he backed from the driveway.

"It's alright, Mom. I told Carrie we had plans for tonight and I'd see her in the morning." Annabella leaned back and stared out the window, the wintery landscape sweeping past. "Besides, she just wants to pick my brains and not use hers for the test. I've already done most of *my* studying."

Richard grinned at Evelyn. "It will be just fine, dear heart." He turned his eyes back to the road.

ANNABELLA MOVED TO THE center of the car, straddling the hump on the floor. She patted her tummy. "That was really good. We should go there more often." She glanced at her mother, sitting close beside her father. "No offense to you, Mom, but the lasagna I had was much better than waiting for spaghetti to cook."

Evelyn laughed, the sound carrying through the dark vehicle. "None was taken, my dear. It was nice to not cook dinner and have to clean up afterward."

Annabella watched as her father glanced at her mother. She could see him smile and mouth the words, "I love you."

Richard cleared his throat. "I'll agree with all of the above. And now, you can get to your homework while your mother and I snuggle on the couch."

Annabella leaned forward, putting her arms on the back of the front bench seat. She breathed deeply of her father's aftershave, warm memories of watching him shave before church floating through her mind. "I thought you both had something you wanted to tell me?"

Richard lifted his eyes to the rear view mirror. "Oh, that's right. I almost forgot."

Annabella laughed, sitting back. "That's just fine. You both can keep me in suspense."

Richard turned on the radio, twisting the knob through the stations. A fast-paced, older song came on and Richard lowered his voice, singing dramatically. He missed the notes and was so off-key that Evelyn and Annabella started laughing.

"Dad, come on! I know you can sing better than that. I've heard you in church."

"I always sing my best in church and you should too, my dear. I'm just not as gifted in times like these." He began going through the stations once more.

Evelyn laid her hand on his arm. "Stop, stop, that's our song!"

Richard put his hand back on the wheel. He nodded. "It is."

Annabella smiled as she watched her parents sing along, her father in perfect harmony. *They love one another so much. I hope I can have a love such as theirs some day.*

"Our lives are as one, have only begun. Let me hold you now, until the setting sun. I'm drifting…drifting…drifting away. Please follow me dear, to a place that is near, I'll love…"

The headlights of the oncoming vehicle filled the interior of the Ford, and Annabella heard her mother scream.

"Richard!"

RICHARD REACHED OUT AND took Evelyn's hand in his. He gave her a wide smile, the cleft in his chin deepening. "She will be fine, dear heart. God will watch over her until she's with us again."

Evelyn nodded, her red hair glorious in the brilliant light surrounding them. Peace settled upon them, wrapping around, and His Presence enveloped as a warm, comforting embrace. The music soared, the most beautiful sound, as they were reunited with well-remembered souls…three new, yet so familiar, faces among them.

They had found that place in their hearts and now it was home.

Author's Note

I could not end this series without a personal note from me! It has been such a pleasure to write these four books about Rubyville and the four Barton women that were a part of it. I loved the research on each era…the clothing, the slang that was used, the automobiles, and the issues that were faced during those times. It has given me a better understanding and appreciation for what others have lived through before my time.

I wrote *Drifting with You (Richard and Evelyn's Song)* while writing this story. I wanted a very simple song that would have gone with the 'Big Band' era. Something that could have been played as an instrumental and danced to, but also had words. Personally, I feel that songs in that time period had a more romantic and upbeat feel to them. I wanted to convey that to you, dear reader, with this song. I have the tune in my head, and I hope you are able to get the general feel.

This story also included reference to songs to set the stage. Most were old hymns that we have all sung during our lives. We can find comfort and truth in them, as they praise our Lord and Savior.

And lastly, but most importantly, I have written the last scene with what I believe is true when we pass from this life into the next…if we are saved. Of course I have taken some liberties since no one knows exactly what will take place. But we *will* be in God's Presence if we have accepted God's gift of salvation, and we *will* be with those Believers that have died before us. There are many verses in the Bible that give us a bit of a peek.

John 14:2-3 New American Standard Bible (NASB)

²In My Father's house are many dwelling places; if it were not so, I would have told you; for I go to prepare a place for you. ³If I go and prepare a place for you, I will come again and receive you to Myself, that where I am, there you may be also.

Luke 23:39-43 New American Standard Bible (NASB)

³⁹One of the criminals who were hanged there was hurling abuse at Him, saying, "Are You not the Christ? Save Yourself and us!" ⁴⁰But the other answered, and rebuking him said, "Do you not even fear God, since you are under the same sentence of condemnation? ⁴¹And we indeed are suffering justly, for we are receiving what we deserve for our deeds; but this man has done nothing wrong." ⁴²And he was saying, "Jesus, remember me when You come in Your kingdom!" ⁴³And He said to him, "Truly I say to you, today you shall be with Me in Paradise."

1 Thessalonians 4:13-18 New American Standard Bible (NASB)

¹³But we do not want you to be uninformed, brethren, about those who are asleep, so that you will not grieve as do the rest who have no hope.¹⁴For if we believe that Jesus died and rose again, even so God will bring with Him those who have fallen asleep in Jesus. ¹⁵For this we say to you by the word of the Lord, that we who are alive and remain until the coming of the Lord, will not precede those who have fallen asleep. ¹⁶For the Lord Himself will descend from heaven with a shout, with the voice of the archangel and with the trumpet of God, and the dead in Christ will rise first. ¹⁷Then we who are alive and remain will be caught up together with them in the clouds to meet the Lord in the air, and so we shall always be with the Lord. ¹⁸Therefore comfort one another with these words.

Revelation 21:4 New American Standard Bible (NASB)

⁴and He will wipe away every tear from their eyes; and there will no longer be any death; there will no longer be any mourning, or crying, or pain; the first things have passed away."

John 3:16 New American Standard Bible (NASB)

¹⁶"For God so loved the world that He gave His only begotten Son, that whoever believes in Him shall not perish, but have eternal life.

Drifting With You
(Richard and Evelyn's Song)

I'm drifting…
Drifting…
Drifting away.
Drifting with you,
To a place that is new.
I'm drifting…
Drifting…
Drifting away.
Drifting with you,
On an ocean so blue.
Our lives are as one, have only begun.
Let me hold you now, until the setting sun.
I'm drifting…
Drifting…
Drifting away.
Please follow me dear, to a place that is near,
I'll love you 'til then, until eternity ends.
I'm drifting…
Drifting…
I'm drifting away

THE COMPLETE Rubyville SERIES

BY DEBORAH ANN DYKEMAN

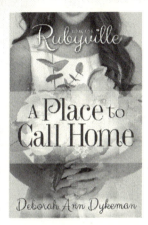
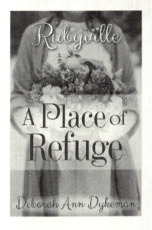
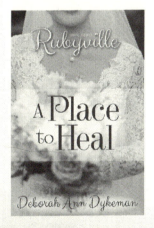
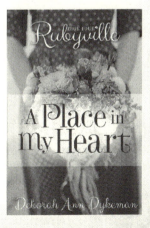

Books available on www.Amazon.com
The entire series available this fall.

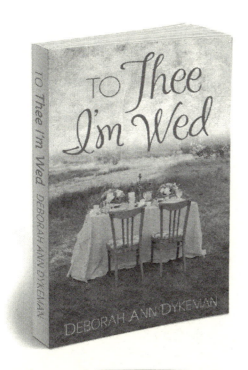

Also by DEBORAH ANN DYKEMAN

Jason and Kathy Miller are brimming with hope and excitement for their future together as husband and wife on their wedding day in June of 1983.

Twenty years later life isn't so carefree anymore. Three children, several pounds, and graying hair have dampened enthusiasm, and Kathy is feeling it. Caring for a home, husband, and teenagers isn't always as fulfilling as a woman would want it to be . . . and that's where problems begin for the Millers.

Kathy now travels a road she would never have considered walking as a young, exuberant bride. Jason struggles along, clearing a path through the thorns that have become their marriage. Will a new baby repair all the damage done or shred the last ties binding them together?

Available on www.Amazon.com

Made in the USA
Charleston, SC
15 March 2017